WHISPERING FOG

THE ADVENTURE OF THE AEOLUS, *KEEPER OF THE WIND*

To Olivia
Best Wishes
Diann Shaddox
10-24-2015

WHISPERING FOG
by Diann Shaddox

ISBN 13: 978-0-9912805-3-7

Cover art copyright 2014 by Joe Miles
Cover Design and Book Layout by Custom-book-tique.com

Visit our Web site at www.eaglequillpublishing.com

Printed in the United States of America

First paperback edition

WHISPERING FOG

THE ADVENTURE OF THE AEOLUS,
KEEPER OF THE WIND

DIANN SHADDOX

EAGLE QUILL
PUBLISHING

OTHER BOOKS BY DIANN SHADDOX

A Faded Cottage

This book is dedicated with love to my son Rick who died suddenly on May 20, 2014 from an aggressive brain tumor. He will always be in my heart.

CONTENTS

Acknowledgements

I would like to say thank you to Mary Hill "Hilly" Dewey, my editor. Thank you for your encouragement, kindness, your patience, and the many hours you have spent working with me. I will be forever grateful for everything you've done.

To Joe Miles. Thank you for creating and bringing to life the ship, the Aeolus, for the front cover of Whispering Fog.

CHAPTER ONE

HARBOR TOWNE, MAINE

Monday, October 13th, 1959

oices called my name. I couldn't answer. My throat was chocking me. I couldn't scream anymore. My beating heart pounded in my ears as my body plummeted through the misty air, not graceful as a seagull diving for a fish in the sea, but more as a ragdoll with arm and legs flapping wildly. Weightlessness had taken over. I couldn't stop myself. I became frozen in fear. Total darkness was all around me until a bright...

Johnny waved his hand in the air trying to get the attention of the young girl deep in thought sitting across the kitchen table from him. The flickering flames of the birthday candles sparkled in her eyes.

"Belinda," Johnny called out. His long body leaned across the table gently patting the formica top with his fingers. "Well, have you made your wish?" He chuckled, tapping even louder on the tabletop. "You'd better blow out the candles before the cake catches on fire."

Belinda pulled her eyes away from the shimmering flames of the candles. She felt a chill in the air and tugged her new, pink sweater up around her neck, her birthday gift from her father. She shivered, a shiver that started from the bottom of her feet ending when her head quivered, bringing her thoughts back. She swished away the curls of long blonde hair from her face. Quickly, she leaned her head over the two-layer white icing cake, with its green buttercream swirls piped on the sides. Taking in one long deep breath, she blew out the twenty multicolored-striped candles leaving a swirling cloud of smoke.

"Happy birthday Katelynn Belinda Brady," Johnny said proudly. He carefully lifted each of the candles from the birthday cake that he'd purchased along with the birthday meal from Miss Sophia's bakery and deli.

Johnny's tall body reclined against the back of the kitchen chair making it squeak. His eyes stayed fixed on Belinda. He'd been in love with Belinda all of his life, and the gossipy women around the small town of Harbor Towne, Maine, including his mom, had wondered why the two hadn't married. The hairs on the back of his neck prickled as he continued to stare wondering the same thing. It wasn't because he hadn't tried, but every time he brought up marriage, Belinda would discreetly change the subject. Now that she'd turned twenty, he believed things would change or at least he hoped they would.

Belinda smiled back at Johnny noticing he was deep in thought. She knew she couldn't resist the tan face of the butternut haired boy, who'd been her best friend, her confidante, since the first grade in Mrs. Jones's class. She'd never had many friends growing up in the small town of Harbor Towne and living miles from town on Franklin's Cliff next to the tall lighthouse, didn't help her socially. It seemed the girls in her class at school had always been jealous of her and the boys were afraid of her because she was too headstrong. Except Johnny, he knew she was stubborn, bullheaded, and nothing anyone said or did would change her mind. But, today her impetuousness was waning and she didn't like how that feeling felt.

Johnny stood from his chair. He hurried to the cabinet hanging next to the sink and pulled out two of his mom's plates with blue flowers on the edges. The knife slid into the cake. He stopped briefly waving the knife in the air as his eyes peered out from under his long hair. "That must've been a hell of a wish – it sure took you awhile."

"I'm sorry Johnny," she replied. Her fingers strummed nervously tapping her nails in an odd rhythm on the table. "My dream I had last night keeps haunting me."

"Ohhhhhhh, the dream about falling?"

"Yes."

Johnny leaned over the table and stared into Belinda's eyes. "Awwww, you know what a dream about falling means. You've lost control of something in your life and you're trying to grasp, cling to something or maybe someone…"

"Johnny," she interrupted, "no more therapy sessions and I haven't lost control. I'm fine."

"I can't help it, I am a psychology major. Remember, I'm here to help."

She smiled back at him. "You know my mind won't stop thinking about what happened last night."

"What about it?" he questioned with a puzzled look on his face. He sat back in the kitchen chair. "Oh, it's about the strange lights and sounds you heard out by the lighthouse; you need to let it go. That's just superstitious rot."

"I can't," she shivered again tugging her sleeves of her sweater down to her cupped hands. "It gives me the chills when I think about it – there was something that…." Her voice trailed off as Johnny moaned.

"Ur," grunted Johnny, "you've just got a very strong imagination and living on that cliff by the tall lighthouse all of your life isn't helping." He wanted to add, *and you need to marry me and move away from that lighthouse*, but he bit his lip stopping the words from coming out.

"I know my imagination is going wild, but…" "Belinda," Johnny interrupted still holding onto the large knife covered in soft moist cake, "there wasn't anyone out on the water that late at night, especially in a thick fog." His head shook no. "Tales of a whispering fog swallowing ships and people are only tall tales from sailors who've been living too long at sea and drinking too much rum." He drew his shoulders back against the slats of the straight back chair. His eyes squinted giving her a strong look. "The stories aren't real. Maybe the movie we watched at the drive-in last Saturday night stirred up your imagination."

"No, the movie didn't bother me and I know real from fiction," she snapped back at him getting annoyed. She studied Johnny's exasperated face and knew she was pushing his patience telling her tales about what she'd seen on her cliff last night. A foolish feeling came over her; it was silly to be so concerned about a silly dream and a foggy night. She'd spent hundreds of foggy nights on her cliff, so why did the fog last night worry her? Maybe her Granddad Elias's story about a mysterious whispering fog was making her imagination work overtime and Johnny was correct. No one would be out in the sea on a foggy night. The answer of what happened last night was simple. The shadows she'd seen swishing on the water were from the light of the lighthouse bouncing off the fog, and the soft muffled sounds weren't whispering voices at all, but the sound of the wind whistling up the side of the cliff.

Johnny didn't say anything else and finished slicing two oversize pieces of birthday cake.

Belinda ate every bite of her piece of cake, opened her gift from Johnny, a gold charm bracelet with a perfect replica of a golden lighthouse dangling from the bracelet. She sat quietly at the kitchen table in Johnny's parent's century old farmhouse. Her eyes became hypnotized by the golden lighthouse swinging gently in a pattern on her wrist in the dull glow from the round ceiling light with one of its bulbs burned out.

"Belinda, you're doing it again."

His words floated in her mind and her head shook as she gathered her thoughts. "I'm sorry Johnny." She paused. She couldn't stop herself as the words came out of her mouth. "I keep remembering what your Granddad Evert said earlier when I told him about seeing the whispering fog last night on my cliff. How it appeared out of nowhere and then disappeared just as fast."

"I knew it was a mistake to let you talk to Granddad Evert, he's full of old wives tales."

"But," she blurted out; "he said my great, great grandfather Finnegan Augustus Brady went missing for six weeks in the year of 1846 and when he returned home…" She watched Johnny's reaction. "He told strange stories about the whispering fog rising up the side of Franklin's Cliff and taking him away."

"Yep, but you heard Granddad Evert's explanation of what really happened back then."

"I know, then again…" Johnny interrupted. "Everyone in town said Finnegan ran off with the widow Harris, since she left the same day he went missing, and when it didn't work out with her… Finnegan made up the story of the strange fog, so he could come home with some dignity."

She arched a brow and irritably waved her hands in the air as if they could do the talking. "That's just speculation!"

Johnny leaned his long body back in his chair crossed his hands over his head wiggling his fingers. "Maybe there's some wildness hidden in your family tree," he snickered watching and waiting for a reaction.

"Fiddlesticks," she responded puckering her face into a frown.

Johnny laughed.

"Oh, I give," she declared throwing her hands in the air, "I guess you're right."

"Finally," he moaned lowering his elbows to the table and placing his head in his hands staring at her. "You know you are pigheaded."

Anxiously, she sat quietly for a few minutes and twirled the golden lighthouse charm hanging from her wrist. "Anyway, how could someone just disappear into a fog?" She narrowed her eyes and looked up at him. "And I'm not pigheaded," she snapped."

He laughed showing his crooked grin knowing she had to have the last word in any disagreement.

Later that night, Johnny's black 1954 Ford pickup crept slowly, twisting and turning along the winding dirt road, leaving a trail of dust behind. They were headed to Franklin's Cliff where the Harbor Towne Lighthouse had sat next to Belinda's home for centuries. Johnny gripped the steering wheel tightly, for a moment he gazed over at Belinda sitting on the seat next to him only inches away. He took in her perfect size oval face, soft creamy skin, cute nose and a smile that melted him into a pile of jello. She was the most beautiful girl in the county and had the bluest eyes he'd ever seen. He took in a deep breath smelling the fresh lilac scent of her perfume. His mouth tightened when her eyes lit as the truck's headlights illuminated the tall stone lighthouse in front of them. This Christmas, Johnny was going to ask Belinda to marry him whether she was ready or not, but he knew the truth; he couldn't compete with Belinda's other love, her lighthouse standing tall on the rugged cliff.

The pickup pulled to a stop in front of Belinda's old Victorian home. Johnny quickly jumped out of the truck. Belinda slid past the steering wheel, climbed out of the truck, and stood next to him. He grabbed her shoulders spun her around to face him as he wrapped his arms around her shoulders letting his fingers gently play with her long, blonde hair. "Happy birthday, Belinda," he whispered in her ear. He leaned down and their lips met, as he kissed her with passion.

"Thanks, Johnny, for my birthday dinner and charm bracelet," she said. Her fingers gently stroked his face as she stared into his kind eyes.

"You're welcome. Now, you be careful walking around out here in the dark," Johnny offered. His voice crackled and his face became taut.

"I'm fine out here, stop worrying it's a beautiful calm night, and…" she grinned, "no fog is in sight, but…" Her hand gripped Johnny's muscular arm from years of hard work on his daddy's fishing boat. She whispered in a soft voice. "I wish you'd stay for a while longer and go for a walk with me."

"Don't tempt me," he chuckled. "I wish I could, but it's getting late and I have to be at the dock before sunrise to meet Daddy, and later in the afternoon I have a couple of classes at school. I still don't like you being out here on this cliff all alone." He paused; "maybe you should go inside and forget about your walk." He became quiet and his eyes panned the rocky cliff. "There's a strangeness in the air that I don't like and it seems very muggy, not a normal October night."

"Now, you're the one talking silly, it's always damp by the sea," she answered. Her fingers brought his face down to her face and she gave him a long kiss goodbye. "You sure you can't stay?" she teased.

Johnny chuckled. "Belinda Brady, are you trying to seduce me?"

"Well, is it working?"

"Ohhhhhhh…" His head shook a slow no. "Gotta get going, it's getting late," he replied stepping back from her. He slid from his pocket a wooden handle pocketknife and handed it to her.

"What's that for?"

"Look, I don't like you being out here all alone; keep the knife with you tonight."

"That's your granddaddy's old pocketknife, I can't take it. Johnny, stop worrying I'm fine out here. Remember I can handle myself."

"That karate stuff you do doesn't work." His head swung from side to side. "But a knife will protect you."

"You're sounding silly. I don't need protecting."

"Take it; at least it'll make me feel better."

"Fine," she answered. Not wanting to argue with him anymore, she slid the pocketknife into her jean pocket.

Neptune, her playful Irish setter, ran up nudging her leg. "See, I'm not alone, I have Neptune," she laughed, "and daddy is in the house."

Johnny moaned.

She turned from Johnny and followed Neptune down the path towards the cliff's edge. She stopped walking and waved her arm in the air. "Goodbye Johnny, I'll see you tomorrow when you're finished with school," she shouted at him.

Johnny swung his arm out of the pickup's window and waved goodbye. A trying smile was on his face as the pickup gradually drove away. The old truck's headlights disappeared down the dirt road leaving only the bright lights of the harvest moon blending with the yellow glowing light of the stone lighthouse, as the light circled in a constant rhythm.

Belinda watched the pickup as it vanished into the darkness of the night, already missing Johnny, and wishing he'd stayed with her for a while. However, little did she know that their kiss goodbye would be their last kiss.

CHAPTER TWO

THE TOLLING BELL

In the year of 1793, William Franklin Brady, an architect from Boston, oversaw the building of the white cylindrical Harbor Towne Lighthouse that stands one hundred and sixty feet above the seawater atop a rugged cliff, known as Franklin's Cliff, on the coast of Maine. Its Queen Anne Victorian-style keeper's home sits about twenty yards from the lighthouse with its steeply pitched cedar roof and deep wrap around porch, enveloping the front side of the home.

During the building process, William fell in love with the cliff and sea. He moved his wife and two sons into the home, and became the keeper of the light. Years past and generations of the Brady family have been born, played, cried, loved, and died in the Victorian home next to the old lighthouse with its thin metal staircase leading up into another world; a world where you could stand and see out into the great Atlantic Ocean, heaving as if it were breathing.

Six generations later Franklin Seth Brady, a small man in stature, graying curly hair, now lives in the old Victorian home with his daughter Katelynn Belinda Brady or known to most as Belinda.

Belinda wasn't like most girls her age, interested in getting married and having children. She was a beauty, no denying that, with her long blonde hair and radiant blue eyes, the color of the sea, catching everyone's attention. She wasn't very big, a tiny thing Granddad Elias used to say. But Belinda wasn't a china doll sitting pretty on the shelf. No sir, she was a tomboy. She knew the cliffs surrounding this harbor better than anyone did. Belinda was a different sort and the sea was her love. It had captivated her since she was a little girl. Maybe it was because she had lived her entire life on this one cliff next to the soaring stone lighthouse.

Katelynn Belinda Brady was as headstrong as her mother had said the day she was born, and her dad believed she was so like her mother, Rebecca, who died when Belinda was eleven years old. Belinda knew she was more like her father, both captivated by the lighthouse and sea.

Seth Brady sat that evening in his comfortable overstuffed chair in the living room of the old Victorian home hearing the motor of Johnny's old black pickup leaving down the dirt road. His eyes stayed fixed on the barometer hanging next to the front door. It was normal. Last night the barometer had dropped unexpectedly, but only for a short period of time and then as quickly as it dropped it returned to normal. Seth wasn't one to believe in the tall tales of the sea. He had always wanted to be a scientist and needed real facts to verify unusual occurrences, but tonight doubt was growing in his mind. He couldn't figure out how the barometer had dropped so quickly last night and how the thick fog had only covered Franklin's Cliff and then disappeared in a matter of minutes. There had to be a reasonable explanation and he was determined to find the answer.

He stood from his chair and paced the living room. He stopped at the plate glass window that looked out from under the front porch to the outcropping of the cliff. His eyes focused on his daughter taking her walk and then his eyes moved back to the barometer as it began to drop. "No," he moaned, nervously lacing his hands together, "it can't be happening again." He lifted out his sterling pocket watch, flipping it over to read the initials engraved on the front of it, *FAB*. He made his way to the bookshelf next to the stone fireplace. His trembling hand lifted a worn leather Bible from the top shelf. Pages flipped open to the center of the book showing a folded stack of yellowed papers with the name Finnegan Augustus Brady, 1846 written on the top page. He sat back down in the chair by the fireplace and began to read the pages written by his great grandfather Finnegan hoping he'd find his answer of the whispering fog.

Meanwhile out on the rocky cliff, Belinda made her way along the winding path headed to the edge of the cliff with Neptune at her side. She wasn't worried about the strangeness that had occurred last night, since thoughts of Johnny swirled in her head. Remembering their kiss, she believed it was time to let her feelings for Johnny show. Overhead the seagulls cried and wheeled in circles searching for fish in the churning seawater of the Atlantic Ocean.

Without warning, a hazy mist swirled surrounding her body and strange whispers floated in the air. Neptune growled with his head erect and his ears up. She shivered, an odd sensation moved up her spine. She tightened her pink sweater around her neck feeling the cool dampness in the air. The weather had abruptly changed.

Her granddad Elias's age-old tale of a whispering fog, tumbling like a creature eating everything in its path, marching closer and closer to shore began to swirl in her head. The tale was about a sailing ship called *The Black Shadow* that had sunk in the waters not far from Harbor Towne, Maine in the year of 1765. Her voice echoed out to sea as if it was swirling to meet the fog as she sang *The Tale of The Black Shadow...*

***

A voyage from across the sea *The Black Shadow* it did sail,
Laden with its treasure as the fate begins its tale.
The sky was blue the air was cool the water's they were calm,
On its course to Harbor Towne its massive sails were hung.
A mystifying, monstrous fog was a looming out to sea.
The fearless crew fought long and hard as the sea began to heave.
The monstrous fog swirled in the air the troubled ship just disappeared.
Echoing screams crossed the sky amid the ship's bells somber cry.
Silence fell in the early dawn the enormous sailing ship,
The Black Shadow, it was gone.
The sky was blue the air was cool the water's they were calm,
The massive rocks had won the war with debris left along the shore.
There was many a tear shed there was many a broken heart,
There was many a lad so brave that night that found a watery grave.
Many tales have been told when the fog begins to roll,
Alone they call the brave young souls soft whispers from the deep below.
Guarding the sea all through the night warning seafarers of their flight,
The cries continue without end until the morning light begins.

***

For generations tales have been told that on unnatural foggy nights, many fishermen out on the sea have heard heartbreaking cries coming from the deep ocean waters. The fishermen believe the tormented voices, known as *The Spirits Walking*, were from the crew of *The Black Shadow* and they were warning ships out in the dense fog of dangers, leading lost ships to shore and to safety, not letting the whispering fog, take any more men.

Neptune's growl intensified.

Belinda stared out to sea. "You can hear the strange voices, too – they're whispering, very softly. It's happening again just like last night. I don't understand what they're saying – they're faint, but the voices seem to be calling out, *beware*."

Her eyes stayed in a steady gaze taking in everything around her. Her head shook. "No, Neptune." The dog's chocolate brown eyes peered up at her. "It can't be the men from *The Black Shadow, The Spirits Walking*."

She shivered as her hands rubbed together slipping them into her jean pockets. "Come on Neptune, there's nothing out there. It's as Johnny said; the sounds are coming from the wind whistling up the side of the cliff and our imagination."

Making her way to the rugged cliff's edge, ignoring the whispers in the fog, Belinda sat down on a round rock that was curved like a chair. The gentle swirling breeze brought an iciness to the air. She shifted her position on the rock, her arms crossed, not sure if it was from the cold or the strangeness in the air. The cool mist kissed her pale face giving her cheeks a rosy glow. Neptune lay on the ground by the smooth rock, panting with his ears erect always on guard. Belinda tasted the sea salt on her lips. Her eyes closed, and her head leaned back listening to the sounds of the night. The waves hitting and crashing against the large boulders at the bottom of the cliff made hissing noises, exploding with power.

The voices in the misty air began to mumble louder. Her eyes opened. No it couldn't be. It was as if the voices were whispering "*Belinda*." Her body winced. Her eyes searched across the dark water. The images out in the sea seemed to be alive swaying in the air with unearthliness while the fog crept closer to the shore, engulfing everything in its path.

"Neptune!" she yelled, "Look, there's a strange shape out in the water!"

Her body stiffened. Using the sleeve of her sweater, she wiped the mist from her eyes.

She waited for the bright light from the lighthouse to circle around. "It has to be the shadows from the light of the lighthouse; there couldn't be anything that big out in the sea, not this late at night."

She leaped from the rock darting to the cliff's rim. "No, that can't be! Do you see it boy, its huge! Wow! The object is moving."

She carefully placed her foot on the edge of the cliff. Cautiously, she leaned over the side peering down into the dark seawater below. "Oh, it has a shape, a silhouette of something enormous and the object is coming closer to the bottom of the cliff, but I can't quite tell what it is."

Belinda crouched down next to the edge of the cliff gripping a squatty tree in her right hand trying to keep her balance. To get a better view, she stepped down onto a small ledge carefully positioning her foot against a rock.

"It's a ship!" she shouted, her left hand swaying in the air. "Uh-oh – this can't be – a ship like that could easily be ripped apart by the jagged rocks."

Her body tensed, and her eyes stayed fixed on the huge shape below at the bottom of the cliff. "It's unbelievable, boy. Look, it's a ship from years ago – a magnificent and glorious ship. It has soaring beige sails flapping like bird's wings. The ship is standing tall in the rough water. Oh, no – the fog is moving in fast and it's beginning to swallow up the sails." She moaned. "I hope not like *The Black Shadow*."

Her hand tightened around the trunk of the tree. She stood quietly listening...

"DING, DING," softly rung, echoing up the side of the cliff. Her body shuddered with the toll of the ship's bell crying out with eeriness, an unnatural and unsettling feeling. "The bell is announcing the ship's position, so there has to be a real ship at the foot of the cliff."

The whispering voices became louder, jumbled together, as they flowed up from the deep water below her.

Belinda stared at Neptune. "Can the whispers really be from the crew of *The Black Shadow* warning me of the ship in peril?"

Her heart pounded in her chest. She quickly let go of the tree and climbed back up to the top of the cliff. She raced along the winding path to her home to get her dad, Seth.

On a mission, she flung open the kitchen door stormed inside the old, two-story wooden Victorian home. Her father was sitting in his favorite chair in front of the huge stone fireplace reading some old papers. His hand reached up and smoothed his wild, gray hair from his eyes as he stared at his daughter standing in front of him.

The fire crackled, flickering light against the walls in the room making dancing shadows.

"Dad!" She paused gasping for air. "There's a large old ship sitting at the bottom of the cliff – close to the rocks!"

"What did you say, Belinda?" Seth asked, placing the yellowed pages back into the Bible and laying his thick framed reading glasses on the round end table.

"I said there is an enormous ship with old sails and huge masts sitting near the bottom of the cliff in the whispering fog."

His eyes flew to the barometer hanging on the wall showing an all-time low. "Whispering Fog?" Seth said in a low mumbled voice, "that can't be."

"Yes, Dad, the fog is whispering, and the ship looks like a pirate's ship. It's ringing its bell to tell us it has set its anchor. Hurry, we need to help them." She wiped the mist from her face. "You need to sound the lighthouse's foghorn, someone might be hurt." She quickly spun around and ran out the back door of the house.

"Slow down, Belinda, you need to be careful," her father yelled, grabbing his coat off the hook by the kitchen door following her down the long path to the cliff's edge. "Where's the old ship, I can't see anything?" he called out catching up with her.

"It's, right there," Belinda shouted pointing her arm. "The ship's set anchor and lowered its sails, so it couldn't have moved. You need to let the crew know we're here. Dad – they might need our help. Don't you hear the ships bell?"

"Honey, a ship like that couldn't be that close to the rocks. The waves and rocks would tear it apart."

"Please Dad," Belinda begged, "just in case they're hurt, you need to go to the lighthouse and blow the foghorn! I did see the ship – I know what it looks like."

He leaned over the side of the cliff. "Honey, I can't hear any ship's bell ringing."

The fog was moving in faster creeping and crawling up the side of the cliff like a monster on the prowl.

"Dad, it's an unbelievable ship," Belinda pleaded. "Its dark blue on the bottom with beige sails and the ship was standing tall, so very tall."

"Calm down," he said staring back at his daughter with the same blue eyes.

"I know there's a ship down at the bottom of the cliff, we have to help them!"

Her dad stood back up, wiped his eyes and gave her an unsure look. "You go back to the house, I don't want you out here," he said in an assertive voice he never used, "there's something wrong. I'll check everything out, but I think it's a whale or something else, not a ship, and I don't hear any whispering voices coming from the fog."

Just as she'd asked him to do, her father turned and hurried down the path to the lighthouse. His head swung back and forth muttering to himself. "The fog isn't whispering, it can't be a ship out in this mess and great grandfather Finnegan was just plain looney." But, the realization hit Seth; he knew Belinda didn't make up stories about the sea. If Belinda saw and heard something, it had to be there.

Belinda knew she had seen the old ship and someone might be hurt. Her body teetered over the side of the steep cliff, knowing what she needed to do.

CHAPTER THREE

AEOLUS

Belinda's trembling hands wrapped around the short tree growing on the edge of the cliff. She had to know what was down in the water at the foot of the cliff. Was it a whale or really an old ship? She knew she should've gone back to the house as her father asked, but she never was one to listen to anyone. It wouldn't take her long and she'd be back before her father would be done with the lighthouse and he'd never know.

With the tree clasped tightly in her right hand, her head turned around and she peered over at Neptune. The dog's barks echoed into the misty night blending with the mysterious voices calling to her. "I'll be fine boy, but I have to find that ship."

Why hadn't her dad heard the strange voices in the fog or the tolling bell from the ship? Her body shuddered. She was letting her imagination grow wild. The whispering voices couldn't be from the sailors that had drowned hundreds of years ago – *The Walking Spirits*. If they were real voices, then could the ship in the waters below be a ghost ship? She'd heard tales from her granddad Elias about ghost ships. Ships that had sunk, reappeared and sailed on the open sea with the crew believing they were still alive. She shook her head no; it was just more tall tales like Johnny had said and ghost ships couldn't be real.

Belinda knew every step of how to get to the bottom of the cliff. This was something she'd done many times, but not late at night or in a thick mist. She took one slow step placing her right foot on a slippery rock. Her thoughts spun in her head. She knew at the bottom of the cliff were huge jagged rocks pointing up to the sky along with the raging waters of the Atlantic, but she wasn't letting that stop her.

Cautiously, she made her way down the high cliff. She stopped moving. She could hear the foghorn from the lighthouse; her dad had done as she'd asked. The loud foghorn sang in a rhythmic sound resonating as it called out to the ship. Her right foot found the next large rock protruding from the cliff. The muscles in her arms tightened as her hands gripped the rocks. "*DING, DING,*" rang out from far below and echoed up the cliff. *Yes, there's a ship in trouble at the base of the cliff.* She calculated each step in her mind before she moved even an inch. Slowly, she positioned one foot at a time onto the slippery rocks.

She shuddered, hearing the roaring waves as they churned and crashed against the rocks far below. The whispering fog had stirred up the sea making it angry and violent. The vicious waves sent chills through her body and the tingling she'd felt earlier in the evening was growing, causing her body to tremble. Her hands were drenched from the cold spew from the waves and the rocks were becoming even more slippery to grasp. She wiped her hands on her soaked jeans as she held onto jagged rocks. She sighed. She'd made it half way down the gigantic cliff, but she understood the next half of her descent would be even more treacherous.

Without warning the rock under her right foot cracked. She gasped feeling the rock breaking into pieces and tumble down the side of the cliff, leaving her foot dangling in midair!

She let out a piercing scream that echoed across the sea.

Her heartbeat pulsated a drumming in her ears as her right foot worked feverishly trying to find another rock. But the rocks were too slippery and she was losing her battle. Desperately she tried to hang on gripping the two rocks with her hands.

"HELP!" She shouted in bloodcurdling scream. "Please, someone help me!" A lump swelled in her throat chocking her. She knew her father couldn't hear her cries for help over the roar of the waves.

Her right foot pawed at the cliff trying to find another rock or tree stump. Her white knuckled fingers tightly held onto the wet rocks in a claw like grip, but slowly her fingers began to slip. Suddenly the rock under her left foot snapped breaking from her weight. Frantically she grasped the wet rocks with her hands as her body hung suspended from the side of the steep cliff.

"NO!" she screamed, "please, someone help me!"

She fiercely fought trying frantically to hold on to the rocks. Nonetheless, her fingers began to slide inch by inch and her body dropped, with what felt like excruciating slowness. In reality, she was dropping down the side of the cliff at a fast speed. Her mind was in slow motion, not able to calculate what lay ahead.

She heard the sound of the thunderous waves crashing against the base of the cliff and felt the foggy mist twirling around her. The realization set in that she'd be hitting the rocks below, and her life would end in a matter of seconds. She was petrified and not able to scream anymore. Her thoughts swirled thinking of her father; he'd never know what happened to her.

Plummeting down the side of the cliff her fingers clawed at the small bushes on the side of the cliff. The plants pulled out roots and all. Faster and faster, she flew down the sheer cliff feeling the powerful salt-water waves coming closer. She said a quick prayer.

She'd soon be hitting the rocks or the deep black water. The truth was, hitting either one she wouldn't survive.

She stopped sliding! Blinded by a bright light she didn't move. She smelled a musty earthy odor. Her eyes blinked as they adjusted to the light from an oil lantern sitting on a boulder. Her head shook back and forth not believing what she was seeing. She had to be hallucinating.

Standing, holding her in his arms was a tall young man in his late twenties with long jet black hair hanging down his back. The man gently set her down on the boulder next to him. Belinda struggled to stand, pulling herself upright. She wiped the mist from her eyes with the back of her hand.

She looked up into the man's deep black eyes, making the hair on the back of her neck rise. It was as if the world had stood still. The night had become quiet, the fog had lifted; a picture perfect indigo night sky was overhead. Twinkling stars, looking like small crystals, sparkled and the only sound was the ship's bell ringing, not the foghorn. The sea was calm and tranquil waves lapped at the boulder she was standing on. Her body ached and her skin stung as the salty waves sent splashes of cold water at her.

What had happened? Her body shivered and a wave of dizziness came over her. Had she died? Everything had changed. Was this heaven? Her brain was addled, feeling as if it was full of pebbles rattling around like a pinball machine every time she moved her head.

A mounting sense of panic grew when Belinda looked up at the tall, broad shoulders, strong muscular armed man, towering over her. A gold handled pistol hung on his waist. He didn't speak. She looked back up at the cliff where she'd just fallen. Where was the bright beam of light from the lighthouse and the sound of the foghorn?

She gasped and fear coiled in her stomach. Standing next to the large jagged rocks was the tall sailing ship she'd seen earlier. Now the ship sat in bright light of the Harvest moon. A sense of panic stirred inside her; was that a ghost ship? Was the man in front of her a ghost?

Belinda opened her mouth, but words didn't come. There was something different about the night. The whispering voices from earlier in the evening had stopped. The big question was, how did the fog just disappear in a matter of seconds?

She studied the ship; it was alluring, dark, very dark blue with gold trim around it. The name "*AEOLUS*" was on the back of the ship in large gold letters.

The man stood still. He stared down at her.

"Thank you for saving my life," Belinda whispered trying to get her voice to speak. "My foot slipped on the wet rocks and I couldn't hold on."

The man stood stiff. He didn't know what to think of the tiny young woman standing in front of him drenched like a wet dog with her long hair dripping water on her face. Her scared eyes, like a wild animal being hunted, stared back at him. He finally spoke, with a very British accent. "What is a young lass like you doing, climbing down a tall cliff in this fog?"

"I saw the ship earlier this evening and I heard your bell ringing, stating you were sitting down by the rocks. I believed you were in trouble." Belinda elaborated taking a step back from the man.

Her eyes took in what the strange man was wearing. His clothes were from years ago. He had on brown short pants that only made it to his knees, black wool socks that came up to the pants leg, and black shoes with square toes. He also had a blue striped shirt, a short brown jacket without a collar, and a black handkerchief tied around his neck. His long black, straight hair was tied with a thin black cloth in a bow at the back of his head.

The crew aboard the tall ship was dressed just like the man. Belinda's head shook as she tried to make some sense of what had happened. Maybe the ship was from a reenactment of the old sailing days, or maybe there was a pirate movie being filmed nearby.

"Is anyone hurt onboard your ship?"

"Nay, my crew and I are fine," he replied. "We wouldn't be in this mess if it wasn't for the dreadful fog. Lass, what were you doing on that cliff so late at night?"

"I live on the cliff in the old Victorian home next to the lighthouse," Brenda blurted, her teeth chattering. Her head tilted to the side staring up at the young man, studying him just as he was taking her in.

"You speak nonsense," he responded, mouth agape. "What Victorian home or lighthouse are you talking about?" he questioned squinching his dark eyes.

"The tall white lighthouse, the one up there on top of the cliff," she answered pointing with her arm. Her head leaned back searching for the light. "Maybe the fog is still too thick up on the top of the cliff and is obscuring the light from the lighthouse," she added. She was getting agitated with the man and was wondering why he was asking such ludicrous questions.

"There isn't a lighthouse up there. I'm afraid you must've hit your head when you fell down the cliff." His back arched his face became taut with creases growing on his brow. He gave her a look like she was insane.

"Yes! There is a lighthouse," she argued stomping her feet swinging her arms wildly in the air pointing up the cliff. "I live up there on top of the cliff in my home next to the lighthouse and my father is the keeper of the lighthouse."

"Lass, we had trouble coming into the harbor in the wretched fog this evening because there isn't a lighthouse in this harbor," he answered so sure and so confident making her even more agitated.

Her hands gripped into fists. "I've lived next to the lighthouse my entire life! You must be crazy!"

"Nonetheless, the men in town have discussed building a lighthouse and I hope they do very soon. It has been touch and go all evening."

Belinda glared at the man; he was as loony as the night. He was the one talking nonsense about building a lighthouse.

The man stepped forward. "You need to come onboard, we need to get you some dry clothes," the man demanded in a strong voice. His head turned to the side and he became quiet for a second. "What are you wearing?"

"What do you mean what am I wearing? I'm wearing new jeans and a new sweater that I just got for my birthday today." Her eyes squinted. "I don't think you know much about clothes – look at what you're wearing," she snapped back at him.

He didn't speak, however his eyes were doing the talking giving her a burrowing stare. His large rough hand reached down and seized her arm, gradually pulling her to the small boat that was waiting next to the massive rocks.

"Let go of me!" Belinda yelled, jerking her arm free from his firm grip. "I'm going home!" She felt the pocketknife in her jean pocket and thought about pulling it out. But that'd be silly since the man had just saved her life and he did have gun.

"Lass, there isn't anything up on the cliff – no one lives up there," he said irritably with a note of steel in his voice. "We must go!"

"No, I'm not going anywhere with you!"

"I need to get you onboard the ship. It's dangerous staying here by the rocks, you might accidently slip and fall into the sea."

"Why don't you believe me?" She sighed. "I do live on the cliff with my father. He'll be looking for me! He's sounding the foghorn!"

The man's large hand again reached over to her. She shoved his arm away. "Who are you and why is your ship here? I've never seen a ship like yours around this harbor before!"

"We've been to this harbor many times, but we've never had problems with the fog like we did tonight; it blew in out of nowhere. We became lost in the fog before we were able to make it to the harbor. That is why we ended up next to the rocks in the shoal; the shallow water was too hazardous to navigate."

He gazed down on her, his head swung sideways giving her a disconcerted stare. "I've never seen fog like that before in all of my sailing or never witnessed anything like it. My crew and I heard soft whispering cries coming from the sea that save us from the jagged rocks. When you started climbing down the cliff the vaporous mist began to disappear, and that was how we spotted you. Our ship is fine, but we have to wait until morning to try and move her. The rocks are too treacherous for us to try tonight."

That was the only thing the man had said so far that made sense. Belinda kept wiggling, but his new grip on her arm was strong and he wasn't letting her go.

"Thank you for saving me, but I need to go back up the cliff, to my father," she offered, thinking she could appease the crazy man by being polite so she could free herself from his grip and get away from the bizarre man.

"Nay lass, I told you there isn't anything up on the cliff. Look up; do you see a beacon from the lighthouse?"

Belinda stopped fighting for a second and stared up at the dark cliff. The night was silent and the only sound came from the ship's tolling bell.

"You will be safe aboard the ship. It's getting colder out."

The giant ship swayed gently from side to side in the moonlight. Confusion and a sense of the unknown spun in her head as a shiver ran down her spine. "*All right Belinda think this through; there has to be a rational answer of why you can't see the light from the lighthouse and why.*" Her eyes stared. "*An old sailing ship is sitting in the deep water down at the bottom of her cliff.*" A large icy wave smashed into the boulder splashing her. She shivered.

"Lass, you're trembling from the cold," the man said, holding a tight grip on her arm as he gently towed her closer to the small boat. "You were almost killed, tonight. You can't climb back up the cliff in the dark, it's too treacherous."

Belinda, for one of the first times in her life, was unsure of what to do. She knew it'd be suicide to try to climb up the cliff and she sure couldn't stay on the wet boulders. Putting her trust in someone was something she didn't do very often. Trusting a stranger, and one who was weird not only in the way he dressed, but in the way he talked, made her feel as if she'd lost control of her mind. Maybe she had.

Reluctantly her head nodded yes; she didn't have any other choice. "I'll go with you, but just until morning. Then, I want you to bring me back here so I can climb up my cliff."

The man didn't answer; he hefted her off her feet into his arms as if she was a child and moved to the edge of the boulder helping her into the small rowboat. He grabbed the wooden oars. Taking deep strokes he was able to maneuver the small boat with ease letting the rowboat float closer to the tall, enormous ship and next to a rope ladder dangling on the side of the ship. "I'll hold the bottom of the ladder as you climb, but be careful, the ladder is slippery," the man warned.

Belinda grudgingly stood from her seat in the small boat.

Quickly the man reached out with one hand holding her arm to help steady her in the wobbling boat. Belinda gripped the ladder in her hands and gradually she began to climb up the side of the tall wooden ship. Reaching the top of the ship one of the crew grabbed her arms, swinging her like a rag doll over the side of the massive ship literally into a new world.

CHAPTER FOUR

IAN

Belinda stumbled. She grabbed the side of the ship trying to steady herself. She felt the wooden ship's side and gave it a thump with her hand. It was real. This couldn't be a ghost ship. The bright glow from the lanterns hanging around the ship blinded her for a few seconds. She blinked adjusting her eyes as they drifted across the wide deck of the ship. She gulped, staring in disbelief at the old-fashioned ship. Her small body swayed back and forth with the movement of the tall ship from the force of the waves. She looked up. Way above her was where the large beige sails had hung earlier in the evening flapping in the wind, now tied tightly against the tall posts, secured for the night.

The young man climbed over the side of the ship. The crew used a winch and brought the small boat to the edge of the ship, and tied it off; swiftly they pulled up the rope ladder.

The man, a few inches shorter than Johnny, stood by the side of the ship, took a couple of strides with his long legs, and crossed the ship's deck. He gently took a hold of her elbow. "Lass, come this way to my cabin. You need to get cleaned up and some dry clothes on – do you need anything?"

"I'm fine," she jerked her arm from his grip, giving him a gimlet glare. Her right foot patted the deck in a strange rhythm as she gripped her hands tightly on her hips.

At least thirty or more men, in unclean clothes, were peering out every nook and cranny of the ship. They began to jabber in a mumbling roar. A stringy haired man, handlebar moustache, frizzy beard, and clothes hanging loose on his pencil thin body, stepped up. A razor thin scar marred one side of his face from his cheekbone to his jaw giving him an even nastier persona. "Ya don't mean ya are letting de lass stay on de ship, 'tis bad luck an' she's a Jonah?" His voice was icy as he shot Belinda a hard glare.

"Yay, Gerald, I say who stays on the ship and 'tis not bad luck; besides the lass will be leaving in the morning," the dark haired man responded in a cold voice standing taut as a violin string ready to snap.

An older man, with a bushy beard and scruffy moustache stepped from the crowd of men, cleared his throat and everyone became quite. "'Tis rubbish ya are saying, Gerald, the lass brought us good luck in the wretched fog, an' we owe her."

Mumbles, like a wave of voices began again growing louder across the deck.

"Santos is correct, when the lass appeared on the cliff the fog disappeared and we found a safe refuge." The tall man shouted to the men as the mumbles silenced. He turned around to face Belinda. "Lass, it's too cold out here for you to stay on the top deck."

Her blue eyes scorched the icy air staring up at him. "Well nonetheless," she waved her arms in the air. "I'll just stay right here and wait until morning, and then I'll go back up the cliff to see my father," she answered, stubbornly. Her feet stayed glued to the deck as the man tried to grab her swirling arms.

The man pivoted around in a half circle gesturing for one of the crew to come to him. "Ian," shouted the dark-haired man, tightening his jaw clinching his teeth together, "come here." His demeanor did not falter as he kept his gaze locked on her.

A short, chubby, pleasant looking older man with a big smile across his face came bouncing towards them. "Aye, Aye Sir."

"Ian, I want you to see to this lass," the dark-haired man exclaimed in a politely sardonic voice. "I can't seem to understand her. Please, take her to my cabin, clean her wounds, and see to whatever she needs."

"Yay Sir," Ian responded, "I'll see ta her."

"I will be with the crew tonight," the dark-haired man added shaking his head back and forth turning and walking over to the crew.

Belinda glanced over her shoulder at the captain. He was justly suspicious of her. She opened her mouth to reply, but quickly shut her mouth with a snap. She could feel the stares; the eyes of all the crew were on her. She turned her face hiding from the men, but her eyes did swing back to the one man named Santos who had defended her. A crooked smile grew on his weathered face and his head ducked in a small nod.

Ian walked up to her wearing the warmest smile across his face. "This way, lass," he said softly gesturing with his hands and doing a slight bow to her. Lightly he touched her left arm. She gave in letting him lead her to a dusty brown colored, weathered door on the front end of the ship.

They entered into a dark, cool room; a whiff of musty stale air took her breath away making her gasp trying to breathe. A chill trickled down her spine. Belinda stood at the door's entrance. Her eyes darted around the room. She couldn't believe her eyes.

Everything was as it was in the old days, just as the outside of the ship. There wasn't any evidence of anything modern.

Ian scurried around the room turning the wheel that lit each of the oil lanterns that were hanging on small metal brackets on the walls, letting their flames illuminate the room in a soft orange glow. Then, the short chubby man began to straighten and tidy things, picking up papers and dirty clothes that were strewn around the room.

"Please lass, sit down, an' relax," he said, his arm pointing to a worn, cloth chair sitting next to a row of windows on the front of the ship. "We all saw how ya fell down that rock cliff. That had ta have been terrifying. What were ya doing on a cliff like that in the middle of the night, if I may ask?"

"I saw your ship early in the evening and heard your bell ringing, thinking you needed help," Belinda answered. She sighed. "I'm waiting now for daylight, so I can go back up the cliff to my home."

"What home?" Ian stopped working and turned his face to her. "Lass, there ain't anything up on the cliff."

"Yes there is, my home and my father are up there, and I've lived there my entire life." She stomped her foot giving him a frowning look. "I wish you'd all stop telling me there isn't anything up on the cliff," she pleaded. She finally gave in and plopped down in the old chair.

Ian quickly grabbed a small blanket and gently wrapped it around her. "That's all right, ya need ta get some rest, but first I need ta see ta yer wounds."

"What wounds?" Belinda asked watching the short-legged man continue to bustle around the room.

He stopped moving. "The ones on yer arm," Ian replied, his head nodded pointing at her arms. He walked to an old wooden bureau, pulled open a drawer and lifted out a small square box.

"Oh," Belinda gasped, peering down at the palms of her bloody hands and arms. Her new sweater was covered in blood and her arms and hands pulsated with searing pain. She'd been so terrified falling from the cliff, meeting the odd man and boarding the strange ship, she hadn't realized how badly she was hurt.

"Is that a first aid kit?" she questioned.

The box top flipped open. Her eyes became huge and her body shuddered seeing what was inside. The box was full of cloth bandages. Her stomach churned and she gaged, holding the back of her hand to her mouth, when she smelled the ugly looking, gross ointment lying next to the bandages.

"A what? 'Tis some salve ta help yer arms heal."

"I think I'll be fine," she gulped for air pulling her arms back away from Ian.

"'Twill heal yer arms up fast, y'll see," Ian assured. He smiled at her as he busily scooted a straight back chair directly across from her and sat down. The wrinkles gathered around his sincere wide-set gray-blue eyes and his round face was lit, full of compassion, as his hand gently reached for her arm.

She reluctantly lifted her arms out in front of the man. Carefully, Ian pushed the torn sleeves of her sweater up on her arm. He squeezed an old rag from a bowl of water and tenderly he began to clean the dirt, pebbles, and blood from her cuts and then spread the ointment on her wounds wrapping and tying the old bandages of rags snuggly around her arms.

The oil lantern's incandescent flames shimmered on the walls in the small musty room as Ian meticulously doctored her arms. Her head throbbed and her stomach continued to churn; this couldn't be true. Was she really sitting on an old sailing ship with an eccentric man washing her cuts with dirty looking rags and putting stinky ointment on her arms? Maybe she was dreaming, but the pain of her wounds felt real.

"There," he said lightly patting her arm, "that will feel better in the mornin' an' now ya need ta get some rest," Ian said kindly. He rose to his feet. He reached out his hand.

She reluctantly placed her hand in his and stood from the cloth chair. He led her to another door.

"Lass, the captain's quarters are this way," he said patiently, opening the door showing a small bedroom.

Ian's small feet shuffled into the bedroom and pulled the woven coverlet down on the bed. He quickly lit another oil lamp hanging on the wall, turning the flickering orange flame very low. The short, wooden bureau drawer creaked open and he pulled a long, dingy striped sleeping gown out and laid it on the bed.

"Ya can change inta this nightshirt – out of those wet clothes." His head inclined pointing to the nightshirt. "It'll make ya more comfortable." He then pulled a folded white shirt with a ruffled collar from the drawer and placed it on the bed. "Y'll need a clean shirt ta wear tomorrow – now, is there anything else I can get ya?"

She shook her head no, looking around the room in the dim light.

"If ya need me I'll be outside yer door, ya just call," Ian said kindly, "an' I'll come running."

Her eyes panned the room. "Whose room is this?" Belinda asked.

"Why, `tis the captain's room."

"Who is the captain? I want to speak to him."

"Ya already have. He is the one that saved ya tonight."

"That man that was rude – is the captain of this ship?" she snapped spinning around looking Ian in the face scrunching her eyes.

"Yay, he is one of the fairest men I've ever known."

"Well, you must have not known many fair men in your lifetime, Ian."

"Ya need some rest, lass," Ian said. He wasn't going to discuss the captain anymore. Ian turned and walked toward the door. His head ducked. "G'night. Rest well."

The door closed. The old chair crackled when he sat down near the door.

She checked the lock on the planked door. The new sweater she'd gotten for her birthday slid past her bandages. She sighed seeing the sweater was ruined. She shook the large gown, or sleeping shirt, put it over her head, unzipped her jeans letting them slide off and laid them on the chair's back to dry. She lifted the piecework quilt lying on the bed and shook it, making her sneeze. The staleness of the room was overpowering and it had a horrible stench.

Slowly, she climbed into the old feather bed making the bed ropes squeak, and snuggled down into the gray, lumpy mattress, fatigue taking over. Lying there in the quiet night, she listened to the sea splashing against the side of the ship.

Well, Belinda, you sure have done it this time. What in heaven's name had she thought, climbing down the cliff in the misty fog to find a ship she didn't even know existed? She'd done some dumb stunts in her time, but this one took the cake. She shivered. Her recurring nightmare of falling had come true. She laughed; Johnny would be having a heyday trying to untangle this mess. She had to believe that tomorrow things would be back to normal and she'd take the scolding and lectures from her father and Johnny about thinking before you act. Exhausted, she rubbed her head from side to side against the feather pillow, but eventually the swaying of the ship gently rocked her to sleep.

The morning light spread across the bed coming through the small round window on the side of the ship. Belinda woke disoriented, her brain foggy. She felt the bandages on her arm and looked around the room. She moaned. Oh, her nightmare was continuing. She lifted her head from the pillow letting her eyes adjust to the dim light in the room. She lay quietly in the bed; the room was just as the old days. The bed and furniture were vintage pieces, nothing modern. Trinkets and an antique clock sat on a wooden shelf at the back of the room surrounded by a small spindle rail. Sitting at the end of the shelf was an old looking beige picture in a silver frame of a tall, thin man standing next to a dark haired, dark skinned woman. The woman sat in a velvet chair holding a small boy who was about two years old. The curly, light brown haired man had the same chiseled shaped face as the captain. Next to the door, a wavy glass, oval mirror hung over the short bureau and a wooden straight back chair sat at the end of the bed holding her jeans. Not much space was between the bed and bureau. The room was so different from her oversized bedroom in the old Victorian home.

Belinda jumped out of the small wooden bed that was tightly secured against the sidewall of the ship. Her fingers rubbed the top of the bureau. *"Could use a touch of lemon-oil and a good cleaning in here,"* she thought, wiping the dust off of her fingers onto the nightshirt. She lifted the long white ruffled shirt from the end of the bed slipping it on along with her dried jeans and tennis shoes. She felt her arms; they'd hurt during the night, but did feel better. Her reflection in the wavy mirror grimaced back at her. She was a true mess; dark circles were under her eyes and her ponytail hung crooked to the side. She really could use the bathroom, needing to pee, but wasn't sure where it was. She'd be home soon so she'd be fine.

Quietly, she opened the small cabin door and stepped into the main room, the one she'd come into last night. An odd, square wooden plate loaded with food and a funny shaped two-pronged fork were sitting on the large table in the center of the room. Next to the plate was some strong, hot coffee in a wrinkled tin mug.

She pulled out a straight-backed chair from the table. Her stomach growled while she scooped the food as fast as she could into her mouth.

A series of taps struck the cabin door sending out a dull and hollow sound throughout the room. Belinda winced when the door swung open with a creak. She leaped from the table. Ian silently walked into the cabin with a big grin on his face. "Aye, lass, good y're awake. I was just coming ta check on ya."

At that moment, the ship lurched, tilting to the side.

"What's happening!" she shouted nervously, grabbing the edge of the table trying to stable herself from the swaying of the ship.

"We are setting sail, 'tis mornin' an' the captain is getting us away from the rock cliff, as soon as possible."

"What," yelled Belinda? She ran to the cabin door flung it open and out onto the top deck.

"Weigh anchor!" came the cry from the dark haired captain standing at the huge ship's wheel.

The massive chain with the gigantic anchor creaked and water swished from it as the crew finished tying the anchor off. The beautiful beige sails began to rise from their tied positions. The captain spun the huge ship's wheel and the ship began to move tilting to the other side. Men scurried past Belinda busily preparing the ship, not paying any attention to her.

Belinda's temper flared as she dashed across the deck to the captain. "I told you last night that when morning came I wanted to climb back up the cliff," she yelled! Her arms frantically waved in the air. "Where are you taking me?"

"Blast it lass, would you please stop yelling and waving your arms like a windmill flying through the air?" said the captain with incredulous disdain. A muscle twitched in his temple as he tightly gripped the ship's wheel, staring down at the wild girl in front of him.

"No, I won't calm down! I told you last night I wanted to climb the cliff to go home." Her eyes drew up to his dark and intense eyes. "Don't you understand anything?"

His dark eyes narrowed and his thin lips gathered. "Yay, lass I understand I had to get this ship away from those rocks. When the sun came up I had to move her – you'll be fine, and would you please quit yelling."

"Why didn't you wake me and take me back to the bottom of the cliff," she shouted, "and where are we going?"

"You ask a lot of questions," he snapped.

He raked his long fingers through his hair showing his dark eyes. "I'm going to do my job if it is okay with you. I have a load of cargo and a crew of men that depend on me doing my job. I can't wait for you to climb your cliff."

"Then, where's the ship going?" asked Belinda, her voice teetered on the verge of cracking.

"We're headed into the bay of Harbor Towne, Maine like we were last night when the fog mysteriously came in and then seemed to just disappear," he answered his dark face growing redder.

"Harbor Towne – oh, that's alright," she said nervously biting her lip. "I'll get a ride back to my house from ole Joe at the dock."

"Good, so you're through yelling?" the captain asked squinting his dark eyes. He looked down at her and the redness of his face disappeared.

"For a while," Belinda added, looking up at the tall, dark skinned man. He was a different sort; not only his dark, reddish-brown skin so different from the rest of the crew with their lighter freckled skin and light hair. He did have patience, but was obstinate. He was also clean-shaven where most of the crew, or at least the older ones, had

37

long ratty looking beards. She didn't understand why the captain was so hateful. Taunting her last night and arguing that her home and lighthouse wasn't on her cliff.

Ian was standing by the door of the cabin, grinning broadly. Belinda turned from the captain, hurrying past Ian back to the room to finish her breakfast. Ian didn't say a word to her and just followed her into the cabin.

"This is good," she said taking another large bite of her breakfast polishing off the food in record time. Belinda looked over at Ian watching as the man continued to clean the room. "What was my breakfast called?"

Ian stopped working and smiled at her. "yer meal is called scrapple; 'tis cornmeal an' headcheese."

"It's very tasty," she nodded in approval, looking up at the round man who was moving quickly around the room. "Thank you Ian for breakfast." She wiped her mouth, stood up and meandered around the room trusting this whole episode would be over soon. She'd be home in time for lunch, understanding her father would be worried about her, but everything would be all right when she got home and things would be back to normal.

Ian spun around with a big grin covering his face. "Would ya like ta watch this beautiful ship dock at the harbor?"

"That sounds nice, Ian," she said, "and thank you, for all of your help doctoring my arms – they do feel better."

"Y're welcome lass," Ian added in a calm voice that had a bit of British and southern accent. "Oh my, I should change the bandages on yer arms before we get ta the harbor an' dock."

"That's alright. I'll let my father take care of my cuts. Thank you anyway for all of your help," she added crossing her arm and tucking them away from Ian.

"'Tis no trouble lass," Ian assured. He walked back to the chest and picked up the small wooden box along with the stinky ointment.

Ian led her over to the cloth chair by the front windows and squatted down in front of her. Reluctantly, she held out her arm. He slowly removed the bandages that were saturated in blood, but the cuts and scrapes were beginning to heal. He added more stinky ointment and put clean bandages or old rags on her arms and hands.

"There my dear, that should heal satisfactorily," he said, tenderly patting her arms. He picked up the ointment and dirty bandages and scooted his chair back.

"Ian, I need to go to the restroom."

"Restroom?" he questioned with a puzzled look.

"Yes, the bathroom."

"Lass, I don't understand."

"I need to pee," she said getting agitated. This was ridiculous. She looked around the room. She was on a ship and most of the men sounded British. "The head, the loo," she added.

Ian's head nodded yes. "Aye, a necessary."

"A necessary?" *What the hell was a necessary?* She nodded her head yes, whatever Ian wanted to call the bathroom was fine with her.

"Yer chamber pot is in the captain's quarters."

Ian led her into the captain's quarters over to the chair sitting in the corner of the room. He lifted the seat or the lid.

She gasped shuffling her feet backwards falling against the side of the bed. Her body shook and her fingers pinched her nose. She now had figured out where the horrible odor in the room was coming from. There, sitting inside the chair was a commode or chamber pot in a wooden box.

"No, this isn't right; don't you have a modern bathroom?"

"Modern bathroom?" he blurted, "What such a thing is that?"

"That's ok; I'll wait until we get to the dock. Ole Joe has a decent bathroom," she said slamming the seat of the chair shut.

Ian shrugged his shoulders. He turned around and left the room. "Now, are ya ready ta go an' watch this lovely ship dock?"

"Yes Ian, that'd be nice," she answered nodding her head she agreed.

Ian led her out on the top deck over to a wooden box where she could sit and watch the ship as it sailed into the harbor.

Belinda watched the irritable captain who was standing at the wheel maneuvering the vast ship to port. The captain tightened his eyes staring back at her. She shot him a nasty look, but held her tongue, at least for the time being. The tall ship sailed pass the huge cliff she'd been on last night. She loved this bay and she'd maneuvered her own small boat into the port many times past the same cliffs.

The cliffs all look beautiful after the misty night; so grand with the morning sun shining bright on them and casting shadows against their sides. She was surprised she couldn't see her lighthouse. Her excitement grew. She stood and walked to the front edge of the ship leaning over the side.

The captain gave her a big glare and Ian rushed over. "Please, lass sit back down on the box until we get the ship docked. 'Tis dangerous fer ya ta stand that close ta the edge of the ship, ya might accidentally fall overboard."

She nodded her head, understanding that Ian would never disobey the captain. She turned around and scrunched her face at the captain. He was treating her like a child or one of those women in town that she despised, who could only sit pretty as a china doll in a rocking chair on the front porch.

She was amazed watching the captain as he brought the vast ship into the port steering it precisely without new modern technology.

Her heart began to race. Her body shifted uneasily on the box and her hands anxiously twisted together.

No! What was happening? The boats and ships in the harbor were from years ago, nothing modern. The ship was nearing the other tall sailing ships as it docked, but they were all from the past just like this one – something was wrong.

CHAPTER FIVE

1788

The crew dropped the scuffed, wooden gangplank against the ship leading to the pier. The captain covered the distance between them in two strides and stood next to her. "Ian will be escorting you back to your home. I appreciate you trying to warn us last night. I'm sorry it has been so difficult on you."

"Thank you for helping me," Belinda said in a calm voice, her eyes peered up into his dark eyes. She knew the captain had apologized and he did save her life last night. Patience hadn't been one of her stronger attributes. She gave the man a long steady gaze. "Captain, my name is Belinda, and thank you again for saving me when I fell from the cliff."

"'Twas my pleasure, Miss Belinda, my name is Sinjin," he added with a hint of smile on his face showing his dimples.

Belinda whispered, "Sinjin."

"I hope you find your home and your father very soon – good bye," he said in his precise British accent.

He didn't seem like your ordinary captain, he was so uncharacteristic for a captain of a sailing ship – so proper. He carried himself with an air of confidence; too much confidence for her liking. She gave in and smiled back. He was very handsome with his broad shoulders and muscular arms and so different from anyone she'd ever met. She sighed inwardly hoping she'd never see him again.

Sinjin did a bow, and as he walked back to the crew she saw a look come on his face. He was as thrilled as she was, for her to leave the ship.

"Are ya ready, ta go home, lass?" Ian questioned with a big grin on his puffy face.

"Please Ian, call me Belinda."

"Sure lass, I mean Miss Belinda," he answered with a chuckle.

Ian's laughter was infectious making them both laugh.

"Alright, Miss Belinda," he said briskly, softy holding onto her arm as they headed down the worn plank to the dock.

She stopped and pulled her arm away from Ian. She didn't move. She stood frozen on the dock. "Oh, Ian where's the ship's store and old Bob, the dock's Irish setter, Neptune's father? Something's wrong, old Bob is always ready to meet new comers to the dock; and where is Whiskers the cat? He'd never miss a chance for food; he's always waiting for a treat when a boat or ship comes in. This isn't right," she mumbled, shaking her head.

Belinda held onto Ian's forearm as they continued to make their way up the hill to the town. When they reached the top of the hill, she spun around in a circle taking in everything. She looked back where she'd come from and where she was headed as her mind swirled faster than her body.

"*Alright…*" she moaned, "*Belinda get a grip.*"

A tiny rustic town stood in front of her, but... What had happened? Maybe she was dreaming, or had hit her head as the captain said. Maybe she did fall down to the rocks and was still lying there on the boulder hurt and unconscious. Could this be a dream? She pinched herself. "Ouch, that hurt," she snapped.

Ian stood quietly watching her with a questionable look on his face.

Her eyes stared down the street. *No this is definitely not my town,* she thought. She wanted to scream! Nothing was the same; small-planked buildings lined the cobblestone road. Her mind whirled and she thought it was going to explode as a pounding sensation was drumming in her head. This had to be a dream and she'd wake up soon. She stared at the small wooden buildings parallel to Main Street. It was odd that the tiny buildings were in the same place where Stan's Hardware, Miss Johnson's Dress Shop, the Dime Store, and the feed and seed store should be, but nothing familiar was there. Further down the road were tiny homes huddled together next to a small whitewashed church with a short steeple that contained a church bell. Where were the paved streets, gas stations, noisy cars and trucks, and stoplights hanging from poles in the intersections?

"Ian, aren't we near the cliff I fell from last night, Franklin's Cliff. We sailed into the harbor; into Harbor Towne Bay this morning – right?"

"Certainly, Miss Belinda, 'tis Harbor Towne, but I don't know of a cliff named Franklin's Cliff," Ian assured, pointing toward the sea. His brow wrinkled and his eyes squinted looking at her with a worried face. "Miss Belinda is something wrong, are ya alright? Ya look pale."

"Ian, this isn't my town. I don't know where I am." She wasn't going to cry, but she felt confused. Even in the cool air sweat trickled down her back. Her head continued to throb, and loneliness was overcoming her. She felt as if she had gone insane, maybe she had gone mad, or maybe she'd died.

The buildings along the street were from the past, years and years ago like in her history books. They were built out of timber and were frame with clapboard siding, and sloping saltbox roof additions.

But they looked new, like they'd just recently been built. The town was a miniature town and there weren't any cars or trucks around, only dirt and cobblestone roads with horses and buggies riding back and forth along the roads. There wasn't anything modern in the entire town.

Ian ushered Belinda up to the first building nearest the docks. A wooden sign hung above the porch, with the name *Hudson's General Store* painted in red crooked letters, squeaked as it gently swayed in the breeze. She moaned, remembering Mayor Hudson's family had owned a general store that'd opened in the early 1700's when the town was established. She'd seen old pictures hanging in the general store that looked just like this building, but that couldn't be.

Belinda stepped on the wooden planked porch and peered in the front window of the store. Wooden bins and barrels full of merchandise sat around the tiny room. A Merchant stood next to a counter talking to a small group of men who were dressed in clothes of the past. They wore long sleeve shirts with vests, and funny shoes like those that the ship's crew wore. New irregular size candles draped over ropes dangled from the ceiling across the room, and oil lamps similar to the ones on the ship, hung on the sidewall; everything from the past.

A brawny man, face big and round with jowls like a hound dog, stood on the porch of the general store talking to a short fat man. The burly man stopped talking and grinned down at her. His eyes flowed from her head to her feet but slowed down as he gazed at her chest. "I see, Hudson, ye got some new merchandise in de store," he said with his head cocked to the side examining her. "I jes might have ta purchase some." The burly man let out an atrocious laugh as his hand came down to grab her arm.

Belinda's mouth sprang open. Ian jerked her from the porch and away from the man. Her head flew around, her eyes giving the short-necked man a mean glare. "Ian, how dare that man talk like that in front of me, treating me as if I were an animal for sale. Where's the police station?"

"Miss Belinda, we don't want any trouble, ya need ta be quiet."

"Well, I don't want to cause any trouble, but Ian, I haven't seen that building or store before. Where did it come from?"

"Miss Belinda, that store has been right here since we've been coming ta this port an' our ship delivers merchandise ta the store. Let's keep walking y'll see something familiar ta ya. Ya must still be confused; maybe ya did hit yer head when ya fell down that cliff." The look on his face told the whole story that she must be crazy, but he was very kind and didn't come right out and say it.

They left the general store and Ian threaded his way through the crowded street with people busily going in and out of stores. He stopped for a few minutes to peer into a shoemaker's building, an apothecary, a workshop, and even a small tavern that was hectic with men coming and going. Women wearing homespun vintage dresses and carrying baskets full of vegetables from the open market hurried past them, but nothing was familiar to her.

Belinda stopped walking and whirled around staring up and down the street. Her head shook back and forth

"Miss Belinda, we'll find yer home, don't worry, maybe y'll see someone ya recognized," he said as he puckered his mouth apprehensively.

All right, there had to be a rational explanation. The ship had gone into another cove and someone had recreated the port into the old days of the past. It was all realistic and the town even had the stench of animals and horse manure, not the fumes from the exhaust of cars and trucks. Now she'd just play along with Ian since she figured the ill-tempered captain was playing a joke on her for yelling at him.

"What year is it Ian?"

"What Miss Belinda?" Ian asked curiously.

"What year is it Ian?" she asked again.

"`Tis 1788, Miss Belinda, are ya alright?"

"Did you say 1788, Ian?" She grabbed her head letting it shake back and forth trying to get control of her feelings. *Now, calm down Belinda this can't be real.*

"Yay, Miss Belinda, `tis 1788," answered Ian with a bizarre look.

She felt dizzy and her stomach was queasy, but she had to remember this was a joke the captain was playing on her. She pondered what Ian had said. It couldn't really be 1788. Someone must've found a place to recreate the old shipping days for tourists or maybe someone was going to make a movie here. That had to be the answer and this was the replica of the town.

"Are ya alright, Miss Belinda? Let's go ta the boarding house an' get some food. I can hear the church bells ringing an' we need ta eat. `Tis twelve o'clock," he added.

"That sounds fine, and then we need to go to my home on the cliff. My father will be worried about me." She stopped walking. "Ian, I still need to pee. Is there a bathroom near here or a necessary?"

Ian nodded his head yes and crossed the road. Belinda slowly trailed behind him. He spun around and grabbed her arm jerking her, just in the nick of time, out of the way as a man yelling obscenities on a galloping horse barreled past, missing her by only a few inches.

She coughed swinging her hand in the air swishing away the cloud of dust that the horse's hoofs had kicked up. "That son of a bitch!" She tightened her hands into fists waving them in the air. "You dumb-ass watch where you're going!" she shouted wiping the dust from her face and clothes.

Ian's eyes grew wide. He stood rooted to his spot with a stunned look on his face. "Miss Belinda," he snapped in a high voice.

"Sorry Ian, but that man almost killed me."

"Yay an' ya do need ta be more careful. This way Miss Belinda," he called out headed in a quick pace dashing in between some buildings.

Belinda stopped walking and gasped. Directly in front of her was a little wooden shack, an outhouse. She'd seen a few old outhouses that were still left around her town. One old leaning outhouse was at Miss Margret's house on Ansley Street, but no one used them anymore.

"Don't they have bathrooms for the tourists and workers?"

"Miss Belinda, what is a tourist?"

She shook her head. Ian needed to get away from the ship more often and learn things. "Never mind," she said pinching her nose as she rushed inside the tiny framed house. She couldn't wait any longer and her options for finding a modern bathroom were running out.

Ian led them back to Main Street. Belinda lagged behind Ian and looked up at the sign on the building that they were standing in front of, *Miss Neil's Boarding House*. The planks of the porch moaned when Ian stepped up on them. He opened the front door and she walked inside.

Belinda stood for a second in the doorway staring. The scraped pine floors were scared from men's boots and a massive stone fireplace was against the back wall burning logs, crackling and flickering light throughout the dark stuffy room.

Women dressed in long cotton dresses, white aprons, and white caps on their heads sat in straight back chairs around the room. A woman, vigorously spinning thread on a spinning wheel sitting in the back corner of the room, looked up when they entered the room. A couple of the women stood staring at her and left the room in a huff. She smiled to herself thinking of the image of her wearing a large men's shirt, torn jeans with her hands and arms bandaged to her elbows.

Ian gently took her elbow leading her into the small dining room and to a long table with benches along each side next to the front window. Belinda sat down at one end of the bench. She looked around the room seeing a vintage cupboard in perfect condition positioned against the back wall laden with food. She took in a deep whiff of air smelling the aroma of vegetable stew and fresh baked bread.

"Miss Belinda, I'll get yer food. What would ya like ta drink?"

"Ice tea sounds nice, Ian. A good tall glass of tea would be refreshing."

Ian clinched his jaw and peered down strangely at her and the woman cleaning the room spun around. "We do not have tea," the woman answered in a huff.

"'Tis alright, Miss Neil, she meant that she'd have some cider," Ian quickly added, "right Miss Belinda?" His head ducked in a nod.

"Yes, cider will be fine, Ian,"

Ian walked to the cupboard picked up a wooden dish and placed a pewter bowl on top. He lifted up the ladle from the porcelain tureen slowly dipping the thick stew into the bowl. A large woven basket of fresh warm bread wrapped in a large white tea towel sat in the center of the table.

Ian placed the tin cup full of cider next to the bowl of stew. Belinda felt the eyes from Miss Neil burrowing into the back of her head. She couldn't believe that they didn't have ice tea and Miss Neil didn't have to make a federal case about it. Ian fixed his bowl of stew picking up a mug of ale. He really was earning his pay and she hoped he was paid extra for putting up with her.

She buttered a piece of bread and peered up at Ian. "How long have you been going out to sea?" she asked taking a bit of the fresh bread.

"I have spent most of my life on voyages since I was a young boy. My father was a seafarer all of his life," he answered slurping his stew. "Sailing is in our blood. Our family has always been able mariners, an' we love the sea."

Belinda kept chewing the bread, nodding her head yes, she agreed.

"I been livin' on a ship darn near my whole life an' I could not think about livin' inland," he added with a far off look taking another gulp of his ale.

"I've heard that when the sea brings you in and you fall in love with it, then it'll never let you go. You are a part of the sea for the rest of your life."

"'Tis true Miss Belinda," he added slurping up the last drop of stew in his bowl.

Belinda turned her head to the window. Just like the western movies at the drive-in, men rode horses up to watering troughs next to the wooden sidewalk, leaped off and tied their horses to the hitching post. Other men helped women, dressed in long calico dresses, down from buggies. Everything was realistic – even the children were dressed the same as in the movies. This town was very authentic down to the oil lamp lighting. She leaned her head over next to the window searching the landscape. It was odd there weren't even any telephone or electric poles in the town or out in the countryside.

How could this town have been built so close to where she lived and existed without her hearing about it? She'd eventually solve this dilemma, as soon as she made it home. Her father would explain everything. He would have a logical answer. She just hoped the captain would have a good laugh and this would be over soon.

The vegetable stew with fresh baked bread covered in homegrown berry jam was delicious and she ate every bite of the stew plus a couple of pieces of bread.

Ian's face beamed watching her eat all of her stew, as he finished his cup of ale, but he never said a word about how much she ate, always a gentleman. "I'm glad ya enjoyed yer dinner; it was good root vegetable stew. There is some apple pie, if ya'd like."

"Ian, you get some pie. I'm enjoying sitting here looking out the window."

He scooted his chair back scrapping it against the pine floor and crossed the room to the cupboard. He sat down and began to gobble his large piece of homemade pie smacking his lips. He grinned taking the last bite of his pie, and leaned back in his chair. Now it was time to pay.

She leaned over the table next to Ian placing her hand on the table patting it lightly. "Ian, I don't have any money, what do we do?" she questioned anxiously.

"I'll pay don't worry, Miss Belinda. I'm glad ya enjoyed yer meal," He said kindly.

Ian pulled some strange coins out of his pocket and spread them out in his hand.

"Ian, what kind of money is that?" she snapped staring down at his hand.

"Well," he said taken aback, "this is a piece of eight, or doubloon, an' this one 'tis a shilling that I am going ta use ta pay fer our meal. I also have a half-cent, half-dime, an' a dime, an' oh, here are a couple of "bits" an' a "two-bit.""

"What is a bit?"

"A two bit is 25 an' a bit is half. I should think, Miss Belinda, ya would know that. Are ya shor' y're alright?"

She stared at him as he paid Miss Neil. Belinda knew she was pushing Ian's patience, but he was the one playing the joke on her. He took her arm leading them out of the dining room through the boarding house and out onto the porch.

He stopped moving. His head swung back and forth looking up and down the street. "Which way do ya live?" he asked kindly letting go of her arm.

"I live on Franklin's Cliff, the cliff that I fell from last night."

He began to walk across the street. "Well," he announced. "'Twill take some time ta get that far back out ta the sea."

She followed close behind Ian as he crossed the road. This time she paid attention, dodging men on horseback and buggies rumbling past that were racing down Main Street. Her eyes became fixed on the sign on the building in front of them, *The Livery Stable & Blacksmith*.

"Ian, I can take a cab and my father will pay the driver when I get home," she called out dashing over to him.

Ian stopped walking, letting her catch up. "A what? What did ya say? That's all right we'll be fine they have a buggy ta use." He quickened his pace.

"I," she called to him, "can take a taxi cab home, and then you can go back to the ship."

"The captain said I was ta stay with ya until ya are home safe with ya father an' I'll never disobey the captain's orders."

He stopped next to the livery stable's huge doors and a hefty man approached him. Ian extended his hand to the man for a shake. They spoke for a few minutes and then he handed the man one of the coins from his pocket that he had just shown her. The man pivoted around and did a loud whistle. A young boy about thirteen years old led out a spotted brown and white horse pulling a black leather buggy from the livery stable.

She sighed knowing Ian was stubborn and she couldn't change his mind. Anyway, this could be fun and it would be interesting to watch her father's face when they arrived at her home in an old fashion buggy.

The burly man scowled helping her into the buggy as his eyes stared at her clothes, just like all of the other people in town. Ian climbed up into the buggy's seat making the buggy wiggle back and forth. He picked up the reins and gave them a little whip and they took off down Main Street through the center of town.

Nearing the edge of the small town the horse began to trot, riding pass homes and the whitewashed church, and turned east onto a dirt road lined in squatty trees. The day was calm and a soft breeze blew from the sea as Belinda sat listening to the horse's hooves clip clopping in a soothing rhythm. Her body relaxed against the wooden seat believing she'd be home soon. This episode would be over, and it would become a tale she'd tell Johnny on their walks on her cliff at night.

Ian tugged the reins and the buggy jerked to a stop bringing her thoughts back to the present. "Where do we turn from here Miss Belinda?" he questioned.

Her eyes scanned the countryside; she didn't see anything that looked familiar.

"The blacksmith at the livery stable told me how ta get this far out ta yer cliff, but he said there ain't any roads past this one an' nothing was out this way. I'm sorry he said there ain't a lighthouse on the cliff. The men in town are talking ta an architect in Boston about building a lighthouse on the cliff; they hope very soon."

Her heart raced. Something was wrong. The landscape seemed the same, but everything else was different. "Turn left, keep going straight and we'll see the lighthouse soon."

The buggy kept traveling through the tall grass weeds straight to the outcropping of the cliff.

"Stop!" Belinda yelled.

Ian jerked the reins and the buggy jolted to a stop. She leaped from the buggy running as fast as she could to the ledge of the cliff. She knew this cliff rock for rock – that hadn't changed. This was her cliff. She'd walked around this cliff most every day of her life. She spun around in a circle taking in everything, but the house and lighthouse weren't there. A knot of fear grew in her stomach and air sucked from her lungs. Belinda wiped a bead of perspiration from her forehead.

She raced through the tall weeds to the cliff's edge and peered down. She stood at the exact spot where she had been last night, before she slid down the cliff to the ship. She stomped her feet. Yes, this was the same ledge and the path that she'd used all of her life, but... Where were the lighthouse and her home? She scanned the cliff. Her eyes landed where the lighthouse should be standing.

She yelled, "No!"

What had happen and where was her father. Maybe she was dreaming or maybe as Sinjin said she'd hit her head and needed to wake up or maybe she'd died. No, she wasn't dead. She wiggled her arms; if you're dead can, you feel your body? A dream – that had to be the answer. This was a dream or nightmare and she would wake up soon and everything would be back to normal.

She moved to the round rock shaped like a chair that she'd scratched her name in when she was seven. She studied the rock, but there wasn't a name on it. It had to be her rock there wasn't any other answer. She turned and looked back at where the lighthouse and house had been last night. Even the large tree in the front yard of the house was gone.

"Dad, where are you?" she yelled loudly. Nothing happened. "Dad!" she continued to shout.

She sat down on her special rock and thought about the lighthouse and a touch of panic grew inside of her. Her pulse beat hard and fast in her neck. Her body stiffened. Her ancestor William Franklin Brady, an architect from Boston who Franklin's Cliff was named after, didn't build the lighthouse on Franklin's Cliff until the year of 1793. Could she really be back in time to the year of 1788 and could the architect the men in town were talking about be William Franklin Brady? Then, if that were so, the lighthouse wouldn't be here.

Was she really in the past? How could something like this happen? How could she get out of this nightmare and get home? She had to have gone mad; no one could travel though time. Her head began to spin looking up at the fluffy clouds floating in the sky and her body twirled and dropped to the ground.

CHAPTER SIX

THE MYSTERIES OF TIME

S injin stood over Belinda gently placing a wet rag on her forehead. His eyes took in her long, silky yellow curls swirled around her beautiful creamy face and her tiny body dressed in such strange clothes. He'd never seen a woman wear men's breeches. The white shirt swallowed her, but he could see the outline of her body underneath, her small shoulders, the curves of her round breast and her tiny waist. Her smooth long fingers gently lay placed on her stomach. She hadn't moved for the last hour softly breathing. Her demeanor was intriguing – both fierce and delightful.

Belinda's eyes slowly opened. Her hand swung to her throbbing head. Her brain was muddled and hazy. She remembered the world spinning and looking out at her cliff, but it wasn't her cliff anymore. She pulled in a deep sigh. She was now back on the ship in the captain's quarters, lying in the feather bed that she had slept in last night.

Sinjin quickly turned his head to avert his eyes from staring down at her.

She bolted upright. "What's going on?" she shouted shoving his hand and a rag from her head. "What's happened to me?" Her body tensed and her sore muscles screamed in pain.

Sinjin stood up straight and swallowed hard. "Would you please stop yelling, you'll be fine, but you aren't going anywhere and I don't have an explanation of what's happened to you," he said in a disconcerted tone. "Now, do you believe me that there isn't anything on the cliff?" he questioned in a strong voice staring down with a look of bewilderment on his face.

"No! My home is on Franklin's Cliff – don't you believe me?" she insisted starting to sob. She couldn't find her home nor her town or her father. That was her rock and cliff, but the lighthouse and home weren't there. Where was her father? Tears kept coming and she couldn't stop crying. She turned her face from Sinjin.

His dark eyes glared down on her with a doleful look. Sinjin cleared his throat struggling to find the right words. "I've never heard of Franklin's Cliff and I won't argue with you anymore about a home on the cliff." He laid the wet rag on her forehead. She pushed his arm back from her shooing him away. Sinjin stepped back from the bed. "I thought if you went back to the town and saw the cliff it'd make you understand that there isn't anything on the cliff you fell from. I thought it might make you remember where you lived."

"I don't know what's going on. Ian said the year is 1788. Is that true or are you joking with me and trying to teach me a lesson for yelling at you this morning about taking me back to my cliff?"

"I'm not doing anything but trying to help you. `Tis the year 1788 and there isn't a lighthouse on the cliff, please believe me."

She leaned her head back against the wooden headboard. "I live in the year 1959 and there is a lighthouse and a keeper's house on the cliff. I live with my father and my dog Neptune. My father is the keeper of the lighthouse. I have lived there my entire life." She studied his face. It was difficult to see his expression clearly in the dim light of the oil lamp.

"I know you believe that there's a lighthouse on top of the cliff, just as I believe there isn't a lighthouse."

"Then, how do you explain my clothes and shoes? Look at my new charm bracelet that I just received for my birthday. You don't have anything like this," she blurted out showing him her bracelet that Johnny had just giving her.

His finger rubbed against his chin and a small muscle twitched working overtime on his brow. "Yay, you were wearing strange attire when you arrived in the mysterious fog."

"My time of 1959 is so different than yours; we have airplanes that fly high in the air like birds next to the clouds, and telephones that let you talk to people from across town, motorized vehicles, trucks, and cars that you can travel in without horses, and record players, and radios that play songs. It's a wonderful time."

"You say in your time people fly like the birds? 'Tis more than my mind can absorb," Sinjin said overwhelmed. He became quiet taking in the young girl in front of him. He rolled his shoulders to release some of the tension growing down his back. He'd never been around many girls in his life, since he'd grown up on the ship with the mates and gone to an all-boys school in London for a few years. Dealing with a tall sailing ship was a lot easier than dealing with a female, and he was sure this female was going to be trouble.

Belinda laid her head against the soft pillow. Her hands continued to grip her head pulsating with pain. She was still incredulous as she wiped the tears in her eyes. Could she really have gone back in time; the words struck a chord deep inside her that it couldn't be true. Maybe she was still dreaming or maybe she'd died? She kept pondering. What does it feel like to be dead or do you feel anything?

"Ian brought you some chowder; he is very worried about you. After you finish your meal, you need some rest. You've had a shock and maybe falling down the rock wall was harder on you than you thought. You need to keep up your strength. We'll solve this riddle," Sinjin assured offering a weak smile. Those black eyes peered down at her. "You are welcome to stay on this ship until you sort this out. You fell off the cliff trying to save us, so the crew of the ship owes you our lives. When another mate saves the life of someone, the other one owes him his life, forever."

She felt so disorientated; her fingers trembled as they moved a strand of wild hair from her face. "I didn't do a very good job trying to save you and you didn't even need saving, plus you also saved my life. But, I'd like to stay here until I can come up with an answer." Again, she didn't have any other choice; fate had made her decision for her.

"It won't be a problem and I'll move into the great cabin to give you my sleeping quarters," Sinjin assured. "Now you need to get some rest. You've had an exhausting day." He turned to the bureau and carefully handed her the warm bowl of chowder. "Finish your chowder." He stared. "You don't want to disappoint Ian. Good night, Belinda," he softly whispered, quietly closing the door.

She finished the chowder, snuggled deep into the feather bed trying to hide from the world. Her mind kept replaying the night before. She couldn't fathom the absurdity of it all of why or how she'd fallen into the whispering fog or what her life was to be like living without her father and Johnny. She had to believe tomorrow she'd wake and everything would be back to normal and she'd be back in her own time and the dream would be over, but she just hoped it wasn't a nightmare.

Sleep finally came to her. Waking the next morning, her eyes stayed closed for a few seconds hoping she was in her bedroom in the old Victorian home. The mustiness of the room told her she was in the captain's quarters and everything was the same as it had been last night. She lay there wishing with all her being that she was back in her time with Johnny and her father. But, it wasn't to be. Her life had always been one of wonders, never a dull moment, but this time her impetuousness of climbing down the cliff in the misty fog had become a nightmare and she didn't have any way to fix what she'd done.

She scrambled out of the lumpy bed peering out the door; sitting on the large table was her breakfast. She picked up the spoon eating the bowl of porridge while her eyes explored her new home.

Ian quietly opened the door a wide smile spread across his face. "Good mornin', Miss Belinda. I hope ya slept well?"

"Good morning, Ian. Yes, I did and I do feel better. Thank you for all that you did for me yesterday and thank you for the breakfast."

"Y're welcome, what would ya like ta do today? Do ya want ta go exploring in town?"

"I don't think that would be a good idea, Ian, so I am going to stay on the ship." She looked down at her torn jeans. "Ian, there is one thing I'd like if it's not too much trouble."

"What can I do fer ya, Miss Belinda?"

"I would like to get some new clothes, if that is possible."

"Yay that won't be a problem. We can go ta the Mercantile Store this mornin'. They have some nice dresses ta fit ya."

"Oh, I wasn't thinking about a dress. I want to wear pants."

Ian jerked to a stop. His mouth flew open.

"I was thinking about wearing what you and the crew wear, if that is alright?" She smiled looking at his reaction. His face twitched nervously. "I'm not used to wearing dresses, and if I am staying on the ship for a while I need to dress like the crew, so I can help. I also don't want to stand out so much."

Ian continued to stare at her, his face sequenced up making creases on his brow. He finally found his voice. "There's extra slops in the slops chest. If'n ya want I can get ya some – if ya shor' that's what ya'd like ta wear?"

"What's a slops chest?" she asked.

"That's where we keep clothes fer the crew."

"That sounds great if you don't mind and I'd like to change my clothes as soon as possible."

"I'll be right back with ya clothes," he answered leaving the room.

Her breakfast was just about finished when Ian knocked politely and opened the door. He walked over to the large table piling clothes on top.

"These will be perfect, thank you Ian. What did you call these clothes?"

"The breeches are called slops, an' they're made from canvas."

She picked up the stiff, wide leg pants that came to the knee, and striped shirt. Tracing the collar with her fingertips she noticed the precise hand finished seams – not machine made clothes. Lying along with the pants on the table was a short vest with buttons running down the front and a pair of long black socks.

"Those are stockings we wear with shoes. This time of year, we all have ta wear shoes. In the warm months, the captain doesn't require shoes. Those are nice an' warm, the captain buys nice stockings."

"If it's alright I'd like to wear my tennis shoes?" she asked, examining the hard leather, squared-toed shoes just as the captain wore.

"'Tis fine, ya can wear whatever ya'd like," he said grinning.

She held up the handkerchief. "Why does everyone wear a handkerchief around their necks?"

"'Tis a neckerchief an' it's used when 'tis hot or ta tie back our hair," he replied.

"Alright, what kind of hat is this?" she questioned, holding the black, triangle, leather hat in her hands.

"'Tis called the Tri-corn ta wear inta town. There are two jackets, two waistcoats, two breeches, four shirts, two frock coats, two pairs of longer trousers, two pairs of shoes, two pairs of stockings, an' two hats."

"This is all of my clothes?"

"Yay, 'tis what every mate gets when they join the ship."

"This will be perfect, thank you Ian."

She scooped all the clothes into her arms and went to the captain's quarters throwing the clothes on the bed. She slipped off the long white shirt and her torn jeans. She lifted the pitcher full of water off the top of the small bureau and poured some into the wooden bowl. She dipped the rag in the water and squeezed it out. Washing her face, she made the streaks of tears left on her cheeks from last night disappeared. She looked over to the chair in the corner. This was now her modern day bathroom; her indoor plumbing and sink - a chipped round wooden bowl with water, an old rag, and a chamber pot as a commode.

She buttoned the blue shirt and slipped the breeches on. She turned to the wavy mirror hanging over the bureau and began to laugh. She didn't recognize herself in the strange clothes. She stepped back and smiled having to admit her body wasn't real curvy so she was able to hide what shape she did have under the men's clothes, making it difficult to tell she was a girl. She wasn't very tall so the breeches hung down longer than they did on most of the mates. She thought about the ship's crew and how much shorter they were than the men she knew in her time. Sinjin was one of the tallest of the men and he still was shorter than Johnny by a few inches. She reached down pulling the stockings on her feet bringing them up to her knees and quickly tied her tennis shoes.

Belinda looked into the mirror. Dark circles showed under her eyes, but she wasn't worried about her looks. She'd never used very much makeup, only on Sundays when she and her dad went to church. She smiled, knowing she had her mom's smile. She laughed at herself letting her golden hair fall down onto her shoulders. Her head shook staring at the messy mass of spiraling thick, blonde curls that she'd inherited from her father. She also had her father's blue eyes, his nose, and shape of his face seeing him every time she looked into the mirror. She picked up the wide tortoise-shell comb from the top of the bureau, drew the comb through the tangled mess and then French braided her hair, tying it with her black neckerchief.

She slipped the vest on, tugging it to fit; now, she was ready to show Ian. Her hand turned the doorknob on the wooden door swinging it open and quietly walked out into the other room.

Ian, standing by the long table, twirled around to face her. His mouth flew open wide like a baby bird waiting for a worm.

"Ian, you need to close your mouth," she laughed at the expression on his face. "Now," she paused for a second as she nervously tugged on her vest, "it's time to go outside and see what everyone thinks about my clothes." She wiggled, the clothes were itchy and stiff, but she'd get use to them already missing her soft cotton sweater. She jerked the door open, stopped and grinned back at Ian and walked out onto the upper deck. The crew spun around mumbling. They tripped over each other not taking their eyes off of her.

Sinjin standing at the ship's wheel gawked in disbelief. Finally, he crossed the deck to her. "What in God's name are you doing dressed like that?" he shouted. He knew having a female onboard a sailing ship would be trouble with a crew of men, but never in his wildest dreams figured this would be the problem. He looked back at the crew. "Get back to work," he shouted at the men. The crew scrambled racing around the ship, but their eyes were still on Belinda.

"You told me I could stay on the ship, and this is how everyone is dressed, right?" She snapped back at him twisting the edge of the vest with her fingers.

Sinjin's narrowed eyes stayed focused on her. "Yay, but you don't have to dress this way. You can go into town and get some women's clothes. That wouldn't be a problem, and Ian will help you."

"I don't want to wear women's clothes," she said in a matter-of-fact way grinning up at him. "Then I couldn't help with the ship." She stood up straight trying to make herself taller.

He wiped the beads of sweat glistening on his upper lip with the sleeve of his shirt. "What do you mean help with the ship?" A frown line grew on his brow.

"You ask a lot of questions," she said giving him a stare, holding her own. "I want to learn about this huge ship and I can do work just as the crew does. I know all about the lighthouse and how to take care of it, so why can't I help with a ship?"

"I see it won't do any good to argue with you and I'm too busy right now. We'll be leaving the harbor tomorrow and then you and I will talk." He stared with one of his gazed stares he was always giving her.

"Well," she moaned, "can I stay dressed like this?"

"Yay, you can wear those clothes and learn about the ship, but you have to be careful and remember there are a lot of dangerous things on this ship."

"Thank you Sinjin, oh, I mean Aye, Aye, Sir," she chuckled, happy to be getting her way. She turned around and briskly walked back to the room to find Ian. Her hand grabbed the doorknob; she stopped before entering the room and gazed back at Sinjin.

Sinjin shook his head, a frown on his face, but she saw his lips quirk into a smile.

The crew unloaded cargo yesterday and now they were loading new cargo onboard the ship. She knew she couldn't lift the heavy wooden barrels, but she had a new plan.

The cabin door squeaked as she pulled it open. Ian was rushing around the room rolling up charts and picking up the captain's clothes; he stopped and looked up at her.

"Ian, can you teach me about the ship? Where and what things are called? Sinjin," she laughed, "I mean, the captain, said it was alright." Her body slid down into the cloth chair by the window. She sighed. "I know I can't go alone to explore the ship, he wouldn't like that."

"If the captain approves then it shouldn't hurt an' it'd be good fer ya ta know where things are located. I'll be right with ya as soon I finish this chore. Ya jes sit an' don't touch anything," he said, swinging his head from side to side worriedly. He hurried back to his work of putting away charts, journals, and papers on the desk.

She sat on the top deck patiently waiting for Ian to finish his work. Her head leaned against the side of the ship watching the crew prepared for their voyage tomorrow. She couldn't believe she was really sitting on an old sailing ship. She wasn't worried at the present the reason why or how she was here in this time or whether this was a dream or if she'd died. Oh, she shuddered, could she be dead and be on a ghost ship. She finally smiled seeing the crew's eyes following her as she walked around the ship. They were as interested in watching her as much as she was in watching them.

Ian popped his head out the door of the cabin. "Alright, Miss Belinda, come in. I guess we should start right here." He picked up more charts laying them to the side. "We are standing in the great cabin. This is where the captain works an', of course, now sleeps."

Ian pushed the door open to her bedroom "This is where the captain of the ship is supposed ta sleep, but 'tis ya room," he announced. "That is called the berth where ya sleep an' the round window on the side of the ship is the porthole. That is a looking glass an' the only one on the ship," he added pointing to the mirror. "None of the crew is allowed in either room unless the captain lets them in. I'm the only crew member allowed ta come inta both rooms."

Ian puffed up as he began to brag. He looked taller than five foot one. "I'm the cabin boy. The Captain needs someone he can trust an' I have known him all of his life. Ya are very lucky ta be using these rooms an' the captain is very kind. Most captains wouldn't give up their sleeping quarters, not fer anyone." He quickly turned heading out the door, moving around fast for a short, chubby man.

"This ship is called a Frigate. It is a full rigged ship," he said swinging his arms out wide. "She has three masts that have square sails. The topgallant mast is the tall vertical pole, which supports the sails. We have several topgallant masts an' that is the Jib or foresail, the triangle shaped sail forward of the mast."

He bounced across the deck. "Here's the ship's bell that tells when we are anchored in fog. The one ya said ya heard the other night."

Belinda's hand rubbed the iron bell remembering its bong resonating up the side of the cliff.

"The bell tells us when it's time ta switch the crew. Ya are not ta ring the bell unless 'tis an emergency."

Ian's face became solemn. "If ya hears a ship's lonely bell ring in a storm," he did a huge gulp, his eyes grew wide, "then someone aboard the ship is gonna die."

"Oh," Belinda moaned quickly removing her hand from the bell.

Ian's arm gestured to the front of the ship. "'Tis the bow the forward part of the vessel." He continued to swing his arm pointing to the sides of the great ship. "'Tis the starboard an' the larboard sides of the ship. The stern is the rear of the ship. She's a beauty, ain't she," said Ian with a huge smile on his face.

"Yes, she is Ian," Belinda agreed, her eyes panned the ship as she mumbled the names starboard, larboard, stern, trying to remember everything Ian said about the ship.

They quietly walked over by Sinjin and Ian whispered in a quiet voice. "'Tis the helm an' the captain is the helmsman."

Sinjin didn't look up or say anything busily he kept checking his compass.

Ian walked to the bow of the ship leaving Sinjin to his work. "There are two chase guns on the weather deck. The rest of our armament is down below."

"Ian, has the ship ever used those guns?"

"Yay, I'm sorry ta say, many times." He cleared his throat. "We can go ta the quarter deck an' lower deck if ya'd like an' y'll be able ta see the galley."

She followed Ian to one of the ships hatches. They made their way down some steep steps that Ian called a ladder, into a dark musty compartment. She blinked her eyes trying to get them to adjust to the gloominess of the dank interior spaces, the belly of the ship. Oil lamps dotted the narrow corridor's walls bathed in shadows and casting a dim orange glow. Her fingers rubbed the ancient, bare wood of the passageway feeling its roughness. They peered into a small room, the galley. But, they didn't stay long when the cook, a short fat, bald headed man busily preparing the noon meal, wheeling a large knife in the air, grunted and looked sternly at them.

Ian stepped into a tiny room with a tiny bed, a tiny chest of drawers, and a straight back chair. "'Tis my home," he said proudly.

Ian and the captain were the only two mates onboard that had beds. Ian's trundle bed was very narrow compared to the captain's bed. She understood how lucky she really was to be able to sleep in a bed. The crew was sleeping in hammocks, which is what Sinjin was sleeping in now in the great room.

Ian tenderly picked up a small frame from his chest of drawers. "'Tis my daughter, Amanda," he said proudly.

"Ian she's lovely." Amanda had a round face shaped like Ian's, the same gray-blue eyes, perfect smile, and thick curly brown hair. Belinda smiled looking at Ian with his gray, wiry hair believing many years ago he'd had the same brown hair.

They climbed back up the steep staircase and stood on the top deck.

She took in a gulp of fresh air. "Thank you Ian for showing me around, and I agree it is a magnificent ship."

"Y're welcome; Miss Belinda, I'll explain more as we leave the port." He smiled and turned hastily going back to his duties.

Belinda watched the crew load all of the wooden barrels into the hatches on the ship putting them down deep in the hull.

Sinjin stood on the dock talking to some of the men from town. The men were discussing taking their load of merchandise to Boston, Charleston and even as far south as St. Augustine. The men didn't notice her watching them, but Sinjin did and gave her one of his strong stares. She'd learned that stare from their first meeting and it meant she had to follow orders.

Her body fell against the ship's wooden side and slipped down to the deck. "*Wow – so that's where the ship would be heading, first to Boston then to the Carolinas and Florida.*

Her heart sank. She now understood where the ship was headed. She hadn't thought about how far the ship would travel and how long it would take them to get to another port. Could she leave her home and her father? She didn't even know where her home was. She could try and stay in this town, but she didn't have any money or a place to live. Her choice was made. This was to be her life, living onboard this ship, at least until she unraveled this mess. She was going on a true voyage.

Without streetlights, the evening came with swiftness as the crew finished loading the ship; most of them had the night off preparing to go into town. Sinjin, Ian and a few others remained onboard.

The night grew darker. She scooted to the side of the ship peering out at the small town sitting up on the hill. She'd never realized the degree of darkness without electricity or the light from her lighthouse. Now, for some reason this was her world, a world that she didn't understand. How could someone travel through time; was that even possible? She felt lost, so alone missing her father, lighthouse, and the life she had.

Old sailing ships sitting in the harbor were busy with their crews getting ready to set sail early in the morning. A few ships were navigating into port settling in alongside the other ships before total blackness took over. It was as Ian had said. *They give themselves a wide berth between the ships moored ta allow space fer movement of the tall ships.*

She snuggled down in the worn chair in the great cabin tucking her legs up under her. She lifted *The Canterbury Tales,* a book she'd found on the shelf in the cabin, in her hands and began to read. It was quiet on the ship with most of the crew in town, but she could hear voices talking on the top deck. She heard Ian's voice above the rest. "Captain, the crew is excited about goin' inta town tonight ta drink their grog," his voice became soft; "we might have some problems."

"Aye," Santos answered, "but 'tis a good thing ta let the crew blow off some steam an' the rum will only stir `em up fer a while. They'll be fine. Lucky went along an' he'll keep `em in order."

"Yay, Santos," Ian replied, "but who'll keep Lucky in order." A mounting of laughter came from the men.

Her eyes tired. Too many thoughts swirled in her mind so she laid the book on the small table next to the chair.

Lying in her bed in the captain's quarters, she heard the crew coming onboard, talking, laughing and singing, knowing they had enjoyed their grog. Her mind continued to replay what had happened over the last couple of days, trying to make some sense out of everything, but there wasn't any logic or answer. Whether this was a ghost ship or real didn't matter, since she was really going on a journey on an old sailing ship. She truly didn't understand what that meant, but was soon going to find out.

CHAPTER SEVEN

SANTOS

The tall ship began to sway, waking her in the early morning barely past dawn, just as it had done that first morning when it was sitting down at the bottom of her cliff. She leaped out of bed grabbing her breeches and top. Quickly dressing she hurried out on the top deck to watch the crew maneuver the huge ship out of the bay not wanting to miss a single minute. Now, the ship was *getting under way*, as Ian had said. She watched in amazement how the crew and Sinjin swiftly maneuvered the ship with such preciseness.

Her eyes misted over blurring her vision when she stared at her wonderful cliff. A sense of yearning, of longing, plagued her as she watched the ship sail past Franklin's cliff and maneuvered out into the open sea. She looked over her shoulder. Out of the corner of her eye, she saw Sinjin watching her reaction.

"Are ya alright?" Ian questioned in a sympathetic voice.

"Yes, Ian," she answered her voice trembling. She still couldn't believe that her lighthouse and home weren't on the cliff. Tears built in her eyes; her heart was breaking, but she wasn't going to let anyone see her cry. She turned her face to the cliff, wondering when and if she'd ever be going home. Her body tensed and she whispered in the calm morning, *"goodbye Daddy, Johnny and Neptune."* She hoped someday to see them again.

Ian reached over and put his arm around her seeing the pain in her face. He had been caring, even though he didn't understand what had happened, but never asked any questions. His little round nose scrunched. "Would ya like some breakfast? We have some bonded jacky."

"What Ian! What did you say you had to eat?" she answered in a high voice.

"Bonded jacky or sweet cake, sorry, Miss Belinda, I fergot ya did not know the name," he replied grinning from ear to ear.

"That's alright, Ian, I do want to learn what everything on the ship is called. No thank you, I'm not very hungry. I would take a cup of coffee please."

"Yay, I'll be right back, Miss Belinda."

She laughed watching Ian's fat body bounce around on the top deck. He moved with ease with the swaying of the ship in a staggering walk across the old wooden deck. That was something she had to get used to, walking while the tall ship pitched back and forth.

Ian reminded her of her father. They had a lot in common, about the same age and had very similar personalities. Ian was a little shorter and chubbier than her father and bald on top of his head. His curly gray hair around the side of his head stuck out framing his chin and neck. Both men were like two mother hens hovering over her.

Ian's voice was sad when he talked about his daughter, the girl in the picture from his cubby. He hadn't seen his daughter in a few years and missed her dearly. His marriage hadn't worked because he loved the ship so much, and his wife didn't want to share him with the sea. She understood how he felt, missing her father and her life. She knew Ian were taking care of her as if she was his daughter, and it did take the sting of loneliness away.

The early mist lightly touched her face as she sat on the top deck in the warmth of the morning sun.

She watched the cliff grow smaller and smaller on the horizon. Stabbing pains of loneliness grew in her heart and she hoped someday to go back to her time, to her beloved cliff and lighthouse, to her world.

"Ian, I love listening to the crew whistling. What's the song they're whistling?"

"'Tis an old sailing song, *The Singing Breeze*. Miss Belinda, whistling on a sailing ship brings us good luck an' a strong breeze."

"Ahhh," she moaned.

"Miss Belinda is something wrong?"

She chuckled. "No Ian – I can't whistle."

Ian let out a roaring laugh. "That's not a problem we have plenty of mates that can whistle very loudly, especially Lucky, an' he can even carry a tune."

"Lucky?"

"Yay, he's the tall mate right over there."

Belinda's eyes swung to a young man who was working to the side of the ship. The honey-wheat haired man, his hair curled at the nape of his neck, was devastatingly handsome. He had broad shoulders tapered to a thin waist. Lucky turned towards her. She gasped when he dipped his body in a bow and a mischievous grin spread across his strong face. He smiled and then began to whistle a beautiful tune as his icy-blue eyes continued to stare back at her.

Belinda felt her face heating; she jerked her gaze from Lucky to Ian. Lucky was a different sort and she'd never met anyone like him. She'd been able to intimidate the boys in her town, but Lucky made her mind go blurry. Most of the men on the tall ship were crotchety and older, but Lucky was young and seemed sophisticated like Sinjin. Both men were different from anyone she'd known.

However, Lucky had a warm smile and kindness about him. Where Sinjin, even though he too was very handsome, had a coldness about him; a standoffish feeling came over her when she was around him.

Her head shook bringing her thoughts back. The crew was remarkable putting the finishing touches on the huge beige sails hanging on their mast, turning them to push the ship in the right direction as they flapped in the strong wind.

"The haul wind is ta point the ship towards the direction of the wind, or by an' large which means, by inta the wind an' large with the wind; that is what we're doing," Ian offered looking up at the sails. "She is 179 feet long an' 130 feet high at the main mast an' she drafts 13 feet an' has a very wide beam."

"Ian, did you say the ship is 130 feet high at the main mast?" Belinda snapped back in a high-pitched voice.

"Yay it is, way up there," said Ian pointing to the top sails. "That's called the crosstrees. That is where our lookout sits. Or, on up higher in the crow's nest near the top of the mast. The crew takes turns aloft on the platform fer their watch."

"Interesting," she mumbled. Her head leaned back looking up at the crow's nest. "Ian, have you ever been up that high?" she asked not taking her eyes from the tall mast.

"Nay, Miss Belinda, 'tis way ta dangerous," he added, earnestly trying to change the subject. He'd already learned she wasn't like most young women he'd known. She had an air about her a determination, and no one was going to stand in her way. He quickly left her and hurried into the cabin.

The crew hoisted the enormous sails and used the boom at the foot of a sail for tension on the sail. The sails, flapping like birds dancing, had become taut with the wind pushing them. It was like watching a group of ballet dancers in unison.

She remembered standing on the cliff in the misty night watching the fog bearing down on the ship making the sails disappear.

"Oh," she sighed, her eyes stayed glued peering up at the crosstrees as the tall poles leaned with the ship rocking from side to side. She smiled. She had a new mission; she was going up to the crosstrees sooner than later. She knew she would have to climb the mast when Sinjin was in his great cabin and not where he could see her. Now, she was contemplating her plan.

The first part of her plan was she'd find one of the crew to help her go up to the crow's nest. It'd be very different sitting that high, swaying with the movement of the tall ship and it'd be very dangerous. She laughed. First, she needed to practice walking on the top deck and get her sea legs, from the ship teetering back and forth.

An old, agile sailor, with a gray shaggy mustache and fuzzy beard, long curly silver-gray hair tied behind his head, was climbing down the ladder from the crow's nest with ease. He was the man she'd seen when she first came onboard the ship. The short, about five foot five inches tall, sturdy built man glanced over at Belinda. A crooked smile swept across his weathered face and his thick, bushy arched eyebrows squeezed together. He strolled slowly towards her scratching his rough whiskers mulling over his next move.

His light chocolate brown eyes stared downward at her. "Now, what do ya have in mind Little Mate? I see ya are up ta something by the look in yer eyes," he questioned very bluntly. He sat down on a container next to her, leaned back against the side of the ship, and crossed his arms over his head showing a heart shaped tattoo with the name Clarissa on his right arm. "I am Santos."

"Santos, I remember you. You stood up for me that first night when I came on the ship, when the crew wanted to get rid of me – thank you."

"Aye – ya shor' were a drowned rat, standing there shivering in the cold night. I'd never seen anything like that fog an' I still don't know what happened." His bushy head swung slowly back and forth as he moaned. "Ya climbing down that cliff inta the whispering fog made it disappear an' saved our ship from the jagged rocks."

"Santos – I'm Belinda and I am going to climb up to the crow's nest – very soon," she assured him, staring up at the massive sails. She turned her head to face him, waiting for his reaction to tell her no. "I want to learn how you climbed so high up with such gracefulness."

"Awe, I see, Little Mate, now how do ya suppose y're going ta get away with climbing so high without the captain noticing ya?"

"I haven't quite figured that out yet, but I will – you just wait and see," she assured him.

Santos chuckled. His mustache wiggled and his gray eyebrows tugged tight making the lines around his eyes deepen. "Well, I see no reason why ya can't go up ta the crow's nest an' be the lookout fer the ship." He grinned squinching up his face. "But then again, I'm not the one in charge, Little Mate."

"Well," she paused. "Santos, can you can show me what I need to do and how to climb that high?" She stared into his old eyes with the deep crevices around them, knowing he had eyes like a hawk even at his age.

"Yay, if ya really want ta. Tomorrow, I'll assist ya Little Mate. Ya need ta understand y'll get in trouble – eventually," he said teasingly. He stood from the container extending his arms out wide stretching his shoulders.

"Thank you, Santos," she called out, as he walked over to a small group of mates and sat down, still grinning at her with his old eyes studying her.

The salt air and the bright sun burned her face. She watched the sails being whipped by the wind as the ship sailed smoothly over the open blue water. She leaned her head back against the side of the ship smelling the salty sea air. It was quiet, no planes buzzing or leaving contrails overhead. It was all so astonishing watching the land as the ship cruised by so peaceful. There weren't any buildings, just land full of trees and beautiful rock cliffs. The sun shone down with the white fluffy clouds making dark shadows dancing on the sparkling water.

A strange whistle began and Ian came hurrying past her toward the great cabin carrying her and Sinjin's lunch plates. "Miss Belinda, ya meal is ready," Ian called out.

"Ian what was that whistle?"

"'Tis the boatswain pipe ta tell us it's time ta eat."

The two wooden plates sat on the long table overflowing with deep meat pie full of fruits and spices, fritters, bread, and a wonderful tasting piece of gingerbread for dessert.

After lunch, she walked around the ship practicing her balance in a wobbling walk. A few hours later, the sun began to sink lowering in the horizon. An opaque glow settled over the blue seawaters. Burnt orange filled the sky along with crimson colors firing up in the west as the leisurely day was ending. Sinjin steered the ship closer to the coastline. He knew the exact place to anchorage, dropping the small bower anchor on a large metal chain into the deep water, securing the ship for the night.

The boatswain pipe blew once more and Ian came up from the galley carrying their square wooden plates full of fish and rice. Sinjin drank ale and Belinda had a mug of warm cider with a hint of cinnamon, and for dessert again a piece of gingerbread. She sat quietly across the table from Sinjin, contemplating her mission tomorrow of going up to the crow's nest. However, she wasn't discussing her plans with Sinjin seeing his face was taut, his eyes sad, and worry lines were across his brow. He was a different sort of man, a man of few words.

CHAPTER EIGHT

STORIES

After supper, Belinda settled into the chair by the ship's front windows and heard voices coming from the top deck. She peeked out the door. The moon was illuminating the night showing a small group of the crew fishing and singing old sailing songs.

She stepped out the cabin door; the night air touched her heated skin making her shiver. The crew continued to sing. She crossed the deck and stood next to Ernesto, a barrel shaped man. She looked at the man's wild, curly brown hair surrounding his bearded, craggy face with a wad of tobacco pouched in his cheeks.

"Ernesto, do you mind me joining you?"

He grinned and spat black liquid into a pewter spittoon. "Nay."

"It's a beautiful evening – look at how red the sky is." she added.

Ernesto nodded his head yes, shaking his wild hair. "Yea, 'tis a red sky in the mornin', sailor take warnin', a red sky at night, sailor's delight," explained Ernesto grinning showing his a toothless grin.

"Come on over lass, and have a seat," Lucky called out, pulling another wooden box by the side of the ship very close to him.

Belinda didn't move. Her feet seemed to be glued to the floor. Her eyes ducked down to the deck's floor not able to look Lucky in the face. Again, she felt the heat grow on her face, blushing. "How many children do you have, Ernesto?" Belinda drew her eyes from the floor to look at Ernesto's dark, worn face with deep lines across his brow from years of being out in the sun.

"Aye, three lads an' two lasses back down in Boston."

"Don't you miss them being out on a ship so much?" she questioned.

"Sure, but working on a ship is good pay an' I'm with `em durin' the winter when the weather gets bad. Ansel, over there," Ernesto's head pointed to the side, "has six little mates an' comes from Williamsburg. Of course there is Lucky who hasn't ever married; maybe that's why he's called Lucky," Ernesto said laughing.

"So you'll get to see your wife and kids when we arrive at Boston?"

"Yay, I'll stay one night with `em an' on the way back ta Maine, when we stop back in Boston, I'll spend the winter. `Tis not a bad life fer a sailor."

"Lucky, you don't have a wife or girlfriend waiting for you at home?" she asked looking at him, as he stared at her with those enticing blue eyes.

"Lass, I'm not barmy. I don't have any nippers at home and that is fine with me. That is why I have so much jammy," he added light heartily with an ease about him that she liked.

Ansel chuckled and leaned over by her. "He means luck," he offered crinkling up his wrinkled face, making his dark hair and widow's peak hairline even more defined and pointing toward his long nose.

Belinda gave in and sat down next to Lucky. Her head turned from him – she couldn't look him in the eyes. Lucky was just as unusual as Sinjin, not fitting the profile of a sailor for this time-period. He was a few years older than she, more of Sinjin's age in his late twenties. Very British, tall lean with a heart-shaped face, wide forehead, pointed prominent chin, and those piercing icy-blue eyes that made her blush. You could hear in his voice that he was highly educated, not like most of the other sailors. He had fun on his mind and nothing else and he wasn't about to settle down with a wife and kids.

Ansel began to struggle with his fishing pole pulling in a large flopping fish onto the deck.

"Wow! Take a gander at the monster fish. That'll feed us for a while," Lucky shouted.

Belinda sat quietly listening to the mates telling stories about their journeys at sea. She leaned back on the box near Lucky. She looked up at him, he smiled down at her, and she turned her head so he couldn't see the redness darkening on her face. She knew the stories the men were telling were tall tales, just as Johnny had said on her birthday, but she wasn't one to disagree with them; look at her story. The crew knew she was different, but they didn't seem to mind or question where she'd come from and Santos telling them she was good luck was all it took to convince the crew it was all right for her to stay on the ship.

She felt a stare and her head swung around. Sinjin, his eyes fixed on her, sat alone on the other side of the ship. His eyes would swing toward Lucky and a frown stayed on his face. She knew they were great mates, but for some reason Sinjin seemed to be watching her more closely when she was with Lucky.

Santos began working and repairing a sail in the light of the full moon. She carefully observed how he was repairing the sail with preciseness of years' experience as any good meticulous tailor could do. Santos was a very capable sailor, an old salt and had been on ships his entire life. He thought it was great that she was willing to climb high up to the crow's nest. He told her many of the crew were afraid to go up that high in the swaying of the ship.

One of the mates called her a landlubber and Santos leaned back and let out a roaring laughter that broke the silence of the night. "Mate, she's as much of a Jack as ya are."

Belinda moved away from Lucky and squatted down next to Santos. Her face wrinkled in a curious look trying to figure out what a Jack was.

Ian chuckled. He leaned over and whispered, "A Jack is a sailor, an' that's a great compliment ta be called a Jack by an old tar."

She scooted close to Santos proud that he thought of her as a Jack and hoped she earned that title tomorrow when she climbed up to the crow's nest. A few more songs were sung and a few risqué tales were told from the crew.

She looked at Santos. His crooked grin spread across his face. "Hey Mates, watch the rubbish ya are telling," Santos yelled out. The mates became quiet their eyes stared at Belinda.

She laughed. "You're fine, keep telling the tales," she hollered scooting her back against a wooden box. She'd grown up tagging along with her granddad Elias to the harbor dock and listening to the tall tales the fisherman would tell. She smiled to herself. The crew's tales had more kick with words she wasn't used to and words she really didn't understand.

She felt a stare and her eyes were pulled behind her, but it wasn't Sinjin staring at her. Jervis's deep-set hazel eyes leered at her. She cringed. Jervis was a giant of a man. The tallest man aboard the ship with hardly any neck, thick shoulders, a scruffy baldheaded man with repulsive features. His bug-like eyes kept staring at her in an unnerving way. Next to Jervis was Gerald, the nasty scarecrow looking man who wanted to throw her overboard when she'd arrived during the whispering fog. He wasn't happy Sinjin had gone against him and had allowed her to stay on the ship.

"Jervis is a Jonah, an' the captain needs ta rid the ship of 'em," Ernesto said with Ansel agreeing nodding his head yes.

Ian leaned in close to her. "A Jonah is bad luck fer the ship."

"I agree, I don't like him," she whispered back to Ian, "and he and Gerald give me the creeps."

She was nudged gently in her back. She flinched. She jerked spinning around.

Santos laughed. "Well, good evenin' Captain Monty, nice of ya ta join us," Santos said scooping up the black cat into his arms. "Little Mate, meet Captain Monty."

"Wow," she moaned, "a black cat. Isn't that bad luck to have a black cat onboard?"

"Nay," Ian interjected, "a black cat is very good luck on a ship an' Captain Monty is the best mouser we've ever had."

Captain Monty leaped from Santos's arms and scampered up into Belinda's lap.

"Well, he's a smart cat knowing who ta snuggle up ta," Santos chuckled folding the repaired sail and laying it on the deck.

A young, pale faced boy with freckles zigzagging across his nose and wild fiery orange hair curling over his shoulders, sat down next to her. His baby-blue eyes sparkled. He grinned squinching up his face making a crooked smile and showing his jutted, pointed front teeth.

"Hi, I'm T-Tobias, my f-father is Finley, he's sitting o-over there," the young boy quickly announced pointing to a short chubby man with the same fiery orange hair.

"Nice to meet you Tobias, how old are you?"

"I will be f-fourteen in a few months," he bragged.

Santos patted Tobias on the back. "He's a great lad an' been on the ship since he was a tiny thing."

Jervis mumbled obscenities under his breath to Gerald making fun of Tobias's stutter. Tobias started to stand, his mouth opened to talk, but Santos's hand had a good grip on the boy's shoulder. "The Captain will takes care of that Jonah."

Belinda scooted back against the side of the wooden box ignoring Jervis. She began to hum softly *The Tale of the Black Shadow*.

"What's that yer singing Little Mate?" questioned Santos.

"It's *The Tale of the Black Shadow*, it's about a tall sailing ship that sank near my cliff in the water near Harbor Towne, Maine. I'm surprise you haven't heard the tale; it happened back in 1765."

"I remember that tale," Ernesto called out. "Some mates at the tavern in Harbor Towne were talking about the whispering fog." His dark eyes swung to Belinda. "The one ya got caught in the other night. They said *The Black Shadow* sunk in the waters by yer cliff years ago an' the lot of them onboard the ship died. Now, the crew from *The Black Shadow*, the ones that drowned, call out ta help ships jes like us trapped in the whispering fog. We did hear some strange voices coming from the dark water…"

Lucky leaned over anxiously, his hands rubbed together in a washing motion. Ernesto shook his head no, but Lucky gave him a look. "The lass should hear the tale."

Belinda's eyes were on Lucky. "Lucky, what tale are you speaking about?"

"While we were in town we met an elf-like man. He stood a little over four feet." Lucky laughed. "Even Jessie was a giant next to him. His curly dark, gray hair hid his aged face and black dotted eyes peered out from under his wild hair. I'd say the man was a hundred years or more. The man at the pub said over two hundred years."

"Nay, Lucky, this ain't a tale ta be told," Ernesto interrupted.

"The lass should hear," snapped Lucky

"I've seen dat man before," Gerald said abruptly, "he's called Ebenezer."

"Ya know Ebenezer?" questioned Ernesto.

Gerald stood and moved over to Ernesto. "I know he ain't a man, but a ghost."

"Yer talking nonsense, Gerald," Ernesto replied.

"Yay, de owner of de bar says de man appears then vanishes."

"Of course Gerald, ya'd believe 'em," Santos chimed in.

Gerald nodded his head at Lucky. "'Tis true, take a gander at Lucky's face; he knows de man ain't real." Gerald scrunched his wrinkled face. "De locals say Ebenezer's an old sailor an' his ship sank years ago."

"I agree, the man I met was strange, but a ghost," Lucky added, "I'm not for sure."

"Well," began Gerald, "Santos, y've seen ghost ships. 'Tis where Ebenezer lives."

Belinda moaned and stared at Santos.

Santos nodded his head yes. "Yay, I've seen tall sailing ships appear on the horizon, but as the strange ship approached us they'd vanish inta thin air. Nonetheless, we've felt their breeze an' seen the ships wake in the water." He paused. "I've heard talking an' laughter, voices floating in the open sea as the ship seem ta pass by."

"Then," Ernesto snapped, "The man could've been Ebenezer de ghost."

"Go ahead," Santos interjected, "tell us what the man said."

Lucky sat up straight and his eyes darted to Belinda. "'Tis a dark and misty night in 1764, a mysterious fog crept like a monster crossing the sea eating everything in its path. A tall sailing ship was caught in the fog's trap. Early that evening, a young man named Finnegan, who'd appeared from nowhere had boarded the sailing ship. The golden haired man knew how to navigate the harbor and worked diligently through the night saving the ship, *The Black Shadow*, from a horrible plight."

Belinda moaned and whispered, "Finnegan."

"Finnegan, a kind, energetic man, lived on *The Black Shadow* for a while. The crew believed he was an angel from the sea sent to save them. Finnegan used strange words when he talked and told strange stories about the future. His tale was one of climbing down his cliff and falling into another time."

Everyone around the ship became even quieter and all eyes fell upon Belinda.

Lucky continued his story. "The smile left the elf-like man's face as it twisted into a frown."

"Go on, what happened ta the golden haired man named Finnegan?" Santos questioned looking down at Belinda with her golden hair curled upon her shoulders.

"It seemed later in the year the phenomenon of the mysterious dark fog happened again when the ship sailed into Harbor Towne. The crew of *The Black Shadow* worked through the long night, but when the dawn came, *The Black Shadow* and Finnegan were gone. The tiny man never knew what happened to the Irish man named Finnegan, the angel from the sea or why he didn't save the ship the second time."

"I know the ending," Belinda spoke taking in a deep gulp of air. "Finnegan was my great, great grandfather."

"Yay, so the story the old man told could be true." Lucky insisted nodding.

"I believe so," Belinda said with a confused look on her face, "as real as my story. Finnegan told stories around town about falling into the whispering fog in the year of 1846, but no one believed him. He did make it back to his time, so he didn't drown with the crew of *The Black Shadow.*"

The crew gave her a haughty look.

"I wonder how he made it back to his time?" Belinda said in a soft voice. She felt eyes on her. She looked to the side and Sinjin was staring. He had been listening to the story.

"Maybe ya is a ghost like Ebenezer an' yer family boards ghost ships," blurted out Gerald moving over by Belinda. "I knew ya were bad luck."

Lucky stood and stepped in between Belinda and Gerald. "That's absurd, Gerald," Lucky snapped back, "we aren't on a ghost ship, and Belinda saved us from the fog."

"Or, she's a part of de fog, ya just wait," Gerald said moving back to Jervis sneering at Belinda still mumbling in a soft voice.

"Well, the sea won't give up its secret an' y're fine here with us, Little Mate," added Santos.

"Sing, the tale of *The Black Shadow* to us, Belinda," Lucky shouted. "Maybe it has a clue."

Belinda's voice rose in perfect harmony as the crew learned the words and joined in.

***

A voyage from across the sea *The Black Shadow* it did sail,
Laden with its treasure as the fate begins its tale.
The sky was blue the air was cool the water's they were calm,
On its course to Harbor Towne its massive sails were hung.
A mystifying, monstrous fog was a looming out to sea.
The fearless crew fought long and hard as the sea began to heave.
The monstrous fog swirled in the air the troubled ship just disappeared.
Echoing screams crossed the sky amid the ship's bells somber cry.
Silence fell in the early dawn the enormous sailing ship,
The Black Shadow, it was gone.
The sky was blue the air was cool the water's they were calm,
The massive rocks had won the war with debris left along the shore.
There was many a tear shed there was many a broken heart,
There was many a lad so brave that night that found a watery grave.
Many tales have been told when the fog begins to roll,
Alone they call the brave young souls soft whispers from the deep below.

Guarding the sea all through the night warning seafarers of their flight,
The cries continue without an end until the early morning light begins.

***

A couple of hours later Belinda opened the door to the great cabin. Sinjin was working on some charts spread out across the large table, in the blurry light of the oil lanterns. He didn't pay any attention to her. She sat down by the window, not feeling as lonely as she had earlier in the day, looking out into the dark night with the full moon shinning down on the water sparkling like tiny bubbles. She had a lot to think about; if Finnegan's story was true, and she believed her story was real and she wasn't dreaming, then there was a way to go home. Gerald talking about Ebenezer being a ghost and traveling on ghost ships gave her the creeps. She looked at Sinjin. Could this be a ghost ship, and everyone be ghost? Oh, this was too much to comprehend. She had to keep thinking positive; now, there might be a way to return to her time. If Finnegan found the answer so could she.

She snuggled in the chair and sat quietly as she studied Sinjin. He was very handsome, tall, dark skin a strong chin and high cheekbones, so different than most of the crews, but she still wasn't able to figure him out.

She stood from her chair. "Good night, Sinjin," she called out going to the small cabin's door.

He didn't look up. "Good night, Belinda."

She smiled; tomorrow would be an interesting day as she looked back at Sinjin.

CHAPTER NINE

A JACKARO

Another early morning came quickly as sunlight glistened on the water once the sun began to rise. Belinda sat up in bed when the ship began to wobble like a toy in a bathtub. She fell back in the bed moaning. She'd been sleeping peacefully snuggled deep under the stack of quilts. Remembering her plan this morning, she leaped from the bed and dressed in a hurry.

The wooden plate of breakfast, cornmeal pudding, sat on the long table waiting for her. Finishing her meal, she pulled open the cabin door, stepped out onto the deck, and saw Sinjin standing at the wheel steering the ship. This morning was the same as yesterday and after the ship got underway, he picked up some charts to work on and went into the great cabin.

Belinda's head tilted back peering up at Santos sitting high above the ship looking down at her with his special crooked grin. His body flowed with ease in the crow's nest, leaning so effortlessness with the swaying ship.

Santos's wiry body climbed down the long ladder and strolled over by her. "I see y're ready Little Mate. Now, while y're up in the crow's nest, ya need ta keep an eye out fer other ships, whale's, rocks, or anything strange. When it's ya watch y're called the barrel man; if ya see anything call out ahoy."

She nodded, she understood.

"Alright," Santos began, "listen carefully. This is called hand over fist," he said demonstrating how to put her hands tight one after the other gripping the ladder. "It's the best way ta hold on ta the ladder. Y'll get the hang of it, no worries, an' just let yer body lean with the ship."

One of the mates cupped his hands together giving her a leg up. Her hands gripped the rope ladder that was squeaking against the mast. Sweat beads formed on her brow even in the cool morning as she made her way up the ladder. Her body trembled. Her heart was beating faster and faster feeling the mast sway with the movement of the tall ship. She slowed her breathing trying not to hyperventilate, but she became so excited seeing the incredible view that she couldn't get her breath. She sat on the small plank feeling free as the wind hit her face and ruffled wild strands of hair against her neck. She closed her eyes for a second listening to the sails flapping in the breeze.

Her fingers gripped around the spyglass that Santos had given her. Her eyes panned the shoreline's brown, rocky bluffs jutting out to sea like pointing fingers. Deep hidden coves dotted the landscape encompassing the blue turquoise waters of the Atlantic. The white, fluffy cottony clouds formed into cartoon shapes leaving dark shadows on the water and changing patterns as they floated seamlessly out to sea. She'd never seen anything so beautiful in her life.

She thought of Johnny. If he could see the ocean this magnificent maybe he'd understand her love for the great water. Using the tip of her finger she wiped the tears glistening in her eyes – knowing that would never be. She wondered how many old sailing ships had sailed past her cliff in the last hundred years, just as she was doing now, the barrel man staring at her lighthouse taking in its beauty and grandeur. Her eyes studied the horizon. It seemed the blue sky and water came to a sudden end. She understood how so many men had thought the world was flat and if they ventured too far out in the water they'd fall from the Earth. Her body snuggled against the mast. She smiled to herself thinking this was one of her most elaborately concocted schemes she'd come up with in a long time. She sighed, wishing Johnny could see her now. She was enjoying her time so high above the ship, however…

The great cabin door swung opened. Her body froze stiff as a board. Sinjin stepped outside glancing around the deck. For the next thirty minutes, he went about his business and at first didn't become aware of her, but for some reason he looked up.

A red color grew on his dark face and she thought smoke was going to come out of his ears. He screamed for her to get down. The leather cord of the spyglass swung over her shoulder and her hands grabbed the rope ladder, just as Santos had shown her. She could see the crew watching from around the ship's deck with grins on their faces.

Sinjin reached up grabbed her off of the ladder and sat her down next to him. His hand shoved the great cabin door open dragging her inside. The door slammed behind him as he pivoted around to face her, his brown eyes stared downward into her blue eyes.

Sinjin scowled. "What do you think you're doing?" His voice erupted loudly as he shouted and his face became redder. "Are you trying to kill yourself like you almost did the other night on your cliff?"

"No, I am not trying to kill myself!" She stomped her foot and pulled her shoulders back trying to stand taller. "I love to climb and I love heights! I was careful and I'm a good spotter; I have great eyesight! Why won't you let me help?" Her hands swung with each word she was saying. "I'll be very careful climbing and I'll pay very good attention, I promise!" she yelled back at him gripping her hands on her waist. "I'm a great watch for the ship." She kept jabbering. Her eyes squinted at him. "I love it up there, you can see forever."

He stood for a few minutes his mouth tightly puckered and those dark eyes stared. "I don't like you climbing that high; it is dangerous up there." His head shook and he moaned again pacing the room. "I'm not sure this is a good idea, but I know I can't stop you since you're too obstinate. So you'll only stay for two hours at a time once a day. You'll have the dog watch," he proclaimed, his hands flying in the air as if he was swishing a fly away.

"Thank you," she said in a calm voice, grinning at him.

His arms continued to swing wildly in a circle as he left out the cabin door hurrying over to the other side of the ship with the crew.

She proudly followed Sinjin onto the deck into the bright sun and sat down by Santos. Many of the crew ducked their heads nodded and grinned at her.

Santos tilted his head back against the side of the ship. His laugh boomed out to sea. His thick mustache wiggled like a plump gray caterpillar on his upper lip. This time his coffee brown eyes twinkled proudly. "Well I hear ya get ta do a dogwatch," he said. "I knew he'd give in an' y'll soon get ta go up an' stay as long as ya want as barrel man, just be patient. I was correct y'll be a great Jackaro."

"Okay, I've heard about Jack, but what is a Jackaro?"

"Listen ta the song an' y'll find the answer."

***

"There was a silk merchant in London he did dwell
He had only one daughter an' the truth ta ya I'll tell
This young lady she was courted by men of high accord
There was none but Jack the sailor would ever do fer her

As soon as her waiting maid learned what she did say
She went ta her father an' there she did betray
Dear daughter if this be true what I have heard of ya
Jack shall be vanished an' ya restrained ta
Poor Jack has gone ta sea with trouble on his mind
A-leaving of his country an' dearest love behind
She went inta a tailor shop got dressed in men's array
She went onta a boat ta stow herself away
She smiled as she answered they call me Jackaro
Your waist is light an' slender yer fingers neat an' small
Yer cheeks ta red an' rosy ta face the cannonball
I know my waist is light an' slender,
My fingers are neat an' small
But I never changed my ways ta face the cannonball
She traveled all around
Her beloved boy she found
The couple they got married as they did agree
The Jack an' Jackaro lived many years at sea."

***

"Ya see yer name fits, y're a Jackaro."

"How can that be, I don't have a love on this ship, so what does that mean?"

"Oh, my little Jackaro ya do, jes follow ya heart. Ya jes don't know it yet, ya little Jackaro." He smiled and she didn't want to ask any more questions. She could see in his eyes he was up to something. Santos had become her confidant and best mate and he loved the sea as much as she did.

"Thank you Santos for your help," she said excitedly squeezing his arm. "I'll do a good job as the barrel man, you just wait and see."

"I know my Little Jackaro," he assured, standing up from the box to leave.

The day went as the others and she was able to finish her dogwatch. Sinjin didn't look up the entire time she was the barrel man.

The ship set anchor and again the crew fished after supper. She sat listening to the songs and tales; she was becoming a mate after all, a Little Jackaro. She now believed she'd be able to survive living on this ship, but an uneasiness was taking over making her shiver.

CHAPTER TEN

THE BLACK SHIP

For the next few days, each day was the same as the day before, a daily pattern for the crew's lives. She'd seen a few tall sailing ships, with their beige sails taut, on the horizon becoming smaller and smaller as they would disappear from her sight, but it'd been quiet and she'd become complacent.

Sitting high above the tall ship was the best time of Belinda's life, being the barrel man, the lookout for the ship, until one incredible clear day. She was sitting aloft on her early morning watch, the thin pale streamers of white clouds floated by making her feel like she could reach out and touch them. On the horizon she spotted a ship headed straight for the Aeolus. She couldn't make out the kind of ship it was. She could see it was a strange and unusual ship – tall and dark.

"Ahoy, Santos!" she screamed, "There's a large, tall ship with black sails looming out on the horizon heading our way very fast. It has a strange flag flying over it and I can't make out what it says."

"Little Mate," yelled Santos running to the ladder, "come down quickly!"

She climbed down the ladder faster than normal and Santos, a strained look on his face, grabbed the ladder, as the knuckles on his hands turned white, climbing right back up.

Santos shouted his voice ringing out across the top deck of the ship, "Ahoy, pirates coming at us ta the starboard side. Little Mate ring the ship's bell."

A chill ran down her back when she gripped the rope tightly in her hands. Using her entire body she tugged on the thick rope letting the bell ring out loudly. Her heart pounded in her ears with each bong of the bell.

Ansel popped out of the hatch. "Santos, how far away are they?"

"'Tis on the horizon moving at an unwavering pace," Santos yelled back.

The cabin door swung open. "What's going on?" questioned Sinjin.

"Pirates," Belinda shouted seeing Sinjin's eyebrows furrowed as he spun around going back into the great cabin.

The crew, swords drawn and muskets ready, mumbling to each other scattered racing all over the ship.

Sinjin rushed out the door of the great cabin. His long sword hanging by his side clanked as he walked across the top deck. "All hands on deck!" he ordered, "arm the cannons!"

Belinda stood paralyzed. Her head shook no; this couldn't be true. This wasn't a tall tale that someone was telling late at night. These were privateers or buccaneers, thieves, and criminals who were waiting to ambush a ship loaded with cargo and this was real.

"Belinda!" Sinjin barked, giving her his stare and narrowing his dark eyes. "Go to the great cabin, lock the door, and hide. Don't come out no matter what."

Haunted expressions were on the crew's faces as their eyes focused on the pursuer as it closed in on the *Aeolus*. She could see pirates onboard the vessel crouched behind the rails waiting for the ships to come together.

The gun crew, which consisted of Ernesto and Santos, stood at the back of the ship and Lucky stood by the cannon on the bow. His head jerked pointing to the cabin door for her to hurry inside; time was running out.

The doorknob turned on the cabin door, but she stopped for a second watching the massive black ship bearing down on them. She rushed inside the great cabin closing the door and locking it. Her hands grasped together ringing them back and forth terrified, and her stomach twisted into knots. "Please," she whispered, "this has to be a dream and we'll be all right," she prayed in a soft voice; hoping she'd wake up soon back in her time standing on her cliff. She thought her life couldn't get any more complicated, but as Granddad Elias would say, the boiling pot of water she'd gotten herself into climbing into the fog, had just gotten hotter, without a way for her to escape.

Her body trembled as she leaned on the door, wishing she could wake up from this nightmare. Could the crew fight pirates and win? She knew the alternative if they didn't win. They would all be killed.

She'd heard the stories how pirates kill everyone onboard a ship, and then burn it after they've emptied it. Her mind replayed the terror in the eyes of Sinjin. The pirates knew the ship had just taken on new cargo and they were set to win and they didn't have anything to loose.

Cannons fired from the pirate ship. The *Aeolus* shook being hit on the starboard side tilting to the right and knocking Belinda to the floor. She staggered pulling herself from the floor. The cannons onboard the *Aeolus* returned fire making a deafening roar and rattling the windows. She was thrown against the wall of the ship like a ball in a pinball machine. Her head throbbed; she reached up covering her ears with her hands trying to brace her body against the wall. When the next cannon fired from the rear of the ship, she was pitched to the floor and there she stayed crawling around on her hands and knees.

Suddenly the cannons became quiet. A loud thud broke the silence in the deafening quietness and the ship swayed back and forth pushed by the black ship. She could hear the wooden hulls moaned and creak from the stress. She cringed, hearing the yell of the pirates on the starboard side of the ship leaping aboard the *Aeolus*. She crouched behind a chair; there was nowhere to hide, they would eventually find her...

Metal hitting metal and screams of pain were echoing from the deck. She slipped from behind the chair and quietly unlocked and opened the cabin door only a few inches. She peered out the door seeing the large black ship towering next to the *Aeolus*. The massive sails on both ships were swaying in the wind, as they seemed to be fighting for their space.

Scores of tanned faced pirates, a motley crew dress flamboyantly in unusual clothing of crimson, violet, and purple silks, kept boarding the *Aeolus*. Blades clanked; bodies moaned dropping to the deck making her shudder.

A few feet away, a pirate's sword slid into one of the crew's chest causing a crushing sound. Belinda stood paralyzed. The mate moaned, fell to the deck and his terrified eyes peered up at her as he took his last breath.

Piles of dead bodies were growing across the deck. To the starboard side she saw Ernesto, Ansel, Lucky, and Santos fighting, holding their own.

Something caught her eye. Sinjin was battling a grizzly looking pirate near the back of the ship. She gasped; right in front of her was Ian. His round body danced back and forth and his sword clanked against the metal of a large pirate's sword. Ian was still strong at heart, but he was older and the man he was fighting was young and stout.

The pirate's sword thrust in the air bringing it down toward Ian. Ian ducked to the side, but the sword hit him in the arm near his shoulder. The crushing sound of the bone seemed as loud as the cannons that had fired earlier and blood gushed down his arm. His hand went limp and his sword drop onto the deck.

The pirate jerked his sword tugging it out of Ian's arm. Ian's face paled. The pirate smirked, twirling his sword in the air, with the victory only seconds away. Ian's eyes grew wide, a valiant man, but he was going to die a noble man, just as he lived.

"No!" Belinda yelled. Ian wasn't going to die right in front of her. She bolted out of the door and leaped into the air with a whooshing sound, hitting the man in the chest with her feet and knocking him to the deck. The stunned pirate lay still for a second looking up at her. He leaped back up angrily swinging his sword straight at her. "You blasted, son of a bitch."

She swiftly grabbed Ian's sword from the deck's floor, but Tate, a strong mate swung his sword and stabbed the pirate in the back. Belinda's body froze. She gagged watching the blood flow down the pirate's bright shirt. His brown eyes stared up at her as Tate pulled his sword out of the body. The man's thick fingers clawed at her. She stepped back and fell against the door of the great cabin trying to move away from the pirate as he thumped to the deck at her feet.

The sword in her one hand scrapped against the floor as she grabbed Ian with her other hand helping him inside the great cabin. She quickly led him to one of the large chairs by the front windows.

Blood dripped from his fingers onto the wooden floor and his pale face grimaced as he sank into the chair. Getting her composure back, she grabbed a rag off the table putting pressure on Ian's wound. She tied a small rope around his arm as a tourniquet on top of the rag and did a sigh of relief as the bleeding was slowing. His head leaned against the back of the chair closing his eyes for a few seconds.

Holding onto Ian's sword, she cautiously peeked out the door, afraid someone might have seen them earlier entering the cabin.

"Miss Belinda," Ian yelled, "ya need ta stay away from the door an' hide! Get over here by me."

"Ian, stop worrying," she said closing the door.

"Ya need ta hide," Ian added.

"I'm fine, but there are too many pirates and not enough of our crew."

"Please, stay away from the door."

She'd been trained in martial arts for the last few years from one of her daddy's old army buddies, but she wasn't very confident right now, of what she'd learned. Her daddy was worried about her living so far away from town by the lighthouse and wanted her to be able to defend herself, but this was the first time she'd ever had to fight for her life. Her hand felt Johnny's pocketknife in the pocket of her breeches. She slipped it out studying the three blades leaving the longest sharp blade out. Her head shook, Johnny in his wildest dreams wouldn't have thought she'd be using the pocketknife to defend herself from pirates.

The smirks on the pirate's faces antagonized her, and her anger built. She tightened her grip on the sword in her right hand and squeezed the handle of the pocketknife in her left. The door flew open and she rushed outside onto the top deck. She pushed the door closed, hearing Ian's voice yelling for her to come back inside.

A plump, beady-eyed pirate blocked her path. She leaped into the air and her foot knocked the pirate's sword from his hands. Ansel, standing behind the pirate, lunged at him with his sword and plunged into the pirate's back. She gripped Ian's sword in her right hand and the back of her left hand flew to her mouth. She gagged seeing the blood gush from the pirate's chest and ran to the side of the ship throwing up her breakfast. Her trembling body spun around, wiping the spew from her mouth. Thoughts raced in her mind knowing the crew had to win or they'd all be dead. Her white tennis shoes, now red, squished in the blood as she darted across the deck. The crushing sound of swords going into the chest of the pirates echoed in her head, hearing their bodies thump to the deck.

The crew was small but mighty. With the preciseness of their swords they were holding their own against the pirates. Her head pulsated, her body ached, but she wasn't going to let the pirates burn this ship and sink it to the bottom of the sea.

Through the mass of swords swinging in the air, she notice Jervis, standing by the larboard side of the ship, a head taller than most of the men, both crew and pirates. A disgusting smile was on his face and his beady eyes were glazed over enjoying the fight. He'd let out a guffaw laugh every time his sword was thrust into the body of a pirate. She wanted to win this battle, but Jervis's laugh sent chills down her spine.

She ducked and wobbled when a pirate's sword came at her. Her left hand swung in the air slashing with the blade of the pocketknife at the huge pirate's arms. *Focus, Belinda*, she told herself. Men, swords, pistols, and blood were going everywhere, but she wasn't willing to quit fighting. A pirate standing beside her lunged his sword into a mate, his gigantic elbow swung at her hitting her directly in the face. Her eyes blinked, struggling to focus, blood gushed from her nose, and the ship's deck seemed to sway more than usual. Beads of sweat trickled down her neck. Ansel's sword lunged into a pirate and the man's long arm reached out his hand grabbing her vest as he fell to the floor taking her with him. She kicked and shoved his body off of her struggling to stand. Her stomach twisted smelling the sour odor of sweat and the pirate's opened flesh oozing with blood. She shook her head to stay conscious and wiped the perspiration and blood from her face. She swallowed hard and staggered a few paces.

Fighting down a wave of nausea her eyes glanced to the back of the ship seeing Sinjin still in an intense battle fighting the same grisly man, the captain of the pirates. Both of the men's body language was fierce with neither one backing down.

A noise startled her and she twirled around; inches from her stood a broad chested pirate. He sneered jabbing his sword at her. She ducked, squatting down onto the deck, the tip of the sword missing her chest by only a few inches. She leaped back up thrusting Ian's sword at the man's chest and feeling the sword slide into his body. She tugged the sword, dripping with blood, from the body as the man fell with a loud thump to the deck. The sky began to twirl overhead. Her eyes widened, jaw dropped, and her stomach churned. But, something caught her eye bringing her composure back. At the rear of the ship was Sinjin stepping backwards near the edge of the ship running out of room to maneuver his sword.

The pirate's sword lunged at Sinjin; he swayed to the left, sending both of the men tumbling overboard. Belinda skyrocketed across the ship's deck ducking and weaving through the fighting men. She ran to the side of the ship and gazed down into the deep, black water below. She hollered down to Sinjin, but the whooping and shouting from the men fighting drowned out her voice.

Down below in the dark water was Sinjin and the pirate about ten feet apart. Her mouth went dry with fear and tears stung her eyelids. She watched Sinjin swim toward the pirate. His tight fist pulled back striking the dazed pirate in the face. The pirate wobbled for a few seconds and then sank into the shadowy water.

A swirl of red tinted water floated around Sinjin, a calling card for the sharks lurking in the deep water. Time was of the essence so

Belinda quickly hurled a large rope down to the water. Sinjin wearily grabbed the rope. He put his feet on the side of the ship and climbed the tall wall of the ship. She tugged on the rope helping him over the side. He stood next to her, blood gushing from a deep gash on his forearm.

"Sinjin, you're hurt!" she shouted, jerking her neckerchief from her hair and tying it around his arm.

"I'm fine!" His left hand, trying to stop the bleeding, wrapped around his right arm as blood flowed through his fingers. His sad eyes stared down at her. He rubbed his right hand on his breeches and reached over letting his fingers wipe the blood from her face.

She smiled up at him. "I'm fine."

His eyes panned the ship a crease grew on his brow.

The pirates quickly noticed Sinjin had come aboard the ship and their captain hadn't, so they began racing across the deck leaping over the side of the *Aeolus* to their ship.

In a victory stance, the crew of the Aeolus raised their swords swishing them in the air yelling, "Damn their souls!"

"The rats are jumping ship. Bloody hell, they're leaving at flank speed," Lucky shouted running to the bow of the ship.

Sinjin ordered. "Prepare the cannons, fire!"

The *Aeolus's* cannons fired striking the pirate's ship, shaking it from side to side, as it sailed limping away.

Belinda held her hands to her ears; her body trembled not able to move from her spot as the cannons continued to fire.

Sinjin stood on the top deck staring at all of the bodies of the pirates and mates. The *Aeolus* had lost three men that day, a lot more than Sinjin had wanted and the crew had a lot of injuries.

Santos walked up and placed his hand on Sinjin's shoulder, "yer Father would be proud of ya this day."

Belinda swung the great cabin door open and ran to the small wooden chest next to the windows. She laid Ian's sword on top of the chest, wiped the blood from the blade of Johnny's pocketknife, and slipped it into her pants pocket. She slid out the top drawer of the chest containing the small, square medicine box and some rags. She squatted down by Ian and gently cleaned his wound tying a strong bandage on his arm. She found the decanter of ale and poured some into a mug, letting him slowly sip the drink to help ease his pain.

A shadow blocked the door. Sinjin walked into the great cabin. "You were supposed to stay inside like I told you, but you never listen to me." He stopped talking. His dark eyes peered down, and a smile emerged on his face. "Thank you, Belinda for saving Ian and my life today." He reached his hand down helping her off the floor, holding onto her hand longer than he needed.

Ian looked up at her. "Thank ya, Miss Belinda, ya did a splendid job. But how did ya fight the way ya did? Can ya teach me ta fight like that?" he added with a weak grin.

"I learned from one of my daddy's army buddies. I also would love to learn to sword fight as well as you and the crew, if you could teach me – deal."

Ian grinned. "Deal." His head leaned to the side, eyes closed with the ale taking affect.

Sinjin gave Ian a soft pat on the shoulder. "I'm sure glad mate – you're alright."

Belinda tucked the small blanket around Ian and quietly followed Sinjin out onto the weather deck. She had brought the bandages and ointment to help see to the crew's injuries. She rushed to Ansel and started cleaning his stab wound. Many mates had lacerations, a few stab wounds like Ansel, and a few had broken bones, arms, hands and one wrist was fractured. She looked over at Santos seeing his bruised and swollen face. He smiled nodding his head at her telling her he was all right.

She hurried to Sinjin. "You're still bleeding. Let me see to your cut, it's deep."

"My crew needs help first, thank you for helping them, then I'll see to mine."

She watched him walked to the three men being prepared for burial. A couple of the men were using old canvas sails and some sea twine to sew a shroud for the three men for their burial at sea. Two of the dead were young men, Shadrach and Thaddeus, but one of the men Zachariah was older and had been on the ship many years. Sinjin bent down next to the men, his face tight and his lips squeezed together.

The crew was family and most of the men had been on the ship the entire time Sinjin had been captain. Ian had explained that Sinjin's father was the captain of the ship before him and many of the men had stayed on when Sinjin took over as captain of the ship.

The ship was getting back to normal and repairs had been made. All the mates came up on the top deck for the funeral. Belinda stood by Santos.

Sinjin came out of his cabin dressed in a uniform, a black jacket that was longer than the one he usually wore. He was solemn. Ian followed close behind.

One man pulled a tattered Bible out of his pocket and began reading.

Christ our eternal King and God,
For You are the Resurrection, the Life,
And Repose of Your servants,
Shad, Thaddeus, and Zachariah,
Departed this life,

O Christ our God;
And to You do we send up glory
With Your Eternal Father and Your All-holy,
Good and Life-creating Spirit;
Both now and forever and to the ages of ages.
As we commit the earthy remains of our brothers,
Shad, Thaddeus, and Zachariah To the deep,
Grant them peace and serenity
You only are the Lord, Jesus Christ,
To the glory of God the Father.
Amen

After the reading of the Bible and prayer, Sinjin said a few words about each of the men. The crew's eyes brimmed with tears ready to fall down their weathered faces and the memory of this day would stay with everyone.

The crew said goodbye to the men and then each body, wrapped in the old canvas sailcloth, slowly slid over the side of the ship. One man dropped a cross over the side where the last man went into the water.

"Goodbye Zachariah, I'll see ya someday in Davy Jones' locker," one of the older mates whispered, his shoulders hunched, gazing downward over the side of the ship.

Belinda felt empty inside watching the men go to their watery graves. An aroma of death lingered over the ship. A stern countenance covered the crew's faces as they went to work and the ship began to sail. It was a sad day for the *Aeolus*.

She left the crew and went to the great cabin so the mates could talk about their day.

Exhaustion was overcoming her body, not only physically, but also mentally. Her purple, swollen, and tearstained face peered back from the old mirror in the small cabin. Her fingers wiggled her nose. Luckily it wasn't broken. She had a few scratches and bruises, nothing more. This had been more of a fight than she had bargained for and this day would haunt her forever.

Was this real or was she still dreaming? Did she really fight pirates? She slumped down in the large chair in the great cabin next to the line of windows and started thinking. But, how could this be a dream. She'd felt the sword when she thrust it into the pirate's body and she felt the pain of her injuries, this had to be real. She twisted her hands together, questioning whether she wanted to stay on the ship or try to get off. If she got off the ship, she'd have to find somewhere to live until she figured out how to get home. Thoughts swirled in her mind missing the life she had. Her fingers felt the gold charm bracelet — her gift from Johnny that seemed a lifetime ago. Her heart skipped a beat, seeing the gold lighthouse charm was gone. An aching pain of her dreams for the future had now disappeared. She touched her lips remembering their last kiss, missing Johnny holding her and making her feel safe.

Her tired eyes stared out the front windows. The magnificent ocean sparkled in the afternoon sun. The sea was serene after what had happened, not leaving any trace of the occurrence.

A knock at the door startled her. Jessie stood at the door holding her evening meal.

"Come in, Jessie."

"Here's yer meal, Belinda. The Captain is eating tonight with the crew. Is there anything else that I can get ya?"

"No this is fine thank you. How is Ian doing?"

"He's resting. He said ta tell ya he'll be back soon ta take care of ya." The young man nervously cleared his throat. "If ya need anything please let me know." He turned and walked out the door.

She pulled the chair out from under the table and sat down at the oversized wooden table, staring at her food of pancakes and fritters. Her eyes landed on a bonded jacky making her think about Ian.

"*No*," she couldn't leave this ship. Everyone had become her family – Ian, Santos, Ansel, Lucky, Ernesto, and even Sinjin. Like all families, there are hard times as well as good times. She'd make it living on this ship. This was her destiny, and she didn't have an answer of why she'd traveled back into time. She sat quietly eating her bonded jacky and knew it would be difficult to sleep tonight; nonetheless she needed to get some rest and tomorrow would be a new day.

CHAPTER ELEVEN

A TALE OF LONG AGO

A new day arose, November 3rd. Time was slipping by. Waking early, Belinda was eager to climb to the crow's nest and do her watch. She stepped out onto the deck and Ian, his arm in a sling, was sitting on a box watching the crew prepare the sails.

"Good morning Ian, how are you feeling today?"

"G'mornin' Miss Belinda. I'm doing a lot better today than yesterday. I'm able ta move my arm around," he answered slowly raising his arm in the air. "Thank ya fer all of yer help yesterday. D'ya want me ta get yer coffee?"

"No, Ian, I'll get my own coffee." She left making her way down the steep ladder to the galley.

She gripped the handles of the tin mugs of coffee in her hands and carefully handed a warm mug to Sinjin.

"Thank you, that was kind of you, but you don't have to get your own coffee, Jessie will see to you."

"I didn't get my coffee this is for Ian. He's been waiting on me and now it's his turn to be waited on." She handed Ian the fresh mug of coffee. He was speechless, but a huge grin spread across his face as he lifted the mug to his lips.

Belinda scooted next to Ian on a box and leaned against the side of the ship arching her back taking in the lovely ship. The day was serene and calm. She felt a stare and glanced up. Santos stood towering over her.

"How ya doing? Ya did a great job fighting the pirates. I was right, ya are a good Jackaro."

"I'm alright just a few bruises. Santos, how are you feeling?"

"I'm sore – I'm an old mate an' fighting is hard on me, but I'm faring."

"Santos where is your home?"

"This ship 'tis my home," he added with a disheartened look sitting down next to her.

"But, don't you have a city you go to in the winter like everyone else?"

"Not anymore."

She decided not to ask any more question after she saw the look on his face.

"Little Jackaro, many, many years ago I did have a home an' amazing wife an' a beautiful little daughter." He stared down at his shoes. "One winter I came home late in December an' found out my wife an' daughter, who had jes turned two, had died of scarlet fever two weeks earlier. I never got ta say goodbye or tell them how much I loved them." His head ducked. "I've never been back. Like I said before, this ship is my life; I don't have a special city ta go ta," he sniffed, "not anymore." He peered up at her; his dark, old squinty eyes glistened with tears.

"I'm so sorry," she said in a soft voice putting her hand on his wrinkled hand.

He smiled.

That evening Belinda leaned back in the soft chair in the great cabin, her quiet spot away from the crew. She began thinking about this time. It was the end of 1788; George Washington, the first president, would be elected next year in 1789. The United States was just beginning and the capitol was either New York or Philadelphia, she wasn't quite sure which city.

Ian silently came into the cabin. "I'll be bringing yer supper in a few minutes. Is something wrong? Ya look troubled."

"No, Ian I was just thinking about your time and sailing into Boston."

"I see; Boston is a great city," he said with a sheepish grin, "almost as great as Charles Towne. Come, look on the charts," he said pointing his finger. "These are the islands that we'll be sailing past. This one in particular I think ya'd be interested in, Little Brewster Island. It has a magnificent lighthouse located on it. It's situated right here," he said touching the chart, "some two miles east of Boston in the bay."

Belinda's fingers drew lines on the old chart.

He smiled at her. "Y'll learn how ta read the charts in time, they're somewhat confusing."

"Ian, I hadn't thought about seeing so many different places. I've never traveled before and I can't wait to see the lighthouse."

"'Tis called the Boston Light an' was built in 1716. A few years ago in 1776, when the British withdrew from Boston, they planted a time-charge at the lighthouse when they left. The explosion destroyed the top of the structure. It was as terrible sight, but it was rebuilt a few years ago in 1783."

"I've read about the Boston Light. It was one of the first lighthouses along the coastline."

"Aye, it was an' it's been a God save ta many seafarers over the years."

"Oh, I bet they still use whale oil lamps for the beacon. Years ago, my lighthouse used sixteen oil lamps. Will we be able to see the lighthouse up close, Ian?"

"Yay, an' when we sail ta Charles Towne we'll sail right past the island on our way down an' y'll get a closer look." The boatswain pipe blew. "Oh, my," his plump body giggled. "'Tis getting late an' I'd better fetch yer meal the captain will be ready ta eat," Ian called out hurrying to the door muttering to himself.

A few minutes later, the door opened. "Where's Ian," Sinjin committed, irritably. "I thought he'd have been here by now with our meal."

"Oh, I'm sorry. He's late because of me. He was showing me on the charts the islands near Boston and the Boston Light."

Sinjin stood by the table full of charts letting his fingers trace the route the Aeolus was taking. "Yay," he said, pulling a chair up to the table. "He's right; you'll enjoy seeing the lighthouse."

The door pushed open. Ian and Jessie walked into the room and hurriedly crossed to the table. Ian, using his left hand fidgeted with the dishes in Jessie's hands setting them on the table. "I'm sorry Sir, I'm late, an' it won't happen again."

"That's alright, Ian. I'm glad you're helping Belinda," Sinjin said in a calm voice.

Relief came over Ian's face. He took his duties seriously and being cabin boy for the captain of a ship this large was very important to him.

Sinjin began to gobble his food.

"Sinjin, slow down, you're eating too fast," Belinda chastised.

He looked up at her with a scowl on his face. "I have a lot of work to do before we sail into Boston in the morning. I don't have time to eat."

"Well, you're going to choke on your food; you have a few minutes to take a short break."

A smile broke across his face and his head ducked yes. He leaned back in his chair taking smaller bites enjoying his meal.

He laid down his fork by the wooden plate and the straight back chair scraped the wood floor when he scooted it from the table. "Now, work." He sat down at his desk and began to write in a black leather journal.

Belinda noticed a collection of the same leather journals in the cabinet above Sinjin's desk. She curiously studied the feathered quill pen as he wrote in one of the journals in a precise penmanship.

He looked up from his work.

"Oh, I'm sorry, I didn't mean to stare," she apologized. "It's fascinating to watch how you write with the quill pen."

His head tilted to the side with a confused look. "I'm filling out the ship's journal, nothing strange about it."

"Well, in my time we don't use quill pens, we use pencils and ink pens."

"Ink pens?" he questioned.

"Sure, I guess you'd say the quill pens already have ink inside of them." She moved closer to the desk. Her fingers outlined the writing on the top of the journals. "Are all these journals of the ships travels?"

"The entire life of the *Aeolus*; most of those journals were filled out each night by my father. Here," he grinned, flipping a few pages back in the journal. "This is your tale of how you appeared on the cliff."

She leaned down next to Sinjin. She shuddered being so close to him able to smell his musky scent – so earthly so natural, not how Johnny smelled with his special aftershave he'd bought at the dime store. Sinjin quickly leaned away from her, his fingers pointed to the correct spot on the page.

"Wow, you wrote my story in the journal?"

"I certainly did, would you like to read it?" He paused. "I assume you can read."

"Of course, I can read." She lifted the book from the desk and began to read her story that Sinjin had written. It was interesting the words that he used to describe the event, not only the occurrence of the whispering fog, the mystery of time, but her story of being from the future.

October the 13th, `tis the year of our lord 1788, Harbor Towne, Maine: An unusual fog had occurred about nine bells that evening. A tiny lass, a beautiful mermaid with long yellow hair and eyes the color of the sea dressed in strange attire, fell from a tall cliff into the unusual and strange fog that seemed to be whispering. `Tis a strange talk, the lass named Belinda, did speak. She spoke of a tale of the future and that she lived in the year of nineteen hundred and fifty-nine, a tale about a tall stone lighthouse that stood on the massive cliff next to Harbor Towne.

She blushed seeing Sinjin was staring up at her. She quickly turned her face handing the journal back to him. "You left a spot for people to sign their names and tell about what happened that day, but you only have Lucky and Ian's story and their signatures."

His lips pursed together. "Ian, Lucky, and I are the only mates on the ship that can write. A few of the mates can scratch their names or X's but not many."

"I didn't realize that, would you like me to write my story and sign my name?"

"Sure, that would be grand."

She leaned down next to Sinjin his face only inches from hers, but this time he didn't move away. She nervously fumbled with the quill pen in her hand. "I just need to figure out how to use it," she said amused, shifting the pen into her hand.

"Here," he said taking her small hand in his showing her how to dip and hold the pen correctly.

She wrote a short story telling her tale of the whispering fog and then she signed her name *Katelynn Belinda Brady,* and stood up.

He whispered, "Katelynn Belinda Brady, that's a beautiful name."

"Thank you," she said handing him the quill pen. "I will leave you to your work."

He laid the pen down on the desktop and rubbed his tired eyes. "Thank you Miss Katelynn Belinda," he said finally smiling up at her.

She stepped outside onto the quiet deck and sat down by the side of the ship remembering the fresh earthly scent of Sinjin. He was so arrogant, over confident and rude, but somehow he pulled her in. Captain Monty leaped into her lap. Her head leaned back and she peered up into the dark sky full of sparkling vibrant stars, but she felt someone watching.

Santos stood over her cupping his mug of ale in his hands. "Nice evenin' ain't it Little Jackaro."

"Yes, it is, Santos, have a seat."

"Ian told me yer excited about seeing Boston an' the Boston lighthouse," he said in a low voice. The box crackled from his weight as he fidgeted getting comfortable next to her.

"This is thrilling for me to see a city when it's young and I can't wait to see Boston."

Santos sat up gripping his mug of ale in his hands, twirling it nervously in a circle.

"Santos, something is bothering you."

His old eyes moistened nodding his head yes. "There is more, my Little Jackaro that ya should know. I have a tale I don't tell often, one that might interest ya." He leaned back.

***

"'Tis a tale that began many, many years ago when I was a fresh young sailor along with a captain named John Alvery." He wiped a lone tear that tried to escape his eye with the back of his hand. "He was a fine gent, an Earl from England, of high class an' learning. His well-ta-do family had moved ta Boston from England an' he was a part of the upper crust of society. We were two different sorts, he an' I, but as close as any brothers could be. When I was a small lad my family was poor an' they'd come ta the colonies from Portugal. John's family was of nobility an' he was highly educated. I was a few years older, but his family had the money ta set him up as a captain of a sailing ship. He soon learned there was good money in going ta the ports in the colonies. They needed cargo an' he was the one ta supply them.

Years went by, good years, as John an' I traveled from port ta port along the coast. It was the best time of my life," he paused his eyes twinkled, "or so I thought. One winter we docked in Boston. I went ta the dry good store fer supplies. Standing helping another mate was this young girl named Clarissa, a pretty thing with light hair and blue eyes so like ya." He smiled. "I instantly fell in love. We were married a few months later an' my life changed completely. 'Twas something fer this old salt ta settles down with a wife. I was happier than I'd ever been.

A couple of years later we were blessed with a baby girl, my precious Nora. She had light hair an' hazel eyes. I was the proudest Poppa.

`Twas the next winter after my Nora was born John decided ta spend the winter in Boston with me an' my family. John's family lived in Boston, but didn't approve of him socializing with sorts like me." His head shook back and forth. "We docked the large ship an' John moved inta my home. It was the most frigid winter I had ever seen. People were stranded all over Boston in the blizzard an' John an' I volunteered ta help. The snow was coming down foot by foot. We could barely get out of our home – nevertheless many people needed our help.

I prepared one mornin' ta go out inta the deep snow with John ta check on others, but he told me ta stay with my family; that was where I belonged. I reluctantly stayed behind watching my best friend leave the warmth of my home." Santos ducked his head. "John was the kindest man I've ever known.

A fortnight went by an' I didn't hear from him. I informed Clarissa that I had to go find John. I knew the precise direction he was headed. I set my course. I took along provisions an' began my search, but no one had heard nary a word from him. He had not made it ta the small town as he had planned. I made my way home, very saddened.

I feared the worst. Here he was a sailor an' ta die on land was not the death he'd have wanted. I anguished each day that I had lost my best mate.

Time went by. One evenin' after the snow had melted there was a knock at my door. Standing tall was the blue eyed, light haired John, with the largest grin on his face; the man that I had presumed ta be dead. I grabbed his arm an' pulled him inta the house. Standing behind him was this dark skinned Indian woman, with the blackest eyes an' long, braided black hair hanging down her back. I stood in shock. John gently took the woman's arm leading her inta the house.

"Santos, this is my wife Zyanya, and yes she is an Iroquois Indian," John added, his broad grin went from ear to ear. "We were married last week. It is all legal and no one can say a God damn thing."

"John, where have you been? I searched, but no one had heard from ya. Ya had us scared ta death an' I thought ya were a goner."

"Well, my friend, I became lost. I wasn't able to stay on course; land is harder to maneuver than my sea. My horse bucked and I was thrown. Lying out in the deep snow, I lost my sense of time. I had broken ribs and my arm was in horrible shape. I thought I was a goner, too." He smiled. "But, an angel named Zyanya saved me. She took me back to her family and saw to my wounds helping me heal."

My eyes stared at the young woman sitting in the chair by the front window gazing outside.

"Santos, when I looked up into her eyes, I thought I'd died and gone to heaven. I knew I was in love and her family or mine wasn't going to stop us from getting married. Zyanya's name means forever and always, and that is what we are going to have."

"What about your ship? What are ya going ta do?"

"I will do as you have done. You, my friend have a wife and a child. What is the difference, old mate?" He laughed, patting me on the back.

"John, ya know the difference. Where is she gonna live while y're away?"

"We'll figure it out. Aren't you happy, for me?"

I smiled. John had a love for life an' the kindness in his soul showed. Zyanya spoke very good English an' I could see the love she had fer John in her dark eyes. I knew the problems that would be coming from the town's people. It was taboo ta marry an Indian, especially for a wealthy English man. Nothing was going ta stop

John an' I was going ta be right there with him, but I knew his parent's wouldn't be happy.

I hurried ta a chest got some ale out of the top cabinet an' poured two glasses. I did a toast.

"Here's ta a long, safe, an' happy life fer ya an' Zyanya.
May yer seas be calm an' the winds continue ta blow.
May ya sail inta the sunset together,
Until ya each grow old."

Our glasses clinked as we both downed our ale.

"Now, I had thought I would have been invited ta yer wedding, John, but I'll forgive ya, since I'm so glad y're alive."

"Thank you old friend for the toast. Now, I have another favor to ask and I do need to come up with a plan. Would it be possible for Zyanya to live with Clarissa for a while until I find a home for us? I don't have a lot of time before we sail and I have to see to the ship, I have been gone too long. We'll be taking on a full load of cargo down to Charles Towne in a few days."

Clarissa came out of the bedroom. "John, Zyanya is asleep; she's exhausted. She told me ya rode from her village all night ta get here."

"I knew we wouldn't find a place that would let us stay the night, so we had to keep moving," John sighed, understanding the problems he was going ta face.

"John, ya know what you've done. Ya ain't welcome in the Indian village an' Zyanya ain't welcome here," I added. "What are ya going ta do?"

"As soon as we get back from our voyage to Charles Towne, I am moving my new family to a place called St. Augustine. A place we can dock for the winter. It's a nice province that will allow us to live in peace."

"Have ya told yer family?"

He ducked his head. "Nay and I understand they won't approve of my marriage, so I am going to wait awhile," he answered.

I wrapped my arms around Clarissa going ta our bedroom. "I have a question. John would like Zyanya ta live here while we sail ta Charles Towne. 'Tis gonna stir up problems."

She looked up at me with a smile on her face. "Yay, any member of John's family is welcome an' I'll handle the town's people," she said proudly.

"I love you." I beamed giving her a hug.

Nora began ta cry, so Clarissa picked up the tiny bundle of four months, sat down in the rocking chair an' began ta nurse. I kissed Nora on her tiny head an' left the room.

The next few weeks John an' I prepared the ship fer the journey to Charles Towne an' back ta Boston. We said goodbye ta our wives an' started our voyage.

The trip did go by fast an' we were soon sailing back ta Boston. John had a great surprise when we returned home, finding out he was gonna be a father.

John an' Zyanya planned ta leave soon heading ta St. Augustine. Clarissa an' I debated on whether ta leave with them, but we decided ta stay in Boston fer a while longer.

I hugged my wife an' baby girl an' watched them standing at the door, waving goodbye. On the way ta St. Augustine, Zyanya gave birth ta a beautiful brown eyed, dark haired baby boy an' John couldn't have been any happier.

Headed back ta Boston, I had decided ta move my family near John an' Zyanya's home. I had found the perfect home an' I couldn't wait ta tell Clarissa."

Santos fingers wiped wetness from his eyes. "'Twas late December. The ship sailed inta the port of Boston. I hurried home. Tacked ta my front door was a note. I couldn't read well, so I grabbed the note an' went inta my home. It was quiet inside the house an' plates with stale food sat on the table. I searched my home, but I couldn't find Clarissa.

I held the note in my hand an' I ran down the street as fast as I could ta the ship ta find John. I handed him the note. As he began ta read tears streamed down his face.

To Whom It May Concern this is to inform you that the family of this home has become infected with scarlet fever. The woman and child died on the 16th of December. They were buried in the King's Chapel Burying Ground cemetery."

I felt like a knife had stabbed me in my heart. My body slid down onta the deck with my head in my hands an' fer one of the first times in my life I cried. If I had just moved my family sooner they would be alive. John put his arms around me an' cried, ta. My life had ended.

John stared down on me. "Santos, we needed to go to the cemetery. You have to say goodbye."

I didn't know if I could handle seeing the graves of my family, but I did as he asked. I didn't know if I could face my family. I had let them down. Gripping flowers in my trembling hands, we solemnly walked over ta the two mounds of fresh dirt – the graves of the two people I loved more than my life. I bent down an' placed the flowers onta the ground. The pain an' loss was tearing me apart. John bought marble markers fer their graves. That day I said my goodbyes ta my family, my life." He sighed. "As I told ya before, I've never been back.

John insisted I go back ta the house an' go through Clarissa an' Nora's things. I put what I wanted ta keep in a special trunk that Christmas so long ago. I closed the door of my wonderful home fer the last time an' I ain't been back ta Boston.

A few years went by an' John an' Zyanya were going ta have another child. I never let my sorrow affect John's happiness. I knew he loved Clarissa an' Nora an' their deaths had been hard on him. Our plan that year was ta sail down ta St. Augustine an' dock the ship until the child was born. I stayed with the ship while John went ta be with his family.

The next month was normal until one evenin'. John came running up the plank of the ship yelling fer me ta come quickly. I hurried out of the cabin. I remember hearing our steps on the cobblestones, as we ran ta his home. I won't ever forget walking inta his wonderful home hearing the words from the midwife. *The baby an' Zyanya were in trouble, things weren't going well.* That night was the longest in both of our lives. We sat in the parlor with the dim flames in the lamps flickering against the wall an' the old clock ticking slowly, hour after hour – hoping an' for one of the first times in a long time, I prayed.

Early that morning the midwife an' Mama Annie came down the stairs informing us the baby girl had died. Mama Annie took John upstairs ta be with Zyanya. I felt so powerless an' stayed with the little boy. An hour later, I heard John's boots clicking on the steps. His face was drawn, I knew the answer; Zyanya was gone. He lifted his son in his arms telling the boy what had happened. I didn't believe I could handle any more pain after losing Clarissa and Nora, but the pain I felt had doubled that dark day. We had a nice funeral for Zyanya an' the baby girl John named Mary Coreen. John an' I had lost our loves an' our baby girls.

We left that day with so much sorrow. The ship was now John an' his son's home.

The boy was so much like his father, but I knew he was a half-breed an' life would be hard on him. John believed he had the love of his family, which was now the two of us, along with the mates on the ship an' the boy would be fine. The young boy wouldn't be welcomed in parts of the colonies, jes as it was fer Zyanya. John told his family of his marriage, his son, an' the death of his wife an' his baby girl. They didn't want ta have anything ta do with him or his son an' was furious at him fer marrying an Indian woman. I saw the hurt in his eyes an' I told him he an' his son would always have a family on the *Aeolus*."

***

Belinda sat quietly, looking at Santos, knowing she was correct; he was talking about Sinjin and his family.

"Sinjin Alvery is part English an' part Indian. His name means John Alvery an' he is a true blend of his mother an' father. He is so like John in ways, but looks so much like Zyanya. I see her every time I look at him, but I see John when I look inta his dark eyes; his brown eyes are so like John's eyes filled with so much compassion. Life has been hard on him growing up as a half-breed. He's overcome that stigma an' is welcomed in most of the colonies but not Boston. He still has family that lives in Boston, John's parents an' it's their loss not knowing such a fine young man.

I'm telling this tale so y'll understand how Boston is hard on the crew of the *Aeolus*. Memories here are very mixed. Life did go on fer John an' me. Young Sinjin helped ta make life worthwhile fer two, old salty's."

Belinda sat back and didn't know what to say. She hadn't thought about how Sinjin had dark hair, dark eyes, and was British; highly educated. She'd never met an Indian. There weren't any Indians living in Harbor Towne. Most of the folks were Scot-Irish like her family, and a few German families lived out in the country, like Johnny's family.

"I'm so sorry for your loss and Sinjin's loss. I'm glad you told me your tale. Thank you Santos for being such a good friend." She leaned over giving him a hug, with tears running down her face.

He rose to his feet holding onto his empty glass of ale wiping his own tears.

Tomorrow the ship would be arriving in Boston. She was now on a mission; the first place she was going was to the cemetery to place flowers on Clarissa and Nora's graves.

CHAPTER TWELVE

BOSTON

Belinda was up early the next day ready for her watch, but her mind continued to swirl about Santos's tale. She climbed up the mast looking out to the islands way in the distance, as the ship began to make its way into the Boston. When the ship neared the port, Jessie was to take over her watch to navigate the tall ship into the harbor.

She had asked Ian to help her find the cemetery where Santos's family was buried. He worriedly let her know how to get there, but warned her that she had to be very careful. If anyone found out she was a girl, the people in Boston wouldn't take kindly to her dressed as a mate, and her punishment would be great. Women were whipped or publicly shamed and sometimes even put to death for a crime as simple as dressing as a man. Ian explained how men were put in the stocks or the pillory for stealing a piece of bread. She cringed, remembering her history class about the wooden framework that had holes for your head and hands and the whipping post in the center of town. But, none of Ian's fears of the dangers of Boston were going to deter her from going into Boston today.

It was all beautiful, the land and sea. The sea spray hit her face as she leaned back on the side of the ship, looking out onto the many islands. She glanced over at Sinjin seeing the sorrow in his face. She knew his father's family lived in Boston and he'd never met them. She was glad Santos had told her Sinjin's story, understanding the hurt in his face.

The ship neared the small harbor full of tall sailing ships. The large ship docked and the crew began their task of unloading the cargo. They would only be in Boston long enough to unload and reload their cargo and would leave as soon as possible.

She pulled out her tri-corner hat to conceal herself as much as possible. Ian gave her directions to the King's Chapel Burying Ground that had been founded in 1630. She walked to the gangplank. Sinjin stepped in front of her.

"Belinda, where do you think you are going?" he asked firmly grabbing hold of her shoulders and spinning her around to face him.

"I have something I need to do in Boston and I'll be back soon," she answered, looking at the sorrow in his face. Time had moved on for him, but the pain was still there.

"I can't let you go into Boston. You don't understand the people that live there they are so different than you," he insisted worriedly.

"Sinjin," she began, reaching up holding onto his strong dark arm. "I do understand the problem, and that I don't fit in. I won't let them know I'm a girl, I promise. They'll think of me as a mate and that is all. I promise I'll be careful."

"Belinda, it's too dangerous and I forbid you to go," he forcefully said.

She wasn't going to argue with Sinjin. She nodded her head yes, but Santos walked up before she could say anything.

"Are ya ready, Little Jackaro? Let's go see Boston?" he said looking at her with those old tired eyes.

Sinjin stared; he wouldn't say no to Santos. "Alright, Santos you take care of her," Sinjin said earnestly with a questioning look.

"I will my Little Jack don't worry," assured Santos taking hold of Belinda's arm.

"Santos, why are you going into Boston?" questioned Belinda as they strolled down the gangplank. "You said you'd never go back to Boston."

"Ian told me what ya were doing an' I'm smart enough ta know it's time ta go visit." Santos stopped walking and looked down at her feet, his head swung back and forth.

"Oh," she moaned realizing what he was looking at. She still had her tennis shoes on – a dead giveaway that she wasn't a normal mate. She raced back to the ship swishing past Sinjin to her cabin and pulled off her tennis shoes slipping on the strange black shoes. She sighed; the shoes were way too big and flopped on her feet. She grabbed a couple of neckerchiefs and stuffed each one in the toe of the shoes. She looked like a clown walking, but the shoes at least stayed on her feet.

She joined Santos on the boardwalk and he laughed at her shoes. The morning was quiet; not many people were milling about and that was fine with Belinda as the two walked down the cobblestone road on a mission. Her eyes took in historic sites along the road that were in their beginning, their early life, and she would've loved to explore them, but today that wasn't to be.

They hurried into a trading post and Santos bought a large bouquet of flowers costing at least a mate's month's pay. Belinda stood quietly near the door her head ducked and face hidden under the tri corner hat. But before Santos could pay for his purchase, the merchant looked over her way. He bent down questioning Santos. Santos, in a calm clear voice, assured the man that was his son, who had been born dumb and mute. She wasn't sure if she liked being called dumb and mute, but looking at the stern face of the merchant, she'd go with it. The man took Santos' money and stared at him.

Santos with full confidence told the man he and his son were headed to the cemetery to place flowers on the grave of his son's deceased mother. The answer finally seemed to appease the merchant and he turned to another customer. Santos walked outside of the trading post and Belinda quietly followed. He turned right, going north on Tremont Street.

They strolled silently along the street, both lost in their own thoughts. Belinda knew what he was thinking. His Nora would be grown like Sinjin and maybe there would've been more children. He would be home with Clarissa and maybe some grandchildren. She saw the anguish in his face and hoped this wasn't too hard on him. He was an old man.

Another block down Tremont Street she saw the small cemetery on the right side of the road. She had read in her history book about the cemetery and the Freedom Trail and many important people were buried at this cemetery. John Winthrop, the first Puritan governor of Massachusetts and William Emerson, the father of Ralph Waldo Emerson, were buried here in this same cemetery in her time. Now, the most important people were the wife and daughter of Santos.

But before they made it to the cemetery, Santos gave her a grave look. She heard footsteps behind them; inconspicuously she turned her head seeing a tall, thick body man marching towards them. She had to keep a clear head and not panic. Nervously she stood close to Santos wringing her hands tight together.

Santos whispered, "'Tis the constable, ya let me do the talking."

Since she was born dumb and mute she had no other recourse. Santos slowed his pace letting the constable catch up. The realization set in, and Ian's words of warning were coming back to haunt her. If she'd been alone like she'd planned this morning, she'd be in jail now.

Santos talked to the constable, explaining that they were mates on a sailing ship that'd docked this morning. He told the story of his poor wife who'd lived here in Boston, dying fourteen years ago in childbirth, and that he and his son would visit her grave when they were in town. Belinda sighed inwardly, thankful Santos could talk a squirrel out of a nut, and the constable believed his story. Santos ducked his head to the constable and the man turned around and left in a hurried pace down Tremont Street.

Santos entered the cemetery through its black iron gates and walked over to two graves. She stopped next to Santos.

He smiled down at her, his fingers anxiously playing with his bushy beard as his eyes turned from her and peered down at the elegant tombstones.

She read the first one:

Clarissa Irene Barros
A loving wife and mother, now in the arms of God,
Born March 8th, 1736
Died December 16th, 1762

* * *

The other tombstone read:
Eleanor Marisa Barros
An innocent child in the safe arms of God
Born November 21st, 1760
Died December 16th, 1762

Belinda turned to walk away to give Santos some privacy, but his head swung up and he reached out his hand touching her gently on the arm. "Belinda, please don't go. I want ya ta meet my family." Santos had called her Belinda.

He then introduced her and explained to his small family how she had brought him home to them.

She bent down and softly whispered, "God bless and peace be with you both."

Santos placed the beautiful flowers on the graves and she step back. He knelt down and talked for a while with tears streaming down his exhausted face. Santos' body crackled as he stood and wiped his tear-stain face. "Belinda let's go home ta the *Aeolus*. Sinjin will be worried."

She shook her head yes, and they slowly walked down Tremont Street toward the ship, being very cautious of who was around them.

Sinjin stood at the gangplank waiting with his arms crossed. Santos didn't speak; silently he walked passed Sinjin. His tired eyes were staring off into the horizon with a wondering look on his face. Ian sat down by him, but he too sat quiet.

Belinda smiled at Sinjin letting him know things went well in Boston, not telling him about their close calls with the merchant and constable.

She went into the great room, leaving the door open to get some fresh air, and sat down in the chair by the row of windows and tucked her feet up under her.

Sinjin stood across the deck able to see into the great cabin. His eyes focused on Belinda, her long tousled mane flowing down onto her shoulders. Her eyes were staring out the window at the water, day dreaming, and he believed she was dreaming about her life that had disappeared into the mysterious fog. Peacefulness was on her sun kissed face. He knew a beautiful girl like Belinda had to have someone she cared about in her time. She didn't wear a wedding ring, but he could see in her eyes a longing for someone she loved.

Sinjin was correct, Belinda was thinking about the life she was missing; marrying Johnny sometime next year, and maybe someday having a little girl like Santos' daughter. Images with sharp clarity grew in her mind seeing Johnny and her father, with grim faces, standing on her cliff staring down into the water wondering what had happened to her. She felt Johnny's arms around her and their last kiss, knowing he'd be full of regrets for not staying with her that evening and stopping her from climbing down the rugged cliff. She wanted to tell Johnny and her father she was alive and well, but was she? She was making it living on the old sailing ship, but wanted dearly to go home where she belonged. How and why did she fall down the cliff and disappear into the whispering fog and how could she make it happen again.

She closed her eyes hearing Johnny's laughter and seeing her father rocking in one of the rockers on the front porch of the old Victorian home. Her father's wonderful voice would sing along with the radio in the living room. Memories were all she had now, so each night she'd keep those memories of her life fresh in her mind. Tomorrow would be a new day and she just might find her answers.

She felt a stare and her head turned toward the door. She saw Sinjin's dark eyes on her. Nervously, his head swung away, but she noticed a slight smile on his face.

CHAPTER THIRTEEN

CHARLES TOWNE

One early December morning Belinda sat on the top deck reading a book. Tobias scooted in next to her on the floor of the deck. "'Tis it h-hard ta read?" he questioned with his eyes wide and fingers twitching nervously in his lap.

She smiled seeing Tobias' freckled face light up in the morning sun. "No, it's not difficult to read." She tilted her head looking at him as he continued anxiously to fidget with his fingers. "Would you like me to teach you to read?"

"Would ya?" Tobias' head shot up, his face flushed.

"Can ya teach me ta," another voice interjected.

She looked up and Joshua, a fresh-faced young boy about seventeen years old, was peering down at her through the long blonde hair hanging over his elongated face.

"You two really want to learn to read and won't play around?"

"Yay," they both shouted.

"Even t-though," Tobias did a long hum, "m-my Pa thinks reading is a w-waste of time, but I knows better."

"Tobias, Finley doesn't understand about reading."

"Well, can ya t-teach us our numbers?" Tobias questioned his face blushing. "I don't think Pa will care about me learning my numbers."

"Yes, I'll teach you both how to add and subtract. When I go into Charles Towne I'll get a couple of primers."

"Primers?" Joshua asked straining his long turkey neck.

"Books that will help you learn to read."

"T-Thank you," Tobias called out, punching Joshua in the arm as the boys walked away. She smiled watching Tobias walk with his duck-feet slapping the deck like a puppy with oversize paws.

Later in the morning, Ansel yelled down from his watch. "Whales on the larboard side!"

Belinda ran to the side of the ship and stood next to Lucky.

"Take a gander at the two black Right Whales – Mums about fifty five feet long, and the calf is huge too, about eighteen feet. Listen, they're making a whistling sound." He whistled a tune back at the whales.

"Oh, they're gorgeous," Belinda said smiling up at Lucky, wiping the sea spray from her face.

"Yay, they surely are. 'Tis baleen whales and that means they're shimmers so you can watch 'em for a while."

"Lucky, why are they called the Right Whales?"

"They were named the Right Whale because they are the "right" whale to hunt. They'll float when they're killed, so it makes it easy for whalers. The sailors can sell and use the whale oil on their ships; the whales are in high demand."

"They're so beautiful and graceful, oh – I'd love to touch them," her voice rose with excitement. "They aren't paying any attention to us." The mother had two large blowholes in a V shape and would go under for about 15 minutes at a time. They moved very slowly and the ship was leaving them behind.

"Goodbye, have long and safe lives," Belinda called out to the whales.

Belinda spun around to leave. Lucky reached out his callous finger and tenderly swished a wispy, wild strand of hair from her face. He tenderly touched her cheek for a few seconds longer than he needed. He grinned and made his sky-blue eyes light up. Lucky did a bow and hurried back to his work.

Belinda looked to the other side of the ship seeing Sinjin had been watching them. His dark eyes squinted tightly, making frown lines grow on his brow. She wondered why he'd even cared that Lucky and she would be watching the Right Whales together.

The next morning Ian hurried into the cabin his eyes lit with excitement. She peered up at him as she finished her breakfast.

"Miss Belinda, we'll be sailing inta Charles Towne tomorrow."

"Ian that's wonderful."

"We'll be staying awhile; we ain't setting sail until Saturday so y'll have plenty of time ta enjoy my beautiful city."

"But, why are we waiting until Saturday, why not leave Friday?" she questioned.

"Oh, nay, Miss Belinda, we cannot set sail on a Friday, that'd be bad luck. We will be fine setting sail on Saturday," he declared.

"Well, we don't want bad luck, but I didn't know Friday was an unlucky day."

"A good captain worth his salt would never leave port on a Friday," Ian called out hurrying as fast out the door as he'd come into the room.

After Belinda finished her breakfast and stepped outside onto the top deck. Standing inches from her was Jervis, grinning, a sinister grin showing a gap of missing front teeth. His warm, rotten breath reeled of ale and his long scar zigzagging across his left cheek seemed to grow wider. She spun around yanking open the great cabin's door and raced back inside. Before she could push the door closed, Jervis' huge hands grabbed the side of the door jerking it open and barged inside.

"You're not supposed to be in here, the captain won't like it," Belinda shouted backing up into the room.

"That son of a bitch won't know I'm in here if ya be's quiet," Jervis replied moving closer to her.

"Get out!" she shouted gradually moving away from him.

"Awe, a feisty lass, we should have a grand time."

"I said get out of here," she shouted even louder.

Suddenly the door flew open and Tobias stood face to chest with Jervis. "Ya l-leave now," the young boy yelled, gripping his fists into tight balls.

"Ye, bloody yoke needs ta be taught a lesson ta leave men's business alone," Jervis bellowed. The huge man swung his tightly gripped, white-knuckled fisted hand at Tobias' face, striking the boy in the nose; blood spurted everywhere as Tobias slumped to the floor.

Belinda swung her leg leaping in the air, but Jervis, being on guard, struck her leg with his massive arm hurling her onto the wood floor. She slid Johnny's pocketknife from her breeches flipping it open to the longest blade. Jervis squatted down rolling her over onto her back. He leaned next to her touching her face with his grimy fingers. She flew the sharp knife right at his face. His massive hand knocked the pocketknife to the side. "I sees y're a spirited Jade." His callous fingers raked down her neck as he began to play with the top of her blue stripped shirt. Grabbing the material, he jerk and the buttons ripped off.

She could see the pocketknife only a few inches from her outstretched hand. Her fingers wiggled, but the pocketknife was out of her reach with Jervis holding onto her body.

Jervis' beady eyes tightened, a grin shown on his face as he looked down at her exposed breasts. Her face was a couple of inches from his dark, dirty beard and he smelled of ale and sweat. She winced using all her strength to push his huge left hand away from her body. An enormous anger, she'd never felt before, grew inside of her and she wasn't letting him win. She was willing to die if she could take the bastard with her. She fought, kicking her feet and legs, swinging her arms wildly in the air and using her fingers to stab at his beady eyes determined he wouldn't win.

Jervis reared back; he'd had enough fighting. His enormous right arm swung like a hammer coming down to her face, but his arm suddenly stopped inches before it impacted. Belinda's eyes jerked upward seeing Sinjin grasping Jervis' arm, a scowl full of rage covered his face. Jervis shoved Sinjin into the long table and leaped from the floor. Sinjin bounded from the floor and faced the guerrilla of a man. Jervis stood towering over Sinjin brandishing an atrocious looking knife in his right hand. She stared along the gleaming steel past the curved hilt, the rock-steady arm, up into the deadly eyes.

"You bloody bastard, I've had enough of you," shouted Sinjin.

"Aye, Captain, what de blazes do ya think ya can do ta me?"

"I have a mind to throw your carcass overboard and let the sharks have a meal," Sinjin replied.

Jervis stepped forward. His arm swung in the air and his balled fist slammed into Sinjin's gut. Sinjin bent over, his breath came in jagged gasps as his hands grabbed his stomach. Jervis smirked wrapping his finger around the hilt of his knife. He took one long stride, and was quickly next to Sinjin pressing the sharp blade of the knife to his chest. Sinjin's right hand slide to the gold handle pistol hanging on his side; the pistol inconspicuously slid from its holster and fired, ripping into Jervis' broad chest leaving the scent of gunpowder floating in the air. The enormous man's hands clutched his chest as his blue stripped shirt turned red. He muttered unintelligible words when his body dropped to the floor with a loud thump inches from her.

Belinda had never felt such hatefulness for anyone as she did for the man lying on the floor beside her. A dark emotion had consumed her fettered brain. She'd been taught in church to forgive, but this time she couldn't, and hoped the man would die.

Sinjin stood over the man. "You bastard, you paid 'tarnal price for your actions. I said you would be keelhauled and I'm a man of my word, but I do not believe the sharks will even want you for a meal."

Jervis groaned, his coldhearted eyes stared and his chest heaved, and then his breathing stopped.

Sinjin leaned down to Belinda lifting her up to him wrapping his arms around her in a caring embrace. "Are you alright, did he hurt you?" he asked looking down at her, tenderly swishing her long blonde hair from her face.

She could see the fury had left his dark eyes, but the pain and worry had taken its place. "I'm fine," she mumbled straightening her ripped shirt. She heard a moan and turned around. "Tobias," she shouted, seeing the boy huddled in the corner of the room. "Are you all right?"

His wild mop of orange hair flipped forward as his head nodded yes.

Sinjin walked over to the boy and reached out his hand. "You're a great mate, and I'm proud to have you on my ship."

Santos and Finley burst into the cabin and stood in the doorway, their eyes full of anger looking down at the man on the floor. Finley grabbed a couple of other mates and they lifted Jervis' huge body from the great cabin floor carrying him outside. The men swung Jervis' body in the air letting him soar over the side of the ship and disappear into the deep water below.

Belinda grabbed Tobias giving him a hug and held a cloth to his round pudgy nose to stop the bleeding. "Thank you, for helping me, I won't ever forget what you did."

"I'm s-sorry I couldn't stop 'em," Tobias slurred in a muffled voice coming from under the cloth.

"You were wonderful, but I do believe you will have two black eyes tomorrow," she added.

Santos nodded his head agreeing and patted the young boy on the back.

"Really, two," Tobias said excitedly pushing the cloth from his grinning face.

Belinda sat down in the cloth chair by the window. Santos handed her a mug of ale. She took a big swig, feeling the liquid burn as it flowed down her throat, polishing off the ale with gusto. Santos smiled down at her. He covered her with a small quilt and left the room as she fell into a deep slumber.

Early Thursday she hurriedly dressed so she wouldn't miss a minute sailing into the Charles Towne harbor, she wasn't letting the episode with Jervis mess with her plans. Charles Towne had become a city in 1670, and the crew called it the Holy City because of its many churches.

The beautiful ship's sails flapped in the breeze. Her head lay against the hull of the ship. She pronounced the name, *Aeolus*, (ee'-oh-luhs) over and over.

"Ian, what does *Aeolus* mean and where did the name come from?"

Ian stopped for a moment. "The name Aeolus is Greek and means *"Keeper of the Wind."* Sinjin's father, John, named her after a Greek god in mythology. The name came from a book that John read when he was a small lad."

"The name is perfect, *Keeper of the Wind*," she repeated.

Sinjin walked over. "Ah, I hear you're questioning about the *Aeolus*. Aeolus was a son of Poseidon by Arne, daughter of the god Aeolus and he lived on a group of islands in the Tyrrhenian Sea. That was the reason Father named his ship the *Aeolus*, believing that Poseidon would keep her safe and protected at all times when it was out to sea."

She leaned against the side of the ship and could see the pride in Sinjin's face knowing that she had fallen in love with the tall, dark, blue ship just as she had with her lighthouse.

The crew eloquently brought the stunning ship into port. When the small bower anchor was down and the gangplank was ready, she swagger walked to the side of the ship.

"Where do you think you are going?" Sinjin called out in his captain's voice.

She stopped and turned around, shocked that he had notice her leaving since he was so busy.

"I'm going to explore Charles Towne," she snapped, looking into those dark brown eyes. "I can't wait to see the city," she answered annoyed at him.

"Not yet," he insisted, giving her one of those stares.

"Why not? I can't help the crew unload so why can't I go into the town," she argued, getting agitated.

"Just calm down; you can go, however Ian will be going with you. I don't want you to go alone."

"I can handle myself and Ian doesn't have to bother with me," she protested with her hands gripping tightly around her waist.

"'Tis no bother, Miss Belinda, are ya ready ta go?" Ian chimed in, as he bounced up and stood next to Sinjin with a big smile across his face. "Let's go see my Charles Towne. Ya do need ta be careful."

"Alright, Ian, let's go," she declared, grabbing his arm giving Sinjin a scowl look.

She let go of Ian's arm and walked beside of him down the scrapped wooden plank and out past the dock, strolling along the narrow cobblestone roads.

"Oh, Ian," Belinda whispered, gesturing her arm in the air as a lump of emotion lodged in her throat. "Look, the city is decorated for Christmas. It's beautiful with its boughs of fresh holly, and evergreen hanging on the street lamps."

"Well," he snickered, "'Tis December."

"The town looks like it just came out of a Christmas storybook," she assured. She was agog seeing sights that she'd read about in history books coming alive in vibrant colors right in front of her eyes, not in black and white photos.

The buildings were beautiful and the architecture was amazing; women were dressed in long pastel and paisley dresses and men in their short breeches and long socks were bustling everywhere. The homes off of Broad Street and South Battery were alluring standing so polished and new with children playing in the yards. The children's laughter blended with the sounds of clip-clopping of horses' hooves on the roads. It was amazing to think these houses were century old historic homes in her time. The noise of the town was so different from what she was used to; no car engines or horns honking, only the braying of horses. She could actually hear the chattering of people having conversations in the doorways of shops.

Ian and she strolled on E. Bay Street taking notice of small shops along the way. A bakery shop, its doors opened wide, was baking goods for the day letting the aroma of warm, sweet-scented bread flow from the shop out into the street. A fragrant smoke drifted from a smokehouse sending the aroma of curing meat to join with the scent of fresh bread.

She jerked to a stop.

"What's wrong?"

"Ian, I've felt like someone is watching and I think they've been following us. I thought I saw a man spying on us from behind the smokehouse."

"Yay, I've seen the man an' I haven't been able ta make out who he might be."

"You don't think it's the constable watching us?"

"Nay, the constable wouldn't hide, he'd come right up ta question us."

"Well, we do need to be careful."

"Jes keep a good watch," Ian added smiling back at her.

Belinda nodded her head yes, but an uneasiness stayed with her.

They ambled along the wondrous roads and Ian began his tale about the British trying to take Charles Towne. The Aeolus and its crew had helped fight for freedom and supported the colonists, so his story was from experience. Her mind spun, this wasn't a story from a history book; it was real. It was incredible to think that his story was from 1782, only a few years ago, and the Revolutionary War had just ended.

"Well what do ya think of my city?" asked Ian gesturing his arms in the air, as they made their way past all the small shops back to the ship.

"It's an amazing city; I see why you love it here."

"'Tis a beauty, ain't she?"

"I'm glad we aren't leaving until Saturday," she whispered.

"Look over there, that theater was built in 1736," said Ian excitedly pointing with his hand. "We also have the College of Charles Towne that was built in 1770, a few blocks down the road on the left."

Belinda stopped next to one of the street lamps smelling the fresh scent of evergreen; her face squinched with a wondering look. "Oh – I'd love to go inside one of the old mansions. It'd be wonderful." She sighed. "I've heard stories about the large plantation homes and how beautiful they were."

"Well, that could be possible fer ya ta see one of the plantation homes, but ya'd have ta dress differently than ya are now."

"What do you mean, Ian?" she questioned spinning around staring at him.

"'Tis a ball that is held every December in Charles Towne an' it happens ta be tomorrow night – at one of the largest plantations nearby," he said, smiling with his large toothy grin, "'tis called *The Grand Christmas Ball.*"

"You mean I could get all dressed up and go to a dance in one of the plantation homes – how?"

"Yay, ya'd be able ta attend, but ya'd need an escort an' one that is a captain of a ship," he added getting quiet, waiting for her reaction.

Her hands flew into the air. "I see what you are up to, Ian, and there isn't any way I am going to a ball with Sinjin, and he wouldn't go with me, so it isn't working. Thanks anyway." She turned in a huff and hastily marched down the street.

"I was just telling ya how ya could get ta see one of the magnificent homes if ya really wanted ta," Ian hollered at her. "Slow down Miss Belinda." He caught up with her, bent over with his hands gripping his knees, and took a deep breath. "The captain received an invitation last time we were in town. I hand delivered it ta him." Ian paused, wiping sweat beads growing on his brow. "The captain works with many of the plantation owners an' delivers their indigo, cotton, an' corn, an' then exchanges it for supplies that they might need."

"Okay," Belinda spun her body around facing Ian, her arms crossed in front of her. "If you know so much, how would I get a dress? I don't have any idea about fancy dresses in this time or what I would need to wear, plus I don't have any money. I wouldn't even know in my own time what to wear to a grand ball."

"That wouldn't be a problem," he said tilting his head back still grinning. "First, are ya willing ta go ta the ball with the Captain?"

"Only, if he is willing," she paused, "to go to the ball with me." Her head turned from Ian not wanting him to see the eagerness on her face, wondering what Sinjin would say.

"Alright, I will see what I can do, but y'll have ta do as I ask when 'tis time," he chuckled.

"Okay, Ian," she said in an exasperated sigh. "I promise I will do as you say, because I would love to see one of those antebellum mansions when it was first built."

They meandered slowly making their way back to the ship. Something caught Belinda's eye, but not soon enough.

Gerald leaped out from the side of a building, stood in front of Belinda with a pistol in his hand pointed at her heart. His oily hair was slicked back from his face. "I tried ta tell de captain y're bad luck, but 'tis ta late fer Jervis." His face screwed into a point scrunching the thin scar on his cheek, as his stony eyes glared at Belinda.

Ian stepped near. "Gerald, what in the name of God do ya think ya are doing?"

"Ian, ya stay out of dis. I have ta gets rid of this Jonah before we set sail," the man replied, his icy eyes glazed over. "I won't let de lass turn de *Aeolus* inta a ghost ship."

"Miss Belinda isn't a Jonah. Now that scallywag Jervis, he was bad luck."

The pistol clicked. Belinda's eyes grew wide watching Gerald's finger twitch on the trigger. He meant business and he'd hated her from that first day Santos told him she was fine to stay onboard. Now, he was going to prove his point.

The pistol fired. Ian shoved Belinda to the ground. She closed her eyes and smelled gunpowder floating in the air. Hearing a thud her eyes jerked open. She didn't feel any pain as her eyes scanned her body looking for the bullet wound. There, lying right in front of her was Gerald with a pearl handle knife stuck deep into his heart with blood soaking his clothes.

Ian bent over and tugged the knife from Gerald's limp body. He stood back up and grabbed Belinda's arm. "We must get going someone must've heard the gunshot.

She raised her body to her feet and stood on shaky legs. "We can't just leave him like this. Oh, Ian what do we do?"

"He made his bed jes as Jervis. We need ta go." Ian declared dragging her down the street. "The captain will know what ta do."

They walked at a hurried pace north on E. Bay Street and turned racing down the boardwalk. Ian let go of her and tore up the plank, faster than she'd ever seen him run, and over to Sinjin. Sinjin grabbed two men and darted past her, his eyes forward and a frown on his face.

Santos reached over taking her arm. "Come an' sit down, ya looks like y're gonna pass out."

"Santos, I thought I was a goner when the gun fired. Ohhhhhhh!" She dashed across the top deck grabbing Ian's arm giving him a hug. "Thank you for saving my life."

"Everything will be fine. Don't forget we have a ball ta get ready fer," he replied with a strained smile on his face.

She made her way back to Santos anxiously waiting for Sinjin and the men to come back. About an hour passed and Sinjin and the men walked up the plank. Sinjin stopped next to her and bent down. "Gerald is at the bottom of the harbor and won't ever bother you again. Ian did well, but I wish it'd been me to put that son of a gun out of his misery."

Later in the day, Belinda sat gazing at the harbor out the windows in the great cabin trying to remember the good times not the episode with Gerald. She'd learned quickly that living in this time was difficult and you had to move on and not dwell on the horrible things. Her eyes closed. The smell of fresh baked bread and Christmas greenery lingered in her mind. Her head leaned back against the cloth chair thinking about Christmases of the past with her father and friends. Thoughts of Johnny became like an old movie, their times of playing in the snow, building funny shaped snowmen and dressing them in her father's old clothes. Her eyes dropped downward looking at the gold charm bracelet on her arm missing its charm, just as Johnny was missing from her life.

Ian knocked and quickly bolted into the room arms wildly swinging over his head. "'Tis done."

"What's done?"

"Ya are going ta the Christmas Ball!"

"You mean I'm really going?" She gasped. "Ian, Sinjin really wants to go with me to the Christmas Ball?"

"Yay, he unreservedly agreed ta accompany ya, I dare say he was thrilled ya wanted ta go."

"Where – how?"

"Miss Belinda, y'll get ta see one of the most outstanding homes in Charles Towne."

"Ian – whose home?"

"Ya are going ta Drayton Hall that was built in 1742 and has 630 acres. Mr. Charles Drayton, who was Lt. Governor in 1785, owns the beautiful home."

"Drayton Hall…" she mumbled.

"Aye, ya will even be able ta meet Mr. Edward Rutledge who was one of the youngest signers of the Declaration of Independence.

Remember we walked past his home yesterday, the home with the verandah porches ya loved."

Her head nodded yes.

"Mr. Drayton loves his plantation an' I know this should be one of his best Christmas Balls. I've heard he's been working on the gardens an' restoring the plantation after the British stayed there."

She became speechless and just sat in the chair by the window glaring at Ian.

"I'd love ta see the plantation myself," he said sighing. "So y'll have ta tell me all of the details of the home an' garden." He paused. "An', y'll get ta meet some of the most respected leaders in the city."

She finally found her voice.

"Ian, maybe this isn't a good idea after all. I won't know what to say to the people at Drayton Hall. I might say something wrong. I don't want to cause Sinjin any problems."

"Ya don't have ta worry about that, women don't over talk. So y'll just have ta stay quiet." He stopped talking and looked over at her. "Now that might be a problem," he answered throwing his head back in his entertaining laugh.

Her head shook to the side as she chuckled along with Ian.

"Besides the captain won't stay long, he doesn't like ta go ta these things."

"Alright, then I'll go," she announce, a frown line growing on her brow. "If you say so, and you're certain Sinjin wants to go with me?"

"Yay," Ian assured with a grin anxiously waving his arms in the air as he talked. "The Captain is very pleased ta be going with ya."

"I still don't have any money to buy a dress."

"The paymaster will pay ya fer yer work ya done. Y'll get paid a pound or maybe a guinea jes as the crew."

"When and how do I get my dress and whatever else I need?" she questioned. She paced the room fidgeting with her hands twisting them together.

"The captain is buying ya dress an' everything ya need an' is glad ya want ta go ta the plantation."

Belinda stopped pacing and faced Ian. "I don't mind spending my money on a dress. He doesn't have to worry about me."

"He does care an' ya can't change his mind, so don't try. I'll see ta getting ya dress tomorrow an' I'll prepare everything fer ya jes as I do fer the Captain."

"But, Ian I don't understand how to dress in women's clothes – for a party like this."

"I have someone who will help us. 'Twill work out an' y'll enjoy the wonderful dance at the plantation." Ian smiled his bubbly smile and briskly left the room.

She picked up her book off the small table and sat down by the windows, but her eyes wouldn't stay on the page with her mind spinning. *I'm really going to a Christmas Ball in a plantation in the old south in the 1700's.*

Belinda stared at her evening meal and nervously scooted her food around on the wooden plate. Her eyes swung from her food looking back at Sinjin with quick glances, wondering what was going through his mind, but she wasn't going to ask him. Thoughts swirled in her head and for the first time she wondered if Sinjin had a special girl that he was in love with at one of the ports.

Sinjin felt her glances and smiled inwardly not wanting her to know how excited he was to be going with her to the plantation. He looked away shyly when he'd feel her stare. He couldn't or wouldn't show his feelings for her. He'd never cared for anyone and had felt so alone most of his life. He swore he'd never fall in love, remembering the heartache his father and Santos had lived through, nonetheless those blue eyes were tugging on his heart and he had passion flowing through his body; passion he'd never felt before.

Later that evening, Belinda sat quietly for a while on the top deck staring out into the dark night, dreaming. She heard the clock in the great cabin strike eleven – time to get some rest. She'd had enough thinking for one day and tomorrow would be a busy and amazing day.

CHAPTER FOURTEEN

THE CHRISTMAS BALL

The sun shining through the porthole flickered on the walls woke Belinda early Friday. Just as normal each day her breakfast, today a hoecake, was waiting on the table in the great cabin with a hot mug of coffee.

After lunch, Belinda sat watching the crew as they finished loading the ship. Hearing a ruckus, she spun around seeing Ian parading up the gangplank carrying an arm full of packages with a short, chubby woman walking along side of him.

"Miss Belinda, 'tis my sister, Rose, an' she has agreed ta help ya get dressed 'fer the ball tonight."

"Your sister, Ian I didn't know you had a sister," Belinda questioned studying the plump woman standing in front of her with a round face, blue eyes and gray hair twisted up in a bun. "Rose, you live in Charles Towne?"

"Aye, my lady."

Belinda's eyes swung from Rose to Ian.

"Yay, Rose lives near," Ian chimed in, "an' it's nice because I get ta visit her often."

"Rose, thank you for helping me, I hope this isn't too much trouble for you?"

"Oh no, I am happy ta lend a hand. I am excited fer ya an' I'll help in any way I am able. Now, come along an' Ian ya need ta leave us alone so we can get ready," said Rose, hurrying in a wiggle walk into Belinda's cabin.

"I know when I'm not needed. If ya need anything let me know." He placed the packages on the bed turned and closed the door behind him.

Rose energetically undid the packages. Belinda stared at the clothes as she watched Rose place them precisely in a pile across the bed. She then gently spread out a magnificent fairytale dress across the bed, yards of silk rippled to the floor.

"Wow!" Belinda exclaimed. Her fingers softy touched the silky fabric. The fabulous dress was the color of the *Aeolus* – a stunning dark blue with a gold lacy trim weaved around the neck, the bodice, the sleeves, and hem of the dress.

"'Tis beautiful, ain't it? Ian said it was perfect an' I do agree," Rose said briskly. "Alright, we first need ta get ya cleaned up an' then I'll fix yer hair." She moved around the room at ease like Ian, so sure of herself. She poured some water from the pitcher into the bowl.

Belinda pulled off her crew's clothes and picked up the rag in the bowl. She didn't move for a few seconds, taking in the fragrance of lilac in the water. "Rose, how did you know I love the smell of lilac?

Rose smiled and her cheeks puffed up making her eyes like blue dots. "Ian is more observant than most men. He said ya smelled of lilac when he first met ya."

"Ian is sweet," Belinda answered, as she began to wash her arms and legs taking what would be considered her bath.

"Now, Miss Belinda sit down in this chair an' let's take a look at yer hair," Rose urged. She gently took Belinda's hair in her plump hands combing it. "Yer hair is beautiful," Rose said arranging the blonde curly hair meticulously on top of Belinda's head leaving strands hanging down around her face.

Rose began telling stories about Ian. 'I'm Ian's younger sister," she smiled, "by a few years. We grew up close since our father was at sea all of the time," Rose said. "Ian would travel a few times a year on voyages with our father, thus he grew up fast," she added. "His daughter Amanda lives near Philadelphia an' he doesn't get ta see her very often. She is getting married next year an' I hope he will take the time ta be at the wedding. 'Tis hard fer Ian ta leave his ship even fer a short while."

"Well, we'll have to do something about that," Belinda added.

"I think between the two of us that jes might work," Rose said, laughing with the same soothing laugh as Ian.

The ends of hair, on each side of Belinda's face, miraculously snapped into place in swirling blonde curls.

"'Tis perfect," Rose added, patting the hair. "Here is some powder ta use on ya face."

Belinda stared in the wavy mirror in awe at her hair as she applied the powder to her face.

The time came and Belinda began to layer the clothes onto her thin body. First were the under garments – the chemise or shift, like a slip, and then a corset, with hooks and eyelets, which was very tight, pushing her small breasts up making them look larger than they were. Then the final layer was added, the stockings made of silk and the petticoat that had beautiful layers of lace trim ruffles on the bottom.

At last the dark blue, long gorgeous dress, or as Rose called it Belinda's ball gown slipped over the petticoat. She then added a pair of long white gloves and a silky long cloak draped over her shoulders.

Belinda stared into the mirror. She flinched. She didn't recognize herself. Her skin glowed with a soft pearl color and her mouth was red and full from the red berry cream Rose had applied to her lips. A smile came on her face. Johnny had called her a tomboy and he'd be shocked to see her now. Tears glistened in her eyes thinking of her father and Johnny.

Rose opened the door and led them into the great cabin. She stopped walking. "Alright Miss Belinda, one more thing, y'll need ta curtsy," Rose said. Her short round body did a light squat so graceful. "When ya are introduced ta someone, gently curtsy."

Belinda tried to curtsy and fell forward catching herself on the large table in the center of the room. Her dress got in the way each time and she would lose her balance, but persistence won and she was able to curtsy without wobbling.

Belinda faced Rose and did a flawless curtsy. "Thank you Rose, this wouldn't be possible without you." She knew the simple words thank you were inadequate to express her gratitude.

"Ya are kindly welcome. Tonight is going ta be a dream come true," Rose answered, smiling a sheepish grin, "in more ways than one." She crossed the room to the cabin's door sticking her head out. "Ian, 'tis time," she called out excitedly. She turned around. "Are ya ready, Miss Belinda?"

"As ready as I will ever be," replied Belinda swallowing hard.

"Do not worry," Rose answered, backing away.

When Ian walked into the great cabin his face lit with an enormous grin. "Miss Belinda, y're radiant." He opened the great cabin door wide. "'Tis time ta leave," he added, proudly leading her out the door.

Belinda stepped out onto the top deck. The crew whistled and yelled. "Take a gander at that – she's gorgeous!"

Belinda looked to the side of the ship. Santos grinned and nodded his head in approval.

Sinjin walked up and stood in front of Belinda wearing his tall black leather boots, long black coat, breeches, and vest to match. His thunderstruck expression imitated his eyes leveling a sparkling gaze upon her. How was he to keep his composure? His heart pounded and warmth pulsated throughout his body. He felt a stare and turned around; Lucky was watching with a hard gaze that could bore right though him. Jealousy was a malicious evil and it had come between the two men, two great friends that now loved the same women. Sinjin bowed to her. He smiled bringing out his deep dimples. "You are the most beautiful woman I've ever seen."

Belinda curtsied in a very smooth form tilting her head to Sinjin. She felt a stare and turned a glance to Lucky standing to the side of the ship fidgeting with his hands. He finally ducked his head in approval and gave her his wonderful smile lighting up his deep blue eyes.

Sinjin looped her arm in his, giving her a reassuring squeeze and they ambled down the plank with her lengthy cloak swishing against Sinjin's long legs. However, instead of turning left to go into town, Sinjin ushered her to the right strolling down the boardwalk.

He chuckled noticing her reaction. "You look worried."

"Why aren't we going into town and take a buggy?"

"My dear that would take a complete day to travel by buggy to the magnificent rice plantation and the trail isn't one we would want to take."

"Then…" she began.

"Patience," he interrupted, "We will be joining a group of guests from Charleston onboard a small sailing vessel."

"A what?" Her head tilted to the side looking up at him.

"A small mast schooner can easily maneuver from the Charleston harbor up the Ashley River." He laughed. "I sure couldn't maneuver the *Aeolus* up the southward flowing river through all its sharp bends."

"We're taking a schooner?" she questioned.

Sinjin stopped walking.

She gasped. In front of them stood a small gaff-rigged ship with tall mast and only two large sails.

A bearded man about forty years old with coffee brown hair flowing onto his shoulders stepped up next to Sinjin; his head ducked showing respect to Sinjin. "Captain Alvery, 'tis a pleasure ta have ya aboard *The Rose*."

"Captain Edward, 'tis a pleasure for me to join you onboard *The Rose*, she is a beautiful ship."

The captain beamed as he turned to prepare the ship for its short voyage. One of the crew led them to a seat in the center of the ship. Five couples sat quietly, their eyes staring back at the city of Charleston. The women's faces were strained; this wasn't an everyday occurrence sailing on a ship.

Belinda held onto her flowing dress and sat down next to Sinjin bringing her cloak tight around her dress. Her head swung back as her eyes stared upward to the tall mast wishing she was wearing her mate's clothes and could scramble up the mast and see far out to land. Sinjin's dark eyes stared down at her, understanding what she was thinking. He tentatively rested his hand on hers and gently squeezed it with that captivating smile growing on his face.

She leaned her head near Sinjin. "How long will our voyage take?" she whispered.

"About three hours, we have to sail during high tide and then we will be sailing back at high tide. No captain wants to be stranded on the river."

"Oh," she moaned; she wasn't used to thinking about the tides since the harbors they sailed into were deep and the *Aeolus* didn't have any problems maneuvering into them.

The ship pitched to the side as it sailed out into the ocean and Captain Edward effortlessly steered the ship to the mouth of the

Ashley River. Belinda relaxed, leaned back against Sinjin and felt the heat of his warm body next to hers, listening to the sails flap high above and the waves gently splash the side of the ship. A smile appeared on her face hearing the crew whistle while they worked on the sails.

Time passed by quickly and she was enjoying the quietness of the day. The late afternoon sun began gradually to sink in the west leaving shadows along the water. The women's hands were gripped tightly in their laps as they sat tense next to their husbands. The stars twinkled in the sky as *The Rose* sailed along the gently flowing river in the cool evening. The oil lamps positioned along the sides of the ship gave off a light orange glow in the darkness.

The ship sailed around a bend and there to their left was an amazing mansion sitting on top of a hill, lit with candlelight shining out from the windows. Sweet music flowed from the house bringing peacefulness to the early evening. *The Rose* docked. Captain Edward stepped up and shook Sinjin's hand as they departed the ship. They followed the other couples up the stone steps and a path lined with lit lanterns and white and pink azalea bushes.

Belinda shivered as they neared the front of the home.

"Belinda," Sinjin whispered, taking her hand and gently squeezing it, "my dear, you will be fine."

They strolled up the wide steps to the huge mahogany front doors. Flames danced on the wall from the oil lanterns hanging on each side of the doors, and boughs of evergreen were weaved around each lantern.

Two men dressed in dark uniforms bowed and opened the huge doors. Sinjin led her into the large marble-floored vestibule and over to the stair-hall with hand-formed plaster ceilings reaching 27 feet high. Chatter and lifting music flooded throughout the home. A short, thin black man took her cloak and handed it to a young black girl.

They fell in line behind other guests; their hosts were waiting at the end of the line. A small man greeted them with sparkly green eyes.

"Captain Alvery," the man said in an excited voice, "'Tis a pleasant surprise. I didn't presume this day would ever come about. Nevertheless, I am very pleased you decided to join us for this glorious occasion. Let me introduce my wife, Hester Middleton Drayton." The man graciously turned to his wife.

Sinjin did a bow, took Hester's hand softly in his hand as she curtsied. Hester wore a long flowing rose-colored satin dress that matched the color of her puffed up cheeks.

Their eyes turned towards Belinda. "Mr. and Mrs. Charles Drayton," Sinjin announced. "I would like to introduce, Miss Belinda Brady from the northern colonies."

Mr. Drayton took Belinda's hand in his and she curtsied as Rose had taught her. "It is a pleasure my dear and I do hope you enjoy your stay at our home," Mr. Drayton said kindly.

Sinjin bowed to the couple, looped Belinda's arm in his arm and they turned to leave. He held onto Belinda tight as they stepped up a beautifully crafted double mahogany Imperial staircase that met at the top with carved lotus and squash blossom designs woven through it.

They were ushered into the upper great hall, the ballroom, quite spacious enough for hundreds of guest. Elegant oil paintings covered the walls around the room, and smells of fresh baked cakes and sounds of people laughing were soothing. Warm fires in the two hearths on opposite sides of the room, along with hundreds of candles burning in the hanging chandeliers above their heads gave her a warm and cheery feeling inside adding romance and elegance to the night. Boughs of evergreen and beribboned bouquets of holly and mistletoe were laying on the mantels. The musicians standing on a platform to the back of the room were playing waltzes, as couples danced swirling around the room.

Belinda felt a gaze of many eyes on them when they entered the room. Her own eyes swept panning the ballroom, studying the beautifully dressed women and handsome men.

Two men holding onto their wives' arms crossed the room to greet them.

"Captain Alvery, 'tis an honor for you to be joining us. My brother and I were discussing this afternoon how great a job you have done delivering our goods." The man turned to face the woman next to him. "First, and foremost, I would like to introduce my wife, Elizabeth."

Sinjin took Elizabeth's hand and bowed, she curtsied, and her dark green dress spread out wide onto the floor.

The other man stepped up. "My wife Henrietta."

"It is a pleasure to meet you Captain Alvery, my husband has spoken about you so many times," said Henrietta, dressed in a crimson dress with white lace layered over it.

"Mr. and Mrs. John Rutledge and Mr. and Mrs. Edward Rutledge I would like to introduce Miss Belinda Brady from the northern colonies."

Belinda curtsied when both men stepped up and took her hand in their hand and bowed to her.

Edward turned from them. "Excuse me," he said gesturing his arm in the air toward the door they'd entered and hurriedly crossed the room.

In the doorway stood a thin man with piercing blue eyes wearing a white wig, and holding onto a shorter plump woman dressed in a teal dress, Edward greeted the couple and escorted them over to his wife and brother.

The couple then turned their attention to Sinjin.

The man leaned over to Belinda gently taking her hand. "George Washington, my lady, and this is my wife Martha." Belinda curtsied. Her hand trembled as she looked into the compassionate blue eyes of George Washington. Her mouth became dry. She gulped. She couldn't believe she was meeting the first president of the United States.

Sinjin stepped near and took Martha Washington's hand and she curtsied letting her teal dress elegantly flow onto the floor. The men began to talk about politics and the women began to talk of children and travels.

Belinda's eyes stayed on Sinjin as Martha talked of traveling back to Philadelphia. He stood tall and erect, so handsome, arched broad shoulders and narrow hips; looking so different from the other men. She could see his muscles protruding from the sleeves of his jacket from working and living on a sailing ship. His dark eyes slowly swung her way always keeping an eye on her. She smiled and a half grin formed on his face showing his dimples which made her face flush as a fluttering feeling grew inside of her.

When the band began to play, Sinjin turned from the men that were deep in conversation and weaved through the crowd to Belinda. "Would you like to walk around and take a tour of the home and gardens?"

"Yes, I could use some fresh air," she admitted fanning her hand in the air. "The room has become very warm with so many people."

Each room of the home had been decorated after the Greek order; Doric, Ionic, and Corinthian like the upper great hall indicating the importance of the room by the design. The Ionic order indicated that room was more important than the one with the Doric embellishments.

They walked out the front door. Belinda slowed her pace as they strolled down the lantern lit path to the gardens. The fresh cool air with the scent of gardenia bushes hit her warm face. Faint shafts of moonlight revealed an eerie, but mysterious glow across the garden.

"Awe, this is nice out here," she assured feeling a wave of delicious goose bumps on her arms as Sinjin drew her close. Her body melted against his chest feeling his fingers interlacing in her hair. A voluptuous shiver rose from the center of her being as her face flushed when he gave his quick heart-stopping smile. A fire kindled inside her coursing through her body. His fingers tilted her chin back, her eyes closed and his face came down to hers letting their lips meet. The kiss was light and playful. His arm caressed her shoulders hugging her tight. She felt something inside of her growing – a tingling feeling she'd never felt before. She wanted to tell him this was the greatest moment in her life, but that would betray too much of her feelings for him.

Sinjin pulled his head back looking at her glowing face as excitement shimmered in her ocean-blue eyes. She was soft and tasted like spring. He felt his body heating, alive for the first time in years. She was calm, serene and beautiful, incredibly beautiful. Her attention drew back to him and he felt his heart thump slowly. She blushed, a sweet pink color infusing her cheeks. He brought her even closer until he was enveloped by her scent of lilac kissing her lush lips – knowing he couldn't deny his feeling any longer, he was hopelessly in love.

He pulled away – her eyes opened seeing his eyes were staring down at her. Amused, she let go of his arm understanding he always needed to stay in control.

He stepped back from her. He'd felt the sensations grow and couldn't let his feelings for her show – not now, it wasn't time.

The evening was serene as they walked the grounds listening to the soft music as it flowed from the mansion. The moonlight shone down with beams of light filtering through the tall trees surrounding the yard. In the distance, the Ashley River's water glistened and the silhouette of *The Rose* bobbled in the water.

Sinjin leaned down; his hand softly caressed her hair as he looked into her eyes. "I'm enjoying our time out here; nevertheless, I guess we need to be cordial and return to the grand ballroom."

She nodded. Sinjin tenderly held onto her arm and led her up the magnificent staircase and into the upper grand ballroom that smelled of the fragrance of mingled fresh pine and beeswax. A sweet aroma she'd never forget.

"Would you like to dance, Belinda," Sinjin asked kindly, spinning her around to face him.

"I don't know how to dance," she whispered, "like they are doing."

"Just follow my lead," he answered in a soft voice, taking her small-gloved hand in his much larger hand bringing her body close as they twirled around the room gliding across the dance floor.

Belinda felt like her feet weren't touching the floor and she was as light as a feather in Sinjin's arms.

The evening moved on. "I think we should go back to the ship, if that is alright with you?" she questioned seeing Sinjin's tired eyes gazing down at her.

"Yay, we will have to leave soon, while it is high tide."

"I've had the greatest night of my life," she answered, "thank you."

"One more dance and then we will leave."

"That would be perfect," she whispered.

Sinjin stepped back from her, bowed. "My lady," he said as his arm circled around her anchoring her tightly against his chest swaying in perfect harmony with the music, dancing their last dance in Drayton Hall.

The final strains of the waltz died and Sinjin led them from the room and they gradually stepped down the glorious staircase out into the cool night air.

The night was a fantasy, a dream. Listening to the music slowly fade away they made their way down the path to *The Rose*. In the soft moonlit night, Sinjin leaned over and tenderly his head titled down and their lips met. He looked into her eyes and whispered, "This was the most wonderful evening I have ever had."

Belinda cuddled close; she leaned her head on his shoulder feeling his arm tightly around her.

Sinjin's eyes stared off feeling her softly taking in calm breaths next to him in the quiet night as *The Rose* sailed soundlessly down the Ashley River leaving a small wake of water. He had so many unanswered questions. His dark eyes peered down at Belinda. *"Who do you love, my sweet Belinda?"*

The *Aeolus* stood tall in the moonlight as *The Rose* sailed into port docking not far from the giant ship. Sinjin and Belinda followed the other couples down the long boardwalk and casually walked up the plank to the top deck. He held onto Belinda a little longer than he needed when they stopped in front of the great cabin.

Someone cleared their throat. There, on the larboard side of the ship stood Lucky his eyes fixed on Belinda. He didn't speak. He turned and went to the hatch disappearing down the ladder. Sinjin let go of Belinda and they stepped into the great cabin. He whispered goodnight and bowed his head.

She said a soft goodnight to him and opened the door going into the sleeping quarters. She undressed, slipping her beautiful blue ball gown off, putting her nightclothes on and burrowing her body into the feathered mattress. Her long hair fell around her face and her arms wrapped around her. She smiled smelling the spicy musk, a masculine scent, Sinjin's scent. Not able to sleep she kept thinking about the night, hearing the music playing in her head, dreaming of how Sinjin's arms felt holding her snug next to him dancing with the handsomest man in Charleston. Her fingers lightly touched her lips remembering their kiss, their enchanted night.

She woke early at daybreak and hurried to get dress to see the magnificent city of Charles Towne before they sailed away.

When she came out of the cabin, Sinjin standing at the ship's wheel ducked his head and smiled at her showing his wonderful dimples.

Ian brought her coffee and breakfast, and eagerly he began to question her wanting to hear all the details of the night. She described the Drayton's house and garden in every detail, but left out the particulars of Sinjin and her walk in the garden and their first kiss. Her life now had changed and her life had become mixed, nonetheless she was at peace for the first time since she'd fallen from her cliff.

CHAPTER FIFTEEN

ST. AUGUSTINE

Belinda's days of being a sailor were many, watching and learning about the ship as the *Aeolus* sailed south to St. Augustine. She still didn't have any inkling of what had happened to her that foggy evening or why it happened, but she was becoming a mate and enjoying living on the *Aeolus*.

Sinjin had allowed her to stay up in the crow's nest longer, just as Santo said. She'd take the afternoon watch that was between 1200 and 1600 each day. She learned what under the weather meant, as the sea spray would make it up to the crow's nest and she would be drenched when the ship would lean to one side. The first time she was soaked by the sea spray, she heard the laughter from the crew below, including Santos' roaring laughter.

Each day she tutored Tobias and Joshua and they would sit patiently learning their numbers and to read and write. Tobias was learning fast and could already read all the primers she'd bought in Charles Towne.

One day Tobias walked over to her, his face bright red, eyes on the deck. "Miss Belinda, we's d-don't has anyway t-ta pay ya, but I-I do have this. My Pa says w-we pays our way an' don't t-take charity." He opened his hand and lying in his palm were bones.

"Tobias, this isn't charity, but I don't understand what you have in your hands?"

He proudly grinned showing his pointed teeth. "'Tis turtle bones an' m-my grandpappy gave 'em ta m-my pa an' h-he gave 'em t-ta me. They came f-from a special turtle t-that has brought g-good luck ta our family f-fer generations."

"Oh, Tobias, I can't keep them, you need to keep them to hand down someday to your son," she said feeling overwhelmed.

"But Miss Belinda, I-I dons have a-anything else t-ta give ya. What if ya t-takes jes one of 'em, h-how'd that be?"

"I don't need any pay for tutoring you, but thank you anyway," she said taking one small bone from his rough hand.

Tobias' head rose peering down at her and his thin lips puckered.

"Tobias, there's more you want to tell me, isn't there."

Tobias slid the rest of the turtle bones into the pocket of his breeches nodding his head yes. His voice quivered, "I-I no 'tis a dream, b-but I-I want ta become a l-lawyer someday."

"A lawyer, that's why you wanted to learn to read?" she exclaimed delightfully.

"Y-Yay, I met a l-lawyer in Charles Towne – a f-few years after m-my ma died. He had a f-fine office with a l-large wooden desk as s-smooth as a piece of glass – an' he sat i-in a black leather chair an' spoke so e-elegantly," he paused, "I believe that is the w-word, an' his name was o-on a plaque." He puffed up trying to stand taller. "I wants my n-name, Tobias Allen Langston someday on a-a plaque sitting on a desk in a fine office, jes like he had."

"Yes, elegantly is the word," she smiled up at the young boy, "but to become a lawyer will take a long time, a lot of hard work and a lot of money."

"I knows it t-takes a lot of money a-an' Captain Alvery said h-he wills help me an' I can go ta the C-College of Charleston if I-I works hard."

"Then we have a lot of work to do and we'll need even more books," she announced.

"Ya t-thinks I can do it," his hands nervously twisted in circles, "even w-with my stuttering?"

"I think you can do anything you put your mind to do. We'll make it happen."

Tobias' face turned even redder and he ducked his head staring down at the deck hurrying off across the deck to get back to work.

She looked over to the larboard side of the ship. Sinjin was working on some sails when his eyes swung back at her. She smiled; he really was a caring man helping Tobias.

Santos slumped down on the wooden box next to her. "How's my Little Jackaro doing? I see ya got a turtle bone, y's gonna have some good luck. I heard ya had a great time in Charles Towne. Do ya believe me now?"

"Yes, I had a great time at the Christmas Ball," she answered not looking Santos in the eyes. She understood what he meant that Sinjin was her Jack in his tale about being a Jackaro.

Santos grinned. "Look at the lightning from the west."

"Are we going to have a storm?"

"We might, but that storm won't reach us until later tonight. The weather is getting a lot cooler though an' this may be a frigid winter."

Ian came bouncing across the deck and scooted in next to Santos. "Miss Belinda, we will be docking soon in St. Augustine," explained Ian, a huge smile on his face.

Her eyes turned to Santos remembering the story he had told about Sinjin's mother living and dying in St. Augustine. "I can't wait to see St. Augustine." She leaned against the wall of the ship her head tilted back watching the darkening clouds race across the late afternoon sky as if they were in a hurry to reach land.

"St. Augustine is a beautiful province, a fascinating place an' y'll definitely enjoy seeing it," Ian assured as he stood back up. "Well, gotta get back ta work – a lot ta do before mornin'."

Santos' head nodded agreeing. He moaned as he stood. "G'night, Little Jackaro, see ya in the mornin'," he said stretching his arms out wide.

"Good night, Santos," she called out watching his body glide in a smooth form across the top deck to the hatch.

The great cabin door swung open squeaking. She tiptoed quietly into the room not wanting to disturb Sinjin who was sitting, his back to her, at the large table working on his paperwork. His shoulders tensed.

"Sinjin, is something wrong?"

"Oh, Belinda, I didn't hear you come in."

"You were too absorbed in your thoughts. I didn't mean to bother you."

"You didn't and I was thinking about tomorrow not my work. It's a little difficult going into St. Augustine, even though I love the province. That is where my home is, on Aviles Street, and where I lived when I was a little boy. I loved living there with my mum and I still feel her and my father's presence when I am there."

"Santos told me that was your home before your mother died, but I didn't know you had kept the house," she added inquisitively.

"Yay, my father and I kept the house and every year we used to spend the winters there. Belinda scooted a chair from the table and sat down next to Sinjin.

His eyes had a faraway look. "My mum wasn't a sailor and loved our home; she was a true land lubber and loved her garden." A smile emerged on his face as he stood from his chair and paced the room.

"My mum just couldn't get use to sailing on the *Aeolus*. My father would tease her that he wanted to live on the *Aeolus*." He stopped pacing and turned to look at Belinda. "She would look at my father fiercely with her piercing dark eyes and he would laugh and put his arms around her giving her a kiss. They were so much in love." His head ducked squeezing his lips together. "Even as a small boy I could tell. My life was perfect." Sinjin sighed, lost in his thoughts.

She laid her hand on his. She squeezed it reassuringly and smiled. This time he didn't pull away. "I understand how much you miss your family. I miss my mom, and the fun times we had before she died and I will never forget them."

Sinjin lifted her up from the chair and put his arms around her bringing her close. "I'm sorry thinking only of myself," he said. Tenderly his fingers tilted her head back and stared into her blue eyes. "This hasn't been easy on you either, not being able to see your family."

"I'm fine, and so are you," she replied letting her fingers cup his face. "We have our family here and we aren't alone."

Sorrow left his face. "How would you like to see my home tomorrow?" he asked excitedly.

"I'd love to, if it isn't interfering in any way?"

"Nay, I know you will love the house."

A flash of blinding lightning, like a giant flash bulb, lit the cabin and thunder boomed sounding like the cannons firing at the pirate ship.

"Awe, the storm is finally upon us," he declared, his hands fell from her shoulders.

She moved near the row of front windows. "It's so bright, so beautiful, but terrifying in a wonderful way."

Sinjin followed her across the room taking a tentative step next to her. He stopped and stared out the windows. "When I was a child,

I would sit by these windows and watch the show the lightning put on zigzagging down from the dark clouds striking at the churning sea."

She stood quietly next to the windows, inches from Sinjin, watching the gale winds stirring up the water making the sea heave in tall waves as the storm approached.

He turned toward her. "My father would tell me the tale of St. Elmo's fire an omen of heavenly intervention that would save sailors from drowning during a storm."

"St. Elmo's fire, I've never heard of that?" Belinda sat down in the cloth chair listening to Sinjin tell his tale.

"Legend says that St. Elmo died during a blustery thunderstorm just like tonight. He'd told the crew not to be afraid and if he ever died he would reappear in some form, and the ship would always be safe. That night during the storm he fell overboard, and then later in the night, a mysterious light appeared at the bow of the vessel and the ship and crew were saved."

A bolt of lightning lit the cabin and thunder roared. She shivered. Her arms wrapped around her body, Sinjin smiled down on her. "Now, when a bluish white light dances at the bow of a ship during a lightning storm it is known as the St. Elmo's fire and the crew believes St. Elmo will see the ship safely through the storm."

The clock on his desk chimed. Sinjin stopped talking. "Twelve bells, at last, `tis time we need to get some rest. Morning will be here soon," he assured.

"Morning is always too soon for me," she said laughing. Gently he pulled her body up to him. Their bodies touched, her heart thundered in her chest, neither one moved away. She tenderly reached up and cradled his face bringing it down to her. He started to retreat pulling away from her, but she held on to him astonished that such a strong man could be so nervous around her. He finally grinned showing his dimples and he leaned down giving her a lighthearted kiss. Belinda finally stepped away from Sinjin and crossed the room to her bedroom.

She gripped the bedroom's doorknob, but stopped. "Goodnight, Sinjin, and I can't wait to go to your home."

He smiled back at her busily rolling up some of the charts on the table. "Goodnight Belinda and may you have sweet dreams," he answered in a soft voice.

Belinda slid her breeches, vest, shirt, and shoes off and slipped on her dingy sleeping shirt. Her body flopped down onto the worn mattress. She swished her head on the feather pillow. The events of fear and happiness from the last few weeks were all muddled up in her mind like pieces of material laid out for a patchwork quilt her momma used to make. She sighed. How could her life from the past and her life in this time blend together to make a beautiful quilt or would the pieces of her life stay jumbled up strewn onto the floor.

The next morning she sat down at the long table in the great cabin.

"G'mornin', Miss Belinda, did ya rest well?" asked Ian setting a plate with bonded jacky down on the table.

She smiled thinking about Sinjin last night holding her tight in his arms. She looked up. "Very," She assured, "with the swaying of the ship, I'm rocked to sleep each night."

"I hope ya enjoy yer breakfast," he said kindly, putting the rest of the charts away.

"Thank you, Ian." She hurriedly finished her breakfast and went out onto the deck.

"G'mornin' sleepy head." Santos said jokingly sitting down. "I heard from young Jack that ya are going inta St. Augustine with 'em this mornin'."

"Yes I am, and news does travel fast on this ship," she added teasing Santos. "Santos, why don't you come with us? I would enjoy your stories of St. Augustine."

"My tales of St. Augustine are of sorrow an' I don't want ta interfere."

"Well, then you do need to come with us and make some tales of happiness in St. Augustine. This isn't going to be a sad trip, but a trip of joy and remembering the good times."

"I haven't been back ta St. Augustine since we buried John there."

"Sinjin's father was buried in St. Augustine?" she exclaimed leaning over closer to Santos. "I thought he was buried at sea."

"Nay, he wanted ta be buried by Zyanya an' baby Mary Coreen."

"Oh, I didn't know."

"When John became sick we set sail fer St. Augustine an' that is where he drew his last breath an' that was the last time I've been ta the home."

She sighed. "It's so beautiful here," she said looking out to the green land as the ship sailed along the coast. "Are we coming into a bay?"

"We're headed inta the South Channel past the St. Anastasia Island ta the Matanzas River," Santos added.

"I can see why Zyanya loved it here. The weather is spectacular with the bluest skies."

"Yay, it was the perfect spot for them since no one judges ya here not like the colonies up north. They were livin' their dream – fer a few years."

The ship sailed slowly past the St. Anastasia Island and the pelicans and seagulls were circling high above watching for fish.

"What was that?" Belinda jumped from her seat and ran to the side of the ship.

Sinjin called out, "dolphins to the starboard side."

Santos laughed his boisterous laugh. "We are stirring up the fish," Santos explained, "Dolphins like ta follow a ship like ours."

"Oh," she exclaimed, "they're so beautiful and swim so gracefully. I'd love to swim with them."

"Aye that can be arranged, maybe sometime next summer."

"You mean I could really swim with those magnificent creatures?"

"Yay, Sinjin has been swimming with the dolphins since he was a small lad an' would love ta teach ya." Santos leaned back watching her reaction. He laughed. "I think that boy is part fish."

Sinjin stood at the helm and smoothly brought the large ship into the port. Quickly the crew prepared the ship to unload the barrels of cargo.

"Belinda, are you ready – shall we go?" asked Sinjin, combing back his dark strands of hair from his face with his long fingers.

"I'm ready." Her hand reached over tugging on Santos' arm. "C'mon Santos," she urged.

"Santos, would you like to come with us?" questioned Sinjin in a surprised voice.

Santos anxiously rubbed his fuzzy beard. "Little Jackaro," his head pointed to Belinda, "wants me ta go."

"Aye, then let's get going." Sinjin laughed. "You know you won't win the argument with her." He spun around facing Ian. "We are leaving and will be in town for a while."

"Things will be fine, Sir, onboard the ship – have a nice visit."

The three walked down the plank past other large sailing ships, the marina, and small storefronts lining the road going about six blocks.

Sinjin stopped on Aviles Street. "Well, there she is Belinda. What do you think of my home?"

CHAPTER SIXTEEN

AVILES STREET

In front of them stood a large two-story reddish brick home with a black wrought iron fence across the front, white columns holding two oversize porches, one up and one down, facing out to the harbor, 15 Aviles Street. Sweet fragrances floated in the cool morning air from green vines with red, bell shaped flowers woven through trellises, hanging next to the side of the porch.

Sinjin leaned down and his hand swung open the wrought iron gate steering Belinda through to the front porch. She stopped walking and turned around seeing Santos, his mouth puckered, tapping his fingers in a rhythm on the wrought iron fence. His head titled back his eyes on the home and a smile immerged cracking his wrinkled face.

Sinjin softly took Belinda's arm; slowly they made their way up the steps onto the massive porch. Four wooden rockers sat across the porch and a tan wicker swing hung on one end. Colossal flowerpots sat on each side of the steps full of green bushy ferns growing down the sides of the pots onto the planked floor.

Sinjin's knuckles rapped on the large mahogany front door and slowly it opened. Standing in front of them was a plump black woman. She wore a simple beige dress and a mobcap sat atop of her head. The woman stared at them with narrow black eyes then a smile emerged on her round face.

"Lordy mercy, I can't believe my old eyes, dis is some day," she hollered staring at Santos, "now is dat really ya?"

"Yay, Mamma Annie," said Santos putting his arms around the woman as she grabbed him in a bear hug and didn't let go.

"Mason shor' won't believe dis." She let go of Santos. "Child, give Mamma Annie a hug."

Sinjin stepped up by Mamma Annie; she grabbed him with the same affectionate bear hug.

"Now, who might dis be?" the woman questioned letting go of Sinjin, her eyes on Belinda.

"This is one of my crew, Belinda Brady," said Sinjin, "and Belinda this is Mamma Annie. She has been taking care of me all of my life."

Sinjin and Santos walked into the large vestibule leaving Mamma Annie and Belinda on the porch.

"Did I hear ya right, child – Belinda?" Mamma Annie stepped close and her black eyes grew wide. "Lordy Mercy, but ya is a girl."

Sinjin started laughing. "Yay, she is," he called back.

"Why is a young girl like ya dressed like dat?" questioned Mamma Annie.

"I am one of the crew of the ship just as Sinjin said, and it is nice to meet you Mamma Annie."

Mamma Annie turned and looked at Sinjin and Santos with a hard stare shaking her head from side to side not approving.

Sinjin laughed. "I will explain later about Belinda and you will soon learn why she's one of the crew," he added with a grin. "And why she does what she wants."

"C'mon in 'n let me makes ya something ta eats." Her dark eyes swung to Sinjin. "Child – ya looks ta skinny."

"I'm fine, and I'm not too skinny, but I sure would like some of your fresh tea, if you don't mind?" Sinjin asked sitting down in one of the overstuffed chairs in the parlor.

"I wills go an' get some tea fer everyone. First, I gots ta tell Mason yer here," she shouted turning around swishing her wide dress back and forth, muttering to herself, hurrying down a long hallway.

The parlor, with its wide planked cypress floors, was massive. Two oversize windows, framed in long dark blue drapes, looked out to the front porch. Next to the front windows a stunning, stained glass oil lamp sat on a round inlaid table, which was between two flowered print wingback chairs.

Santos stood drumming his finger on the mantle. His eyes peered up at a painting above the oversize fireplace of a tall handsome man standing behind a young dark-skinned woman who was sitting in a chair holding a dark-skinned boy, about four years old. He looked down at Belinda. "Yay, that is Zyanya an' she was really that gorgeous," Santos said, his voice trembling.

Belinda studied the portrait seeing the young vibrant family in the painting so full of life. She smiled, seeing that Sinjin had inherited his deep dimples from his father.

"See, I's told ya I had's a surprise," Mamma Annie declared, her large body swished into the room with a hefty black man in tow.

"Santos, ya son of a gun, it shor' is nice ta see ya 'n I'm glad ya decideds ta come back 'n visit," said the man hurrying over to Santos.

"Mason, it has been ta long," Santos proclaimed, putting his hand out shaking Mason's hand, as they patted each other on the back.

Sinjin stood from his chair and Mason grabbed him. "Son," exclaimed Mason, "it's nice ta see ya."

Sinjin let go of Mason and quickly introduced Belinda.

Mason did a bow to Belinda and a smile flowed from ear to ear. "Son, how longs is ya staying?"

"Oh, we just came for a visit and we have to get back to the ship in a few hours."

"Dat ship." Mamma Annie swung her arms in the air like a wild bird. "'Tis as Miss Zyanya used ta says, ya can gets away from dat ship fer a whiles. Ya is staying de night 'n ya don't argues withs me child," she muttered turning and leaving the room still flapping her arms.

Mason and Santos laughed. "Well it looks like we're staying the night," said Santos patting Sinjin on the back.

Mamma Annie came back into the room carrying a beautiful china plate full of small little cakes and sat them down on the coffee table.

Belinda stood from her chair. "I didn't prepare to stay the night Mamma Annie, so I'll be going back to the ship – Sinjin can stay."

"Nay," Mamma Annie snapped back, "youngs lady I wants ta know ya story 'n ya is staying ta, I wills takes care of ya."

Santos chuckled shaking his head at Belinda. She couldn't win against Mamma Annie.

"Alright, I'll stay," Belinda said, sitting back down in the chair taking a sip of her warm cup of tea. "What is this tea, it's very different?"

"It is one of my mum's herb teas called ginger," Sinjin added, swallowing his tea and eating his fourth little cake. He sat his empty cup down and stood. "Belinda, let's go, I want to show you my mum's garden." He turned facing Mamma Annie. "While we're in the garden Santos will fill you in on Belinda's story."

"'Tis a great idea an' we do need ta catch up," Santos assured letting his finger tap on the mantle of the fireplace.

Sinjin held onto Belinda's arm pulling her close to him. They strolled out the large French doors into the courtyard, which was overflowing with bushes and flowers. A small lily-filled pond sat in the center of the flower garden. He steered her to a bench that sat to the side of the garden under a large, twisted oak tree, a special place to take in the entire garden.

"This bench is where my mum would sit each morning and then would end her days sitting right here. She loved it here in her garden."

"I understand why, it's beautiful and so calm, so peaceful."

Sinjin scooted in very close to Belinda. She felt his warm body against her.

His hands clasped together as he leaned over. "I would always find my mum out here busily pruning her flowers and singing songs in her Indian language. I'd scoot in close to her on the bench and she'd tell me tales about her life growing up in her Indian village. She missed her family, but like my father, they wouldn't talk about their families. My father, after my mum died, would come out here each night and talk to my mum; he believed her spirit was still here. I sometimes feel her spirit and think he might've been right." Sinjin wiped his misty eyes.

Belinda stayed quiet; she reached down and took his hand in hers. Her head leaned against him, staring up into the old live oak's twisted tree branches watching and listening to the many birds fluttering their wings and singing their variety of songs.

Mamma Annie rushed out into the garden thrusting out her hand to Belinda. "Miss Belinda please comes with me 'n we wills get ya settled inta yer bed chamber." She winked at Sinjin gently taking Belinda's tiny hand in her large dark hand.

Belinda followed Mamma Annie up the large wooden staircase down a long hallway into a bedroom on the back of the house. A crystal vase, overflowing with white rose buds, sat on a table in the corner of the room. Fluffy white cotton pillows snuggled against a dark mahogany headboard and the most beautiful quilt, a wedding ring design with all the colors of the rainbow, lay on a rice bed in the center of the room.

"The quilt is beautiful," Belinda added, letting her fingers lightly trace the wedding ring design.

"I's knew ya'd like dis room, dis was Miss Zyanya's favorites room. She'd come in here's on rainy days, 'n sits right der in dat chair 'n quilts. She made dis quilt fer Sinjin ta give ta his bride when he someday gets married."

Mamma Annie opened a door to the side of the room. Belinda froze. Her mouth dropped open. Inside the small room was a bathroom, and sitting in the center was a copper claw footed tub full of water. She leaned over letting her fingers wiggle in the water. She sighed. "Oh, the water smells so sweet."

"Dat's rose petals 'n ya wills feels like a young lady soon. Here – now, let's get dos dirty clothes off of ya an' get ya cleaned up. Des men's don' knows how ta take care of a young's girl, but Mamma Annie do."

Belinda's dirty breeches, vest, blue stripped shirt, and long socks slipped off. She heaved a sigh sticking her toes in the water. She sank blissfully into the tub letting the warm sweet scented rose water cover her body.

"Mr. John broughts two tubs here fer Miss Zyanya as a gift after they firsts moved ta dis house. Now yer clean clothes is lying on de bed 'n I wills be back ta help ya, ya jes relax." Mamma Annie turned and closed the bathroom door.

The bath felt like heaven. Her head swished back and forth and her long hair floated in the perfumed water. She hadn't realized how much she'd miss taking long baths. The rough bar of soap had a little bit to be desired, but it washed the sea salt and grim from her skin. Her body lay against the back of the tub. Her tired eyes closed smelling the fresh rose scent. About forty-five minutes later, she heard Mamma Annie bustling around the bedroom and knew it was time to get out of the relaxing bath. She stood, grabbed the large cloth off the back of a chair, and dried off. She wrapped the cloth around her thin body and went into the bedroom. There, lying on the bed was a gorgeous silky, dark green dress with beige lace trim around the neck and sleeves.

"Here, lets gets ya dressed before ya catch yer death," Mamma Annie declared helping Belinda slip her undergarments and a petticoat over her head. "Miss Belinda, sits right over heres on dis stool an' lets me brush dat hair, it shor' is a tangle mess."

Mamma Annie's hands began vigorously brushing Belinda's long blonde hair pulling it up perfectly on top of her head, letting golden ringlets fall down around her face. "There, nows it's time fer supper," Mamma Annie announced proud of her accomplishment.

"Thank you, Mamma Annie for the bath, it was fabulous, and I know I needed it."

"Yer welcomes, Miss Belinda," Mamma Annie said beaming. Her skirt swished back and forth going through the bedroom doorway and her shoes clicked on the staircase as she briskly made her way downstairs to the kitchen.

Belinda followed Mamma Annie down the staircase. She stopped at the bottom of the stairs and gasped; Sinjin stood in the dining room's doorway dressed in a freshly cleaned jacket and breeches. Sinjin took her hand and led her into the dining room.

Santos was dressed in his clean jacket and breeches just as Sinjin. He stood from the table. "Little Jackaro ya look beautiful," he announced, a gleam in his eyes.

"Thank you and you look handsome too," she offered smiling.

Santos wiped his moist eyes and continued to stare at her. Sinjin leaned over and whispered in Belinda's ear. "That was one of my mum's favorite dresses. It's a dress Santos and my father brought her from one of their voyages. Mamma Annie must have become fond of you very quickly to have allowed you to wear it."

Belinda hadn't thought about where the dress came from, but wearing one of Zyanya's dresses made her nervous.

"Mamma Annie does know how to take care of us," Sinjin assured with a smile on his face, as he slid back a chair from the dining room table and Belinda sat down.

The table was covered in a beige tablecloth embodied around the edges with pink roses. A tall crystal vase full of colorful flowers and two candlesticks with beeswax candles sat in the center of the table flickering light across the walls of the room. Fresh beans, rice, and fish was placed on the table and the three heartily ate every bite of the food.

"Sinjin, where are your parents buried?" Belinda asked in a soft voice, hoping she wasn't opening up old wounds.

"Not far from here, a few blocks down the road in the churchyard. Would you like to go to the cemetery when we're done with our meal?" He asked, staring at her with his dark eyes like Zyanya.

"If you don't mind, that would be nice," she answered softly.

When the meal was done Sinjin stood from the table scooted his chair in and helped Belinda stand. Santos didn't move, nervously pushing food around on his plate.

"Santos, why don't you join us?" questioned Belinda. "It's a lovely evening and I would love for you to come along."

Santos reluctantly stood from the table.

"Now, we need to get some flowers from the garden," she added. But, before they moved, Mamma Annie was back in the room with three multicolored flower bouquets in her arms. She dipped her head as she handed the flowers to Sinjin and smiled at Belinda.

Sinjin held the wooden front door open and Belinda walked out onto the front porch feeling the fresh air on her face. They walked down the steps through the wrought iron gate and turned right. The orange glow of the setting sun shimmered onto the street. Sinjin wrapped his arm around Belinda pulling her close and Santos trailed silently behind them.

The small cemetery was on the next block to the right in the churchyard surrounded by a wrought iron fence similar to the one around Sinjin's home. Thick green vines with white flowers were weaved in and out of the fence's railing.

"When my mum first moved to St. Augustine she planted all of the bushes around the cemetery and church; everything had to have flowers. This is jasmine entwined in the fence," he said as he leaned over and picked one of the white flowers handing it to Belinda. "And those bushes," he said pointing, "are gardenia bushes."

He swung the wrought iron gate open. His shoulders became rigid as he ambled slowly to the back of the cemetery and up to three graves.

The first grave was Sinjin's mother.

Zyanya Alvery
She walked in beauty
A blessed Wife and Mother
Born July 26, 1742
Died February 16th, 1768

The next grave was his baby sister:

Mary Coreen Alvery
A sleeping Angel
Born February 16th, 1768
Died February 16th, 1768

Then it was John's grave, Sinjin's father:

John Harold Alvery II
His last voyage, homeward bound
Caring Husband and Father
Born April 17th, 1733
Died February 3rd, 1785

Sinjin bent down and placed one of the bouquets of flowers Mamma Annie had given him on each grave. Santos stood to the side of the cemetery and stared off into the night.

When Sinjin stood back up from the graves, he wiped his eyes, but a smile spread on his face bringing out his dimples. "Let us go home," Sinjin said, gently taking Belinda's arm. He turned to leave.

"Sinjin, if ya don't mind I think I'll stay a while longer," Santos said earnestly looking down at his old friend John's grave. "I'd like ta spend some time with my old mate."

"Yay, that is fine, Santos and we'll see you in short while," Sinjin said.

Belinda leaned away from Sinjin over to Santos and whispered, "Santos, remember good memories not sad."

Santos' hands anxiously rubbed his wild fuzzy beard and nodded his head yes. "John would definitely approve of that, he never dwelt on sad times."

Sinjin and Belinda leisurely strolled down the street seeing the *Aeolus* to their left towering over many ships in the harbor. They stepped upon the porch.

Belinda pulled Sinjin to a stop. "Sinjin, do you mind sitting out here on the porch for a while? It's so peaceful out here."

"If that is what you would like, that will be fine," he added walking to the swing. Sinjin's feet began to push the swing back and forth, his head tilted down, but his dark eyes peered up. "Belinda," he said in a soft voice, "you sure are beautiful in that dress," his head ducked shyly away from her, "and you smell wonderful."

She lifted his hand caressing it in between her hands. "Thank you," she whispered snuggling her body close to him. The feeling she'd felt in the garden at Drayton Hall had returned, making goose bumps grow over her body and a tingling sensation ran down her back. Sinjin's strong arm brought her closer letting her cuddle even nearer to him. A twinge of guilt came over her thinking she wasn't missing her father, Johnny or her home. She only wanted to sit right here next to Sinjin – forever.

Santos leisurely strolled down the street a contented look on his face. He stepped upon the porch and leaned over giving Belinda a sweet kiss on the cheek. "Thank ya, my Little Jackaro; ya somehow know what is good fer an old salt like me."

"You, my friend have helped me in more ways than you will ever know," she offered in a soft voice looking into Santos' tired but peaceful eyes.

The door opened and Mamma Annie came walking outside carrying a tray with fresh drinks. "I sees de walk was good fer ya," she said smiling.

Santos sat in a rocker slowly pushing the chair back and forth staring out to the harbor, his mind thinking of times long ago. They sat in the stillness, quiet for a while as Sinjin and Santos drank their rum, and she drank her cider blended with warm rum. She felt the potent rum flowing through her body calming her as she leaned against Sinjin. She sat watching the moon as it rose alongside many bright twinkling stars popping and exploding with sparkly lights. It was so peaceful in the small town, no planes, no constant hum of machines or car motors driving down the roads.

The time did come to say good night and Belinda slowly walked up the stairs to her new bedroom. Lying on the bed was a soft clean nightgown. She slipped the nightgown on and gently laid the green dress over a chair sitting in the corner of the room. She tossed back the beautiful quilt, blew out the candle, and climbed into bed pulling it up around her face. The light of the moon was shining in around the edges of the curtains giving off a peaceful glow across the bed, but she was wide-awake tossing and turning. Her mind so mixed with thoughts from her life with her father and Johnny and now her thoughts were of Sinjin and the *Aeolus*.

She scrambled out of bed, put on a robe matching the sleeping gown. She opened the bedroom door quietly, so as not to wake anyone, and tiptoed silently down the stairs sliding her hands tightly along the well-polished mahogany banister.

She stepped outside into the garden. She stopped. Sinjin was sitting on the bench in the moonlight, his head bent down staring at the ground. She turned to go back up the stairs, but he spotted her.

He stood and hurried to the door. "Belinda, is something wrong?"

"No, I just couldn't sleep and I didn't mean to disturb you."

"Nay, you didn't disturb me; come 'tis a stunning night and I'd like some company."

She sat down next to him on the bench.

"'Tis a special place to sit at night and think. My safe haven when I was young when my father was gone on the *Aeolus*, playing and helping my mum with her flowers. Always waiting in anticipation for when he'd come home and stay the winter with us. Now I'm the one that loves to travel on the *Aeolus*, but I need to start coming here more often," he added. "Now with you with me – I can." He looked at her reaction at what he had said. "We can stay here after our last journey up north, if you'd like?"

"I think that's a great idea I'd love to stay here during the winter. I do hope Santos will stay, too," she added leaning against the back of the bench.

"If you ask Santos he won't turn you down," Sinjin's voice trailed off. "Belinda, what was your life like living by your lighthouse…" His head bent down and his fingers anxiously wiggled on the bench's seat. "And do you have someone special back in your time?"

"Yes, I do. His name is Johnny and we've been friends all of our lives."

Her eyes inconspicuously peered at Sinjin. She held back a smile seeing him frown as she talked of Johnny.

"Johnny's a great guy, but he just couldn't understand my love for my cliff and lighthouse. He believed all the stories of the sea were tall tales and not real and I don't think he'd even believe my story now," she answered. "My life was unusual growing up on the cliff near the lighthouse, but I wouldn't trade my childhood for anything."

Sinjin turned his face toward her intensely listening to her story and his frown lines were vanishing.

"I wasn't ever lonely sitting by the sea. Even as a small child I used to explore the cliffs and loved to go down to the water's edge to sit." she paused and looked at him. "Down at the bottom of the cliff where you save me that night. It was my special place to hide from the world. I'd stay there hours at a time watching the tides come and go, looking down into the dark black water wondering what mysteries the deep sea held."

She looked into Sinjin's face and continued her story. "Grandmother Katelynn," she smiled, "who I was named after, my dad's mother, died the year before my parents were married and Granddad Elias was lonely living in the old Victorian home. So – Granddad Elias asked my dad if he wanted to move in and help with the lighthouse, since taking care of the lighthouse was getting harder for him.

My parents moved into the keeper's house not long after they were married. My mom, Rebecca, after she moved to the cliff fell in love with the sea, as she had fallen in love with my father, Seth. My parents lived happily for many years and my life was wonderful. But the year I turned eleven, my mom developed pneumonia and died that winter."

Sinjin's dark eyes gazed at her full of sympathy.

"My father and I lost Granddad Elias the next year after Mom died. The loss of my mom devastated my father and he became a shell of the man he once was. We treasured the lighthouse and sea, but the house did become lonely after my mom was gone. Each night became the same routine – Dad would read at night, and I would go out to my beloved cliff and talk to the sea."

Sinjin took her hand sandwiched it in his. "I know 'tis hard on you not seeing your Dad, Johnny or your cliff, but I'm glad you're enjoying living on the Aeolus and it is your home as long as you want."

She felt his fingers cuddling her hand in a caring touch "Thank you Sinjin and I do love – the *Aeolus*." she gulped; she couldn't believe she almost said she loved him.

His head tilted down; his hand caressed her face and kissed her passionately. Her sweet smell of fresh flowers was making it difficult for him to control himself. She was so beautiful in her robe, so feminine, so different from a mate on the ship. She snuggled close letting her body melt against his chest. She looked up at him and a smile graced her full luscious lips. He wanted to tell her how much he loved her and his dream for her to stay with him forever, but it wasn't the time. He could still hear in her voice, as she told her story, how she missed her life. A twinge of jealously stirred inside him knowing she did love Johnny back in her time. But, he wasn't letting go of her and at the moment, she was his for the night to hold and keep his dreams alive.

They sat for hours in the light of the moon talking and telling their dreams.

Sinjin kept his one dream a secret wondering in his mind what she'd say if she really knew his feelings. They told tales until the early morning, of growing up in different centuries, but so similar with the love from their families.

She lay burrowed under the quilts in the soft clean bed, her mind swirling with thoughts of Sinjin. Her fingers gently tracing her lips remembering Sinjin's kiss and the warm sensations flowing through her body. The tingling feelings had grown last night. Being with Sinjin was so different from being with Johnny. Johnny was her friend, but Sinjin – she smiled to herself – she was in love with Sinjin, a deep passionate love. She'd never felt emotions like that before wanting him to hold her tight and never let her go. She thought about her life, still not able to uncover the mystery of time, but the pain of missing her father, Johnny and her life was softening as each new day in this time past slowly by. Her eyelids heavy with sleep won as she drifted off into a tranquil state of wonderful dreams.

Later that morning the sun shining into the room from around the side of the curtains woke Belinda from a serene sleep of sweet dreams and she reluctantly climbed out of bed. Lying on the chair, instead of her beautiful green dress from last night, were her clean clothes from the ship. She picked up her breeches and brought them to her nose smelling their fresh scent, and twirled around. *"Oh, I love it here."*

She raced down the stairs, but stopped, she sagged on the handrail seeing Sinjin and Santos were sitting in the dining room having breakfast.

"G'mornin' sleepy head," chuckled Santos, as she rushed into the room.

"Good morning, I can't believe how long I slept – ohhhhhhh, the food smells great," she said as Sinjin stood and slid a dining room chair out for her.

"Well you were up late," he answered in a chuckle leaning down next to her as a smile spread across his face showing his dimples.

Mamma Annie came in the dining room and placed a plate of eggs and wood smoked ham in front of her.

Belinda leaped from the chair giving Mamma Annie a hug. "Thank you Mamma Annie for cleaning my clothes, you have been so kind," Belinda offered.

"Miss Belinda, 'twas a pleasure ta have a girl heres ta see ta 'n ya comes back soon," Mamma Annie replied grinning from ear to ear looking down at Sinjin knowing his secret dream.

After the delicious breakfast, Sinjin led them into the living room. Santos looked up at the painting of Zyanya and John above the fireplace. He whispered a soft *"good-bye."*

Mason came into the room shook Sinjin and Santos' hands and then walked over to Belinda. "Ya come back girl; ya shor' made Mamma Annie a happy woman 'n she shor' likes taking care of ya."

Belinda gave him a hug. "I will be back, I promise, Mason."

The three walked to the door and Mamma Annie came rushing over giving bear hugs and wiping tears from her eyes with her apron.

"Now, Santos don' let it bes so long next time comin' home, we is getting ta old fer dat."

"Oh, I won't an' I'll see ya in a few months," Santos said proudly winking at Belinda.

Sinjin, Santos, and Belinda strolled quietly down the cobblestone street headed to the *Aeolus*. Sitting next to the gangplank was Ian watching for them.

"Miss Belinda how was yer visit in St. Augustine?" Ian asked as Sinjin and Santos went to work.

"Come and sit by me Ian and let me tell you my tale of visiting a fairytale home in a magnificent city."

CHAPTER SEVENTEEN

THE BLUE LOCKET

A few days had gone by since they'd left St. Augustine sailing due north. One cool evening Belinda couldn't sleep. She wrapped a small quilt around her and gradually opened her bedroom door so the door wouldn't squeak and wake Sinjin, who was asleep in his hammock in the great cabin. She could hear his soft breaths believing he was asleep. She quietly opened the cabin door and stepped outside onto the deck looking out into the peaceful night. She shivered in the cool night. The indigo darkness had consumed the night with a few twinkling stars overhead. She leaned against the side of the ship looking up into the brilliant night sky as the ship weaved from side to side gently being pushed by the waves.

The stars sparkled; the crescent moon was a spotlight shining down onto the ship watching over as a sentry, guarding the ship for the night. She could see the dark water glistering in the moonlight. She listened as the small waves splashed against the side of the ship. This was her life, this old ship along with the crew, and she didn't know what her life would be like without it. A cool icy breeze stung her face so she tightened the quilt around her neck; Santos was correct the weather was changing.

She heard a squeak and knew the door to the great cabin opened. Sinjin walked outside.

"I'm sorry I woke you, I tried to be quiet."

"No, I couldn't sleep either," he said in quite voice as he sat down next to her smoothing his long dark hair from his face, "I was awake lying in my hammock thinking."

"It's a stunning night isn't it?" she commented, peering up at the sky.

"It is," he whispered back to her, his eyes staring at her not at the stars.

She felt his gaze and smiled up at him.

He scooted near and pulled something out of the pocket of his jacket. He reached down gently lifted up her hand and placed a small object in her palm.

She looked down; a tiny, golden oval locket hanging on a gold chain was lying in her hand. The front of the locket was hand painted a dark sapphire blue, the same color of the ship, and had an enameled golden flower embedded in the center.

"I can't accept this," she whispered nervously.

"Do you not like the locket?" He asked squinching his eyes.

"Oh, no, I love it; I've never seen anything so beautiful in my life."

"Then it is yours. Please take it, Belinda; it matches the blue in your eyes." Sinjin softly whispered.

Belinda's fingers gently stroked the locket lying in her hand.

His eyes stayed on her. "The locket was a gift to my mum from my father. She always wore it. Please, Belinda, wear it all of the time," he paused, "and think of me."

Belinda held the locket up in front of her looking at it in the moonlight, knowing how much it meant to Sinjin. She placed it gently around her neck and he fastened the clip.

Her eyes closed remembering the painting over the fireplace in his home on Aviles Street, seeing this same locket on Zyanya. "I will always wear the locket, thank you Sinjin." She reached up gently stroking his face as she kissed him bringing back the warm emotions she'd felt when she kissed him sitting in the garden of Aviles Street. She had to smile; wondering how Santos knew Sinjin was her Jack on the ship.

Sinjin shyly touched her hand very softly. "Belinda," he whispered, "Santos said that he told you my father's story, about my father's family disowning him and – me."

"Yes, he did and I'm sorry for all of your loss."

"You also know my father's family lives in Boston and how they have never met me." He chuckled, "I know you, and you'd have gone to see them."

"Sinjin, I don't know what I'd have done in your place," she answered. "I know your father didn't worry about what they thought and you shouldn't either. It's their loss not getting to know you." Her head nodded yes. "I would have had to meet them, but you know I have a big mouth." She laughed.

"Would you go with me when we dock in Boston to meet them?" He finally smiled. "You would have to wear women's clothes."

"We might get ourselves in trouble, but if that's what you want to do, I'd be glad to go with you," she assured smiling back.

He became quiet. Sinjin was a man of few words and she could see the pain in his face, his past had been difficult on him.

Later that night she lay in her bed looking at the locket with tears in her eyes, knowing how special the locket was to Sinjin. She'd cherish it always. She heard the outside door to the great cabin squeak knowing Sinjin was back in the great room. She held onto the locket falling asleep dreaming of a new life.

CHAPTER EIGHTEEN

CHRISTMAS

The ship sailed past Charleston on their way to Williamsburg, their last stop before reaching Boston. Belinda looked out to the city with memories still fresh in her mind when Sinjin held her in his arms dancing their last dance at Drayton Hall.

"Belinda," Lucky sat down with his blue eyes sparkling, "are you alright, you seem right knackered, and very far away?" he questioned worriedly.

"Oh, I am fine, Lucky, I just miss being home on Christmas. In my time, Christmas is really something," she sighed, "with decorations and gifts. I loved to decorate our home and I'd even put a wreath on the lighthouse. My father would always cook Christmas dinner and I'd set the table with my mom's nicest tablecloth and dishes." Her eyes rose from the deck looking at Lucky. "I'd bake plenty of cookies and my father would invite a few of his old friends over for dinner. After dinner," her voice rose with enthusiasm, "my father would play the piano, and we'd sing with the fire crackling in the fireplace. It was the best time," she said exhaling as she finished her story.

"Blimey, our Christmas is similar to your Christmas, and I'd love for you to come to my home for Christmas and have a cracking time," Lucky added passionately.

"Your home," her body flinched. "I thought you weren't married, Lucky?"

"Crikey, I'm not," he chuckled, "however my parents and family live in Williamsburg. My parents would love to have you visit and you'd have a smashing time. They have all kinds of Christmas parties and I know they'd love to have you join us and then you would have a new Christmas to gab about."

"That is very kind, but I couldn't leave Sinjin and Santos behind on Christmas, thank you anyway." She studied Lucky. She understood in this time Christmas was an intimate celebration for only the closest family and friends so this was a very unusual invite.

"Santos is a great bloke." Lucky's head ducked not looking her in the eyes. "And the captain is welcome to come along." He hesitated. "If you really want him to join us. We have plenty of room. Please think it over, we will be arriving in Williamsburg in a few days," Lucky urged.

"I will," she called out to him surprised he wanted her to spend Christmas with him, "thank you Lucky."

That night Belinda sat at the large table in the great cabin anxiously pulling a biscuit apart. "Sinjin," she began in a soft voice, "Lucky has invited us and Santos to stay Christmas at his parent's home in Williamsburg. I hate to leave Ian and everyone on the ship, but what do you think – should we go?"

"Well that is something – that Lucky wants you to join him." Frown lines grew on his forehead. He paused and leaned over to her with a questioning look. "You sure Lucky wants me to come along?"

"Sure, why not, he says he has plenty of room."

"Yay, he does, I've been to Lucky's home, and it is very grand. His father is a very wealthy nobleman who was born in England and moved here when Lucky was young. But, I'm not so sure I'm welcome." Sinjin took a bite of chowder, looking up with one eyebrow raised at her reaction.

She sat quietly and nervously twisted the biscuit in her fingers mulling over what he was saying. She kept thinking. Why would Lucky be living on this ship if he were wealthy and why was Sinjin worried he wasn't welcome to go to Lucky's home?

"I see your mind is working overtime," Sinjin laughed. "Lucky is a different sort and doesn't like living on a plantation. It didn't work well for him doing what most would consider normal work." He sat against the straight back chair. "We met when I was delivering goods to his father's plantation and he became fascinated with my ship and my travels. We became good mates and he finally asked to join the crew of the *Aeolus*. I knew his father wasn't happy, but he had four other brothers to take over for him on the plantation and that seemed to appease his father. If you would like to spend Christmas with his family – that would be all right with me. I'll have to think about going, and you'll have to ask Santos."

"You have to go or I won't go," she assured smiling at him. "Is there something I don't know that is going on with you and Lucky; I thought you were friends?"

"Lucky and I are great friends, however…" His frown left his face and he grinned showing his dimples not wanting to tell her the truth. "Alright, one night if you insist," he sighed. "You know you do get your way a lot."

"Good, then, I'll see what Santos says and one night it is. I do need to go into town to get some gifts for Ansel and Ernesto's children."

"Awe, you will have to wear a dress to go to Lucky's home," Sinjin announced with an antagonizing smile.

"That won't be a problem, either. It'll be fun to visit with Lucky's family and see a new home."

"Uh-huh," Sinjin moaned squinching his face again with the frown appearing and his dark eyes squinting as if he were searching for an answer in her face. A jealousy grew inside of him seeing her face light up when she spoke of Lucky. He wanted to grab her and tell her how much he loved her and not to go to Lucky's home, nonetheless she had to make up her own mind, and he would live with her decision.

"You'll see, Lucky says his parents love to have a good time so this will be fun." She finally put the piece of biscuit she'd been twisting in her fingers in her mouth and began to eat the warm chowder.

"Yay, it should be interesting," Sinjin moaned in an inaudible voice.

The next day she sat staring out into the blue water.

"I see some concern in yer face, Little Jackaro, of where we are heading."

She nodded her head yes.

"We're going inta the bay an' then up the James River. It'll take us a while ta maneuver the river, but we have ta go ta Jamestown first an' unload our cargo, then we'll come back ta Yorktown ta dock since its port is larger." He took in a deep sigh. "I hear ya are ready ta meet some new people." Santos seemed to have more to say, but stopped and became quiet.

"Santos, I do hope you will go with us to Lucky's home."

Santos studied her. "An' Sinjin has agreed ta go — ta Lucky's home — an' doesn't object ta ya going?"

"Yes, Sinjin agreed to go with me, why not?" She gave Santos a deep look. "There's something going on with Lucky and Sinjin that you aren't telling me, isn't there?" she questioned.

Santos shrugged his shoulders and didn't answer. He sat quietly looking out to the land as the ship sailed into the bay. His body inclined against the side of the ship, his arms crossed over his head, and finally spoke. "Little Jackaro this invite maybe more than ya bargain fer, but I'll go along."

She gave Santos a puzzled look, but didn't ask any more questions knowing he wouldn't tell any answers.

Lucky was thrilled when she told him she was going to his home for Christmas, and he told her that this year was going to be a special Christmas.

The ship quickly began to unload its cargo in Jamestown, a very quaint and simple town compared to Charles Towne. The cool breeze of winter hit her face as she watched the crew unload the cargo.

The plank was down and Ian appeared. "Miss Belinda, are ya ready ta go," he asked excitedly.

"Yes, Ian, but you don't have to go – I will be fine."

"The captain said ya were going ta buy toys fer Ansel and Ernesto's children an' I would love ta help, it's an outstanding idea."

"Yes."

"We will have a grand time, let us go," Ian announced excitedly, walking down the plank and off the ship.

"Oh, these are perfect." Belinda picked up some handmade cloth dolls with sweet round faces painted on them.

She looked over at Ian, a mischievous grin on his face, and she had to smile watching him. "Miss Belinda, the wooden ships are amazing an' I would have loved one when I was a lad," he said excitedly playing with the wooden ship.

"I hope Ansel is still on board the ship," Belinda called out hurrying down the boardwalk to the ship, packages overflowing in her arms.

"Miss Belinda, slow down," Ian called out, his short legs sprinting in a fast stride behind her.

She laughed and slowed her pace.

Ansel stood anxiously waiting on the dock. She handed him a stack of gifts for all of his children. "Oh, I'm so glad you stayed. Tell your little ones Merry Christmas and a Merry Christmas to you and your wife."

Ansel stood stunned. She reached over hugging him and a smile spread from ear to ear. "Thank ya, Miss Belinda an' a Merry Christmas ta ya," he hollered as he hurried down the boardwalk, waving his free hand in the air, goodbye.

Sinjin had decided they'd leave tomorrow morning to go to Lucky's home. Tonight they were having their own special Christmas dinner with Ian. Sinjin brought the plates full of food from the galley and Belinda decorated the table with candles and garland she had cut from some of the trees near the port. Sinjin, Santos, Ian, and she had a special dinner. She hated to leave Ian tomorrow, but she knew someone needed to stay and oversee the ship. Santos tried to get out of going, believing he should stay with the ship and help Ian, but she wouldn't let him.

The night was serene listening to all of the stories and the cook had made a special rum bread pudding for dessert. After the meal, she jumped up from the table grabbing the Christmas gifts from her bedroom that she'd bought earlier at the general store without Ian noticing.

"Merry Christmas," Belinda called, watching as Ian pick up his new pipe along with some fresh tobacco. Santos lifted out a cigar from a box of cigars, and Sinjin opened his silver timepiece with his initials etched on top.

Her heart pounded when she remembered her father always carrying Finnegan Brady's watch. Finnegan's pocket watch wasn't from the 1800's but was identical to the one she'd just purchased for

Sinjin. The watch was proof Finnegan had gone back into time. She became excited and couldn't wait to tell her father.

Later Santos sat on the deck smoking his cigar and Ian puffing on his pipe. She smiled, watching Sinjin take his watch out of his vest-pocket every few minutes, rub his thumb across his initials and open the top checking the time.

She lay in her bed wondering what her father was doing. Was he preparing the house for Christmas hoping she'd be coming home? A lone tear ran down her face. This was going to be a special Christmas for her and Johnny, and she believed her Christmas gift would have been an engagement ring. How her life had changed becoming so mixed up; understanding she now couldn't accept Johnny's proposal of marriage because she'd fallen in love with someone else. Anxiousness grew, thinking about spending Christmas in a large plantation home, but finally she fell into a deep sleep dreaming about Christmas.

CHAPTER NINETEEN

THE DECISION

She slept like a baby, woke excited to go to Lucky's home, a new adventure. She dressed in women's clothes and hurried out on the top deck carrying her small cloth bag filled with a few clothes. Sinjin and Santos were waiting by the helm.

Lucky popped up from the hatch and crossed over to her, dressed so handsomely in long breeches, clean shirt, vest, and a pair of square-toed black shoes. He stood quietly for a second, his eyes staring at her, but his eyes did a quick flash to Sinjin. His thoughts returned to Belinda. "You, my dear, are lovely." He looped her arm in his. "Are you ready to go to my home and have an incredible Christmas?" Lucky asked leading her past Sinjin and Santos.

Her head nodded yes, as she took a second look at Sinjin with his brow crinkling as he frowned.

A very nice carriage waited at the end of the dock. Lucky held her hand as she stepped into the carriage and then he slid into the seat beside her. Sinjin and Santos sat across from them and Sinjin kept a strong glare fixed on Lucky. Lucky leaned his body next to Belinda with a smile across his face. The ride continued for a while, but finally the carriage turned down a long tree lined road. There sitting at the end of the path, so magnificently surrounded by tall trees, was a red brick, three-story plantation home quite a bit larger than Drayton Hall with its wide veranda spread across the front.

"Well, take a gander at this, what do you think, Belinda?" Lucky asked, as he helped her out of the carriage. "We have seven hundred forty-five acres here next to the James River."

"It's beautiful and I can't believe you grew up here?" Her head tilted back looking up at the massive home.

"Yay, I've lived here since I was a small lad – come let's go inside." He entwined her arm in his, did a quick glance to Sinjin, and ushered her up the huge porch steps to the massive front doors. The two wooden doors swung open. Standing in front of them was an older black man, Chester, the Henshaw's butler.

Lucky and Belinda walked into the vestibule with Sinjin and Santos close behind.

"Master Theodore, yer mother is waiting fer ya in de drawing room," the man announced doing a bow.

"Thank you Chester," Lucky said graciously handing Chester his Tri-corn hat.

Sitting erect in a flowery patterned wing backed chair was a petite woman with sapphire blue eyes, dressed as beautifully as the women were at the Christmas Ball in Charles Towne.

"Mum," Lucky announced, letting go of Belinda's arm darting across the room to the woman, squatting down next to her chair he gave her a kiss on the cheek. "It's good to see you."

Lovingly the woman patted Lucky's face with her small pale hand. "'Tis nice, my son, to have you home."

A man appeared in the drawing room's doorway showing semblance to Lucky; heart-shaped face, wide forehead and the same sharp chin, only the man's hair was salt and pepper gray.

The man stepped next to Belinda and gently took her hand. "Sir Theodore William Henshaw II, my lady."

"Mum, Father this is Belinda Brady," Lucky's strong voice amplified in the drawing room as he stood up from his mother's side.

Sinjin and Santos crossed the room to the woman sitting in the chair. "Mum, this is Sinjin Alvery and Santos Barros. This is my mum, Gwendolyn Henshaw."

"Sinjin and Santos it is nice to finally meet you, I have heard stories told from Theodore, welcome to my home," she said, holding out her hand.

Sinjin took the woman's small hand in his and did a bow. "Thank you, Madame for inviting us to spend Christmas with you and your family – it is very kind," Sinjin said confidently.

Theodore quickly shook Sinjin and Santos' hands. "Santos, blimey haven't heard from you in yonks," Theodore exclaimed giving Santos a pat on the back. "Gentlemen, it is nice to have you stay with us in our home. Now, let's have a drink to celebrate this joyous occasion."

Lucky's mother rose from her chair. "All right, my dear," she said, gesturing her hand in the air for Belinda to follow. "Come and talk with me, and please call me Gwendolyn."

Theodore busily began to pour ale into crystal glasses and the men did a toast, but both Sinjin and Lucky's eyes were on Belinda as she left the room.

Belinda followed Gwendolyn to a sunroom a few doors down the hall from the drawing room. She could hear the men's voices joking and laughing as they enjoyed their ale. She sat in a tan wicker chair across from Gwendolyn. Quickly the conversation began of why and how Belinda came to be living on a sailing ship. A fabricated story began and Gwendolyn soon turned her thoughts to the Christmas party to be held later that night in the massive plantation home and all the people around the county that would be joining them.

A young black girl, dressed in a brown dress with a white apron, brought Gwendolyn and Belinda a cup of warm tea along with a flowered china plate full of small cakes.

"Oh, I have always loved to bake at this time of the year," Belinda added, taking a bite of a round sugar cake.

"You like to bake? That is Quinnie's job, why would you want to do such hard work," Gwendolyn's head tilted to the side taking Belinda in, "and you such an ickle, tiny thing?"

"I love to bake and I have to say my gingerbread cookies do come out very tasty."

"My dear, if you would like to bake, Quinnie would be glad to let you help in the kitchen, that wouldn't be a problem," Gwendolyn added giving her a strange look. "Teddy loves scrummy desserts and gingerbread cakes are some of his favorites."

"I just might take you up on that idea," Belinda surmised. She studied the woman in front of her so prim and proper and wondered if she had ever stepped a foot in the kitchen. She laughed to herself. Gwendolyn might not even know where the kitchen was.

"What idea is that you are talking about," asked Lucky, standing in the sunroom's doorway, the sun shining around his tall thin frame, his icy-blue eyes on Belinda.

"For me to bake some cookies or cakes while I'm here," Belinda added with a grin.

"Oh, I see, if `tis what you would care to do and think you'd have a jolly time, then by all means you can have all the fun you'd like. All of the men are preparing for a fox hunt this afternoon." Lucky smiled and leaned down next to Belinda. "And no," he whispered, winking at her before she had a chance to say anything. He reached out taking Belinda's hand. "Now, my dear, how would you like me to give you a tour of my plantation?" he asked in a gentle voice.

Her hand slid into his rough hand and she stood from her chair tidying her dress and hair. "Sure, that would be fine and I'd like to see this marvelous place."

He sat his glass of ale down on the small table next to her chair, leaned over, and kissed his mother once more on the cheek. "Mum, we will be back in time for munch."

"Enjoy your outing Belinda, 'tis a pleasant morn'."

"Thank you Gwendolyn," Belinda said holding onto Lucky. She stopped by the front door. "What is munch?"

"Our noon meal," he added smiling down on her leading her outside onto the verandah.

A black buggy sat waiting for them in the circular drive. Lucky helped her into the buggy and scooted in close. She sat taking him in. He wasn't a mate of the *Aeolus* anymore, but the son of a plantation owner, who'd attended college at William and Mary.

Lucky placed a soft blanket on her lap. "The air is a little nippy this morning, but I agree with Mum it is a beautiful day."

She positioned the blanket settling into the seat of the buggy. "What did Chester call you when we first arrived?"

Lucky chuckled. "Blimey, I wondered how long it would take you to figure out my name isn't Lucky, but Theodore William Henshaw III. My friends and family call me Teddy so if that is what you would like to do while you are here – then 'tis fine with me."

"Teddy it is, when I am with your family, but Lucky it is on the ship," she answered. "You do seem to have a lot of jammy," she added, laughing. "This place is huge."

The buggy's wheels rolled slowly creaking along a dirt path following the James River. The morning was peaceful, a gentle breeze blew, and the sunlight flickered through the trees onto the flowing water of the river.

He leaned near her placing his arm snuggly around her shoulders.

She shivered feeling Lucky's warm body so close to her.

"Oh, it is beautiful here." She turned her head from him trying not to think about him holding her so close feeling her face warming. "Sinjin said you have four brothers."

"Yes, Franklin the eldest is married and built a home on the north side of the land. Langston who married recently is living here in the home for now and loves to work the plantation. Then, there is Robert and Russell, the babies of the family, who are about to finish college. They are the reason my father let me leave to sail with Sinjin on the *Aeolus*. Living two lives, one here and the one on the ship, does make me nutter sometimes and some people believe me mental."

Lucky, so poised and sure of himself, began telling tales of growing up on the enormous plantation with his brothers and the antics they got themselves into over the years. "Isn't this the top," he gestured swinging his right arm out wide. His left arm stayed tight around her shoulder as his icy blue eyes peered down on her.

"Yes, this is the most stunning place and I can't believe how at ease I feel here," she added turning her head so he couldn't see her blush.

A toll of a loud bell jolted her thoughts back to the present.

"The iron bell tells the workers in the field 'tis time for munch and I'm afraid it is also time for us to be heading back."

Belinda studied Lucky. He was handsome with a sharp nose, and long wavy reddish-blonde hair tied behind his head. His skin was fair, so opposite of Sinjin's looks. He seemed so different today, but she couldn't quite figure out what it was.

Lucky leaned forward. "Tristan, 'tis time to go home. We wouldn't want to keep Mum waiting." Lucky reached his fingers over smoothing the wispy strands of blonde hair that had blown in her face revealing her blue eyes. He'd kept his feelings hidden from Belinda. However at this time, she was on his plantation, and nothing was going to stop him, not even the captain of a tall sailing ship, from showing the passion that he felt for her.

"Yay, Master Theodore," Tristan answered as he did a soft whip and the horse began to move, clip clopping at a faster pace down the long path toward the main house.

Lucky pulled her body closer to him and his arms tightened gently caressing her shoulder. Belinda's mind raced. She'd never thought of him in any other way except a good mate, a friend; but something was different. That's what it was this was — she gasped, a date not a friend showing her around his home. Her eyes swung up at Lucky sitting so debonair, again so confident.

The buggy arrived at the home at the precise time for munch. Lucky tenderly reached out taking her hand and helped her out of the buggy. He led her proudly, his left hand holding tightly to her arm, into the dining room. The men in the room stood next to the dining room table each holding a mug of ale and she could see a few more men had arrived while they were gone. Sinjin stood by Lucky's father deep in conversation, but his dark eyes glanced her way giving her a stare with one eyebrow raised in a questioning look. Lucky gripped her arm tighter as they walked around the room, introducing her to each of the men.

Gwendolyn sashayed, her dress swishing from side to side, over to the dining room table. Theodore stepped next to his wife's side and slid her chair back away from the table, and she gracefully sat down. Lucky ushered Belinda over by his mother, to the side of the table, and pulled out a chair. Sinjin and Santos sat down by Theodore at the other end of the table, but Sinjin's eyes stayed fixed on her.

A couple of young black women, scullery maids, dressed in beige dresses served everyone at the table mincemeat pie with fresh baked bread. When the meal was over Gwendolyn stood and nodded her head. "I am retiring for a kip; I'm right knackered and I will see you gentlemen later." She turned around. "Belinda, you are welcome to rest for a while or sit and read whatever you would like." She tilted her head to the side and smiled. "Teddy will see to your every need."

"Thank you Gwendolyn," Belinda replied, as Lucky graciously helped her out of her chair.

"Father, I will be with you in a while." Lucky took Belinda's arm glancing back at Sinjin. He dipped his head to her whispering, "Are you ready my dear – I will introduce you to Quinnie our cook."

They walked outside the large home and through a doorway to an oversized room, high wooden beamed ceilings stretched across the width of the kitchen. Along the sidewall was an enormous fireplace over ten feet wide and five feet tall, with blackened iron pots attached to hooks that were suspended over the red-hot log fire. Belinda stared curiously at the keeping ovens built into bricks on the right side of the hearth. A puffy faced black woman wearing a long brown dress and beige apron, moved with ease busily swishing her plump body around the kitchen. The scullery maids, who'd served the meal earlier, were cleaning the dirty dishes in a large metal tub in the back corner of the room.

The woman whirled around in a half circle to face them. "Master Theodore?" the woman snapped in a questioning look, "Is there something I's can get ya?"

"Quinnie, Miss Brady loves to bake and Mum assured her that you wouldn't mind helping her."

The young girls did a moan. They stopped working for a second and glared at Belinda. Quinnie stood stiff, her mouth wide open, fanning her face with her apron giving the girls a strong look to be quiet. "Lordy, girl ya want ta work heres in dis hot kitchen when ya don' has ta?"

"Quinnie, I love to bake." Belinda gulped. "If it's alright with you?"

"If dat is what ya want 'tis fine withs me, Miss Brady," Quinnie said still fanning herself with her apron.

"Please, Quinnie, call me Belinda."

"Yes'm," Quinnie said, her small beady eyes squinted studying Belinda.

Lucky smiled and leaned over kissing Belinda on the cheek. Belinda flinched. "My dear, I will see you in a while, have a grand time," he said, turning to leave. Quinnie smiled. Lucky grinned, watching Belinda's surprised expression grow on her face.

"Here's ya an apron," Quinnie said tying the apron around Belinda's thin waist.

Two children ran into the kitchen and slid to a stop. "Mamma, who's she?" they questioned staring at Belinda with large scared eyes.

"She's Miss Belinda an' she's gonna bake with us."

Belinda squatted down next to the children. Both children backed away hiding behind Quinnie. "My name is Belinda, now what is your name?"

"Dis one," Quinnie said as she pulled the little girl about six years old from behind her, "'tis Celeste an' he's Asa." She pointed to the little boy who was about four years old.

"How would you, Celeste and Asa, like to be my helpers today?" questioned Belinda.

Their eyes grew huge and a smile grew on both of their faces. Quinnie nodded her head yes, and the children came out of hiding.

"Quinnie, do you have a good gingerbread recipe I can use?"

"Lordy, yay I's a great gingerbread cake recipe an' I hasn't had time ta make 'em dis year – Miss Gwendolyn has kept me's busy with her small cakes. Here, I wills help get everythings fer ya an' tells ya what ya need."

Belinda pulled up a stool for Celeste and lifted Asa up into a chair. Giggling, the children began to add the ingredients that Quinnie told them to add in a large bowl. The dough dumped onto a large wooden floured surface. Each of the children took turns rolling the dough, and they squealed with delight cutting out the gingerbread with teacups and watched with excited anticipation as the cakes baked.

"All right, who is ready to taste the small cakes?" Belinda asked, as Quinnie placed them on a cloth to cool.

Belinda lifted Asa in her lap and he smiled a toothless grin as she handed him and Celeste each a piece of gingerbread. "Thank you Quinnie, I had so much fun."

"Thanks ya, Miss Belinda fer taken time with mys little ones.

Belinda had another plan in her head. She said good-bye, leaned down hugging the children, and went into the house. "Chester," she called out, "I would like to go into Williamsburg can you help me get a buggy?"

"Yes'm, I wills has a buggy brought around immediately," he answered with a wondering look on his face.

"Thank you." She walked to the front door and out onto the porch.

In a few minutes, Tristan pulled up by the porch's steps in the same black buggy she'd rode in earlier with Lucky. "Where's would ya like ta go Miss Belinda?"

"I would like to go to Williamsburg, to the mercantile shop, please."

"Yes'm," Tristan answered.

She stared out the buggy's window at the small quaint town and saw a silversmith, a printer, and apothecary, but she needed just one special store. She rushed into the mercantile shop and went straight for the homemade toys in the back finding a little cloth doll and a wooden boat. The bumpy ride home took another couple of hours as the horse trotted along a worn path full of ruts and deep holes. The buggy turned onto the tree lined lane and she sat in awe staring at the magnificent house at the end of the drive. She accepted Tristan's hand and gracefully alighted from the carriage rushing into the home and out the back door to the kitchen on a mission.

She squatted down by the children who were sitting in the corner of the warm kitchen watching their mother cook. "Celeste and Asa, Merry Christmas," she excitedly said. She handed them their gifts and their eyes grew wide holding the presents in their little hands.

Quinnie stood rigid by the hot stove in silence.

"Merry Christmas, Quinnie," Belinda said, as she leaned over and gave her a hug. "Oh, tomorrow when I leave I would like to take a large batch of the gingerbread back to my ship for the crew, if that is alright?"

"Yes'm, dat wills be fine an' I wills get them ready fer ya," Quinnie said, her fat cheeks pumped up with a big smile.

Belinda sat in a rocking chair on the verandah looking out over the beautiful rolling hills of the huge plantation. Chester kindly brought her a mug of warm apple cider with a hint of rum. She slowly rocked back and forth thinking about her day while sipping the cider. About thirty minutes later, a large group of men rode horses down the lane toward the house. Sinjin, a smile on his face, was riding along side of Theodore, but she could see Santos, with a grim face, preferred to be on his ship not on the back of a horse.

Lucky leaped off of his horse and rushed up the porch's steps taking her arm and they slowly followed the group of men into the parlor. Gwendolyn gracefully glided down the stairs at the perfect time. Sinjin stood next to Theodore and pulled out his new watch checking the time. He looked over at her and she smiled back at him.

As on cue, women from Williamsburg began to arrive in buggies joining their husbands in the parlor.

Santos hurriedly crossed the room to Belinda. "How ya doing, Little Jackaro?"

"I'm doing just fine Santos. I made gingerbread cakes with Quinnie, the cook, and her children this afternoon. I had so much fun."

Lucky saw her talking with Santos and rushed over. "I am going upstairs to get cleaned up and later we can go for a walk in the garden."

"That would be nice; I would love to see more of this grand home."

Lucky bowed and let go of her hand.

Santos moved next to her. "Little Jackaro, ya need ta be aware there is more on Lucky's mind than ya know," he assured. He turned and walked away not saying anything else.

Before she had a chance to think or go after Santos, Gwendolyn, with a young woman in tow, hurried over to her. "Belinda, my dear, this is Adelyn, Langston's wife."

"Nice to meet you Adelyn," Belinda assured. The young woman began talking about the large wedding she'd had and how many people attended. But, before Adelyn could start talking about the next party Lucky showed up all dressed in his proper clothes.

"Belinda, are you ready to take a tour of the garden?" he questioned.

She nodded yes, and as she walked to the vestibule she noticed Santos watching her very closely.

Lucky wrapped her long cloak around her shoulders and pulled her tight next to him as they strolled down the path to an impressive garden full of tall trimmed hedges. He led her to a bench on a small hill. He then bent down and tenderly handed her a beautiful silver broach in a tin box. "Merry Christmas, Belinda."

"Oh, Lucky, this is too expensive – I can't accept this."

"'Tis a Christmas present, so please take it." He leaned close, clasping his hands together nervously. "I also want to speak my mind and let you to know how I feel about you."

She sighed. Santos was right. She must have been a nitwit not to have noticed what Lucky was up to. She had her clue that their buggy ride wasn't just a friend showing her around his home, but she didn't want to believe it. Now she understood Sinjin's glares at Lucky. The two men were in competition for her.

"Belinda, some people believe I am barmy living on a ship, but I know you understand." He smiled. "My dear, I have to be honest with you, I was taken with you that first day you came onboard in the mysterious fog. You were so different from any woman I'd ever met. I didn't know how to tell you how I felt,' he paused, "until now." He sat down next to her on the bench taking her hand in his hand. "My dear, you can have everything you want and live here on this plantation with me and we could be very happy together." She opened her mouth. He raised his left hand in front of her to stop her from speaking. "Please don't say anything, not yet; think about it, living on a sailing ship isn't for you. You deserve the best." He leaned over gently clasping both of her hands in his. "This could all be yours someday."

When his hand fell down, she sat shocked – words wouldn't come.

He wrapped his arms around her and pulled her close. "Now, we need to get back inside, our evening meal will be ready soon."

"Lucky," she finally found her voice and started to speak...

"No," he interrupted, "we will talk later."

They strolled back into the parlor and she was quickly swept away by Gwendolyn and was introduced to Langston, Franklin and Eva, and Robert and Russell.

Santos hurriedly weaved his way through the crowd of people toward her.

"Oh, Santos," she blurted out grabbing his arm, "you were right, Lucky does have more on his mind. Later he's going to ask me to marry him and to live here on this plantation. I didn't have any idea he felt that way."

"Well, Little Jackaro, ya have a choice ta make livin' here on one of the best plantations in the colonies with everything ya want marrying a plantation owner," he hesitated, "or livin' on a tall sailing ship. Most women wouldn't have a problem choosing," he said with earnest gazing at her with his tired old eyes.

Before she could answer him, Gwendolyn grabbed her arm and led her away from Santos to the sunroom. Sitting there quietly staring out the window into the darkening night was Adelyn. Gwendolyn steered Belinda to a brown wicker rocker next to Adelyn. A cry, sounding like a cat, brought her attention to a thin black woman standing in the doorway with a bundle in her arms.

"Oh, Belinda, you do have another Henshaw to meet," Gwendolyn spoke in a proud voice. "This is our newest member of the family, Langston Henshaw Jr."

The woman holding the baby crossed the room, but instead of handing the baby to Adelyn or Gwendolyn, she laid the bundle, wrapped in a creamy soft blanket, in Belinda's arms. Even in her time, babies weren't a part of Belinda's life. She didn't believe she had the motherly spirit inside of her. Johnny had talked about having a houseful of children and she'd hoped that would never come true. The warm baby snuggled next to her breast as its miniature mouth wiggled wanting to suckle. His tiny blue eyes peered up at her as she leaned close smelling his sweet scent. She noticed out of the corner of her eye the other women watching her, knowing the reason for the baby's visit. They were hoping to bring a longing to her to marry Lucky and have a few babies of her own. Her life living here in this time would be difficult without modern conveniences, but in her time, she wouldn't have a baby nurse or nanny to help her with a child, as she would here. The baby nurse reappeared on cue taking the baby from her arms.

Gwendolyn stood. "We best, be joining the men," she assured, ushering Belinda into the dining room over to the huge table. Lucky sat down next to her with a grin on his face, his blue eyes glaring back at Sinjin. The men's eyes locked on each other. Lucky believed he had won Belinda's hand in marriage.

She knew the men were challenging each other to see who would win. She sat quietly at the exquisitely decorated dining room table and felt as if she were in a daze as everyone talked and talked and the words became muffled in her mind. She became irritated; she wasn't some prize horse being auctioned off to the highest bidder. How dare these two men play games for her affections. Nonetheless, she did have a decision to make.

After the meal was finished, Gwendolyn stood and led everyone into the large parlor and graciously served each person a hot toddy with some small petite cakes. The warm toddy felt soothing as it flowed down her throat with a calming feeling, but her mind wouldn't stop thinking about what Santos said. She did have a choice to make, living in this grand home or an old sailing ship.

Her eyes were drawn to Sinjin standing tall, his dark hair and eyes so different from everyone in the room, holding his own in the conversations with the other men. He felt her stare and turned his face to her. She felt the heat of his gaze. He grinned; his half grin telling her she was fine. There on the other side of the room was

Lucky, with the bluest eyes, standing so poised and confident – one of most handsome and wealthiest bachelors in the county. Any woman in this time wouldn't think twice about their decision and would jump at a chance to live in a beautiful home with servants to take care of your every whim. What now? She knew she was in love with Sinjin, but the life on a ship was difficult at best and Lucky's home was warm and inviting.

The evening was ending and Gwendolyn came up to her. "Dear, 'tis getting late and you look knackered. Why don't we let the men continue talking and I will show you to your bed chamber."

"That would be nice," Belinda said, hoping this day would end soon.

Gwendolyn held Belinda's arm and led her to the curved oak staircase. They stepped upon the bottom step, but stopped when Lucky walked up.

"Good night Belinda and Merry Christmas," he said softly as he kissed her on the cheek, and then leaned over kissing his mother's cheek.

Belinda's eyes turned to Santos, who was leaning on the doorjamb watching.

Gwendolyn graciously showed her to a lovely bedroom, on the front of the home, with handmade quilts layered on the clean bed and green curtains framing the two windows. Belinda dressed into her nightclothes climbing into the bed to hide, but tossed and turned all night. She woke the next day tired, her mind hadn't giving up thinking of the decision she had to make, two men, two choices, each as different as night and day.

She dressed and slowly made her way down the long staircase and entered the dining room. Adelyn and Gwendolyn sat at one end of the long table eating their breakfast absorbed in conversation; baby Langston was asleep in the nursery with his nanny. Belinda stood in the doorway for a few seconds watching them. This was their life not hers, sleeping in late and planning parties. She smiled to herself; she had her answer.

She picked up a plate from the sideboard scooping an egg and bread onto the plate and sat down at the table listening to more party stories.

Lucky quietly came into the room. "Belinda," he asked graciously, "would you like to go for a walk?"

She nodded yes. Gently he took her arm leading her out the backdoor of the house into the flower garden.

Lucky leaned his head down and passionately kissed her before she could push him away. His touch was warm and inviting, but the kiss felt cold, remembering the warm feeling she had when Sinjin kissed her in the garden in St. Augustine.

Belinda gently pushed Lucky away and sat down on the bench. He leaned down bending his right knee. She grabbed his arm. "No, Lucky."

She leaped from the bench tugging his arm bringing him up to face her. Lucky wasn't quite as tall as Sinjin but she had to lean her head backwards to look into his eyes. "This is difficult for me to say. I am so different like you said – and your offer of marrying you is tempting, staying here living in this wonderful home with you and your family, but my home is the *Aeolus* and I'm sorry I can't marry you."

Lucky's eyes were full of pain, his shoulders drooped, and he smiled at her. "I do hope you had a good stay here and enjoyed Christmas. Belinda, if you do change your mind, I will be here, waiting – please think this through. I do love you and I'll give you the world. Please, don't make a hasty decision."

"Yes, I did enjoy my stay and I love this magnificent plantation. Thank you and I still hope we can be friends?" She said clasping his hands in her hands.

"I hope so too, but I think I will be staying here on the plantation for the rest of this voyage. And when you change your mind I will be here waiting when you return," he said full of confidence.

Slowly and quietly, they walked arm and arm back to the house. She hurried up the stairs and into her bedroom and packed her small cloth bag. She heard voices in the vestibule. Holding onto her bag, she made her way down the long staircase, but abruptly stopped halfway down the stairs. She studied Sinjin, deep in conversation with Theodore. He stood so confident and handsome and she knew she'd followed her heart. Sinjin looked up and gave her one of his looks and his eyes swung to the bag held in her hand. She smiled at him. He grinned and did a sigh running a hand across his damp forehead.

Theodore patted Sinjin on the back as they walked out onto the verandah and Santos followed.

Gwendolyn and Adelyn stepped up to her. "I hope you had a pleasant visit my dear and that you will return soon." She smiled knowing her sons intentions.

"Yes, I did have a nice visit and thank you for your hospitality," Belinda said softly. Gwendolyn held her arm and the three stepped out onto the verandah.

Lucky was leaning on one of the verandah's posts his face drawn. Sinjin walked up to him and their hands met with a tight grip. Two men loving the same woman, but words were not said; their eyes did the talking.

Lucky turned from Sinjin as his head leaned down staring into Belinda's eyes. He took her hand in his. "Please, think about what I said and on those cold nights on that ship remember you have a home waiting here for you, and someone who will always love you," he added. He leaned over to kiss her on the lips and she turned her cheek to him.

Quinnie came running out the front door. "Miss Belinda, Miss Belinda, here's ya gingerbread," she hollered, as she handed Belinda a beautiful, large tin filled with the gingerbread cakes. "I's don't want ya ta ferget yer gingerbread," she added, smiling puffing up her chubby face.

Belinda looked down; Celeste and Asa were standing hiding behind their mother's long dress holding onto their new toys. Belinda squatted down and reached her arms out to them and they came out of hiding giving her big hugs. Adelyn did a huff and turned her back, but Gwendolyn stood smiling holding onto her son's arm.

Sinjin leaped up the verandah's steps taking Belinda's cloth bag from her, wrapped his arms around her, and helped her into the buggy. Tristan did a little whip and the buggy began to roll along the drive. She turned around, took one more look at the massive plantation and Lucky standing on the verandah's steps, understanding he was where he should be.

They arrived at the dock and Ian stood on the top deck waiting for them. "Merry Christmas," she shouted to all of the mates handing them her large tin of small cakes as they all grabbed handfuls of gingerbread.

Belinda sat down on her box and Santos walked over. "Well, I see ya made yer choice or did ya," he sighed. "We'll be back in Williamsburg on our way ta St. Augustine, if ya happen ta change yer mind."

"That I won't do, this is my home, and you are my family. I never want to be without you and Sinjin," she added earnestly tears building in her eyes.

He leaned over and gave her a hug. "My Little Jackaro y'll always be my family an' y'll never be alone."

"One more thing, I don't want Sinjin to know about Lucky's proposal," she insisted.

"Well, `tis a little late; Lucky talked ta him a long time ago an' he knew Lucky was going ta ask ya ta marry him."

"He knew what Lucky's intentions were," she snapped, "and he didn't tell or warn me —or stop me from going to his home?"

"Yay, he knew ya needed ta make yer own choice, y're hard headed, ya know." He laughed. "Sinjin shor' was worried, but shor' was happy when ya came out of that house carrying yer bag ta leave. I never seen that look on his face before, the anguish of not knowing yer decision, he did a big sigh of relief when ya walked up. I'm sorry Lucky decided ta stay an' not sail with us. I'll miss him, but he really does belong on that plantation an' watching him with his father proved it." He moaned as he stood. "Now I need ta get back ta work."

"So do I," Belinda said, "I need to change my clothes."

That night at supper, Ian and Santos walked into the large cabin with big grins on their faces. "Merry Christmas," they both said, as Ian handed her the most beautiful sword. "I taught ya ta sword fight an' thought ya might need this someday; every mate needs their own sword."

Belinda took the sword and pulled it out of its scabbard, letting the light from the oil lanterns sparkle onto its slivery blade. She slid the sword back into its scabbard and laid it on the table. "Thank you Ian," she whispered giving him a hug.

"Here," Santos anxiously handed her a package, his worn face lit with a smile. Lying in front of her was a new brass spotting scope. "Every barrel man needs their own spotting scope," he added.

Tears ran down her face. "You two are great, thank you."

"Merry Christmas, an' we're glad ya decided ta stay with us," said Santos, as the two men walked out the door.

"Aye, to not be out done." Sinjin stood from the table and walked over to his desk. "Merry Christmas, Belinda," he said handing her a soft brown package.

She unwrapped the gift and lifted up a beautiful blue shawl in her hands.

"Since you like to go outside in the evenings to sit, I thought you might need this, and it matches your eyes. You do need some nice things in life and this cashmere is soft."

"Thank you, Sinjin." She stood on her tiptoes and gave him a hug. She looked into his dark eyes knowing she had followed her heart just as Santos had said. She did understand what he meant about needing nice things in life. She had given up a life of everything a girl could want in this time to live on a ship. "This is perfect," she assured, as she put the shawl around her shoulders. "I will have to go out on the deck tonight and sit for a while."

"Sounds nice to me," he wrapped his arm around her. "I'm also glad you decided to stay." He leaned in close and whispered, "I love you, Belinda." The words finally exited his lips.

She smiled up at him inclined her heard back and their lips met passionately.

"I love you, Sinjin," she said in a soft voice.

He pulled her body tightly against his. She laid her head on his chest; they didn't move or talk for a few minutes.

They stepped outside. Ian was sitting quietly with his new pipe tucked in his mouth taking deep draws as smoke circled his head.

"Beautiful night isn't it," Belinda commented.

"Yay, Miss Belinda, by the `morrow `twill be rainy, which ain't good 'cause of how cold `tis gotten."

"How do you know it's gonna rain, Ian?"

Sinjin sat down next to her. "Belinda, the moon is telling us."

"What? How can the moon tell you it's gonna rain?"

Sinjin smiled at her. "A ring around the moon means rain is coming soon and Ian's correct it won't be a good thing with the dropping temperatures."

"Well, I agree it is cold, but it's a beautiful night with all the stars twinkling." She tightened her new shawl and relaxed scooting in close next to Sinjin as she quietly listened to Ian and Sinjin tell tales of years of sailing on the *Aeolus*. She was home and this was where she was staying.

CHAPTER TWENTY

THE STORM

Tuesday morning January 2nd seemed different, but Belinda couldn't quite get a handle on what was wrong until she went out on the top deck. She felt lightheaded and chilled by a gust of icy air, as the waves grew and hissed slapping the sides of the ship as if the sea was boxing with the ship. It seemed quiet; nary a whisper was being spoken as the crew busily moved around the top deck.

"Jessie, what's going on," she called out staring up at the man in the crow's nest high above her.

"Belinda, look over there," Jessie shouted, pointing to the low clouds on the horizon. Before she could ask any more questions, one old sailor, Jericho, securing some ropes on the tall mast, interrupted Jessie. "'Tis an ox eye, Miss Belinda an' there's a storm brewing. It looks like a Northeaster ta me."

Santos walked up. "Y're skipping yer watch an' let Jessie stay up there, this ain't good an' the ship could be in danger."

The door to the great cabin flew open and Sinjin stepped outside taking in the dark clouds bearing down on them. "Ahoy, all hands on deck, Avast. Secure the ropes and sails – tighten the bowline. There's a storm coming right at us and we need to prepare, lying ahull, best bower, and sea anchor."

The crew scattered around the ship. She'd learned when Sinjin used the best bower and sea anchor that meant that the ship was in danger and this wasn't a good sign. The crew began lowering all the sails getting the ship ready to drift and then lowered the larger of the anchors, best bower from the bow. The sea anchor was used to stabilize the ship in heavy winds and would help slow down the roll and strong pitch of the ship.

She rushed to Santos who was standing near the larboard side of the ship his sharp clear eyes studying the grey ominous clouds racing towards them. "Why don't we try to get to a port before the storm arrives?"

His head swung to the side shaking no, his bushy gray hair blew in the strong breeze across his arched shoulders. "There ain't an asylum harbor near here Little Jackaro. We're at our best riding out the storm right here an' not trying ta maneuver inta an unknown port with the sea growin' an' winds blowin'. Ya need ta get prepared 'tis gonna be a long day an' night."

"You be careful, too, it's so cold out here," she offered, nervously reaching over to him lightly touching his arm.

Santos smiled at her. "I will, I need ta get prepared, an' the ship will be fine." Fretfully his fingers rubbed his long beard and his hawk-like eyes stayed on the storm as he walked across the deck to the other side of the ship.

She stared at Santos. His shoulders were hunched and he was worrying more than he was telling. She went to the bow and found a spot to sit to watch the growing storm. She cuddled Captain Monty in her lap anxiously patting his soft black fur as he purred. The storm was coming at them at a fast speed just as the fog did that night on her cliff. A strange feeling swept over her just the same as it had when the whispering fog appeared. The sea was angry and this wasn't a good sign for the *Aeolus*. The ship began to pitch swaying dangerously from side to side and the storm was still miles away.

Ian swaggered weaving back and forth trying to steady himself as he cross the deck. "Miss Belinda, the Captain would like ya ta go inta the cabin. The seas are getting rough an' `tis getting ta dangerous fer ya out here on the top deck."

Her eyes gazed over at Sinjin. He looked up from the helm feeling her stare and gave a trying smile, but not enough to show his dimples, only worry lines appeared on his face. She smiled back at him, nodded her head yes and reluctantly stood and made her way to the great cabin's door. She shivered and tugged her new shawl wrapping it tight around her shoulders; the darkness of the storm was bringing eeriness to the afternoon. She stepped into the cabin. The ship pitched to the larboard side slamming her into the wooden walls, reeling her body to the floor. She crawled to the chair next to the row of long windows and pulled herself up into the chair. Captain Monty leaped into her lap and she sat nervously rubbing his head watching the hands on the clock tick unmercifully slow. She remembered what Lucky said about cold nights on the ship and for her to remember his warm, clean safe home. She shook her head. Captain Monty let out a loud meow. "Awe, you know what I'm thinking don't you. No, Captain Monty, you don't have to worry I'm not going back to Lucky's home. This is my home and I wouldn't trade it for anything."

Ian had explained about icing on tall ships and how serious a threat it was. The sea's spray blowing across the deck from the stormy water would freeze immediately on contact with the ship's deck and would make it dangerous for the crew to maneuver. She shuddered. The crew could easily slip on the top deck and fall overboard.

The howling winds sent chills down her back as it whipped and lashed furiously against the ship. The ship fighting against the fierce

Atlantic Ocean was leaning from side to side as it rolled and pitched back and forth like a toy bobbling in a bathtub. She became terrified knowing how difficult it was for the crew to handle the huge tall ship with icing and the blustery winds. She sat in the darkness of the great cabin. The oil lantern's small flames seemed to be licking at the walls in an angry mood. Her hands continued to rub Captain Monty keeping time with the tick of the clock. She listened to the wind crying out in a sad wailing song as the sea hit the ship sending water across the top deck swishing from side to side.

The door flew open sending a strong icy breeze into the cabin. Ian shoved the door closed, his hair covered in ice crystals. He anxiously rubbed his gloved hands together as he quickly moved into the room. His face was drawn and his body drooped full of fatigue and exhaustion. She couldn't imagine how the crew felt, taking turns fighting the freezing waves with no end in sight.

"'Tis between the devil an' the deep blue sea out there. We usually don't get storms like this fer a few more weeks inta winter. This is very odd, but it does happen. I have been caught in a few of these storms in my life. This one is a doozy, but 'twill be over soon." Ian assured, seeing the concerned in her face.

"Ian, how is everyone doing and is there anything I can do to help?" She stood letting Captain Monty leap from her lap.

"The Captain is fine, an' so is the crew. They know how ta handle this storm. The Captain just wanted me ta check on ya."

"Oh, Ian, I'm fine, but I wish I could help."

"Ya just stay where ya are an' that'll be helping enough," Ian answered, wiping the melting water dripping from his hair. He turned around, tugged the cabin door open, and then quickly closed it behind him.

Her body tensed trying to look out the frosty glass of the windows. But the waves were hitting the windows icing the glass in crystal patterns as the ship continued to moan as a wild, hurt animal in terrible pain. She had seen the sea angry, but had never been out in a storm like this before. She understood how terrifying it was to be out at sea on ship in a storm and why her lighthouse was so important to be able to have a beacon to show the ship the way to safety. She sat in the chair by the windows, tugged her shawl tighter around her shoulders, bringing Captain Monty close and listened to the howling wind.

Something was wrong. She hopped from the chair throwing Captain Monty to the floor; he did a loud meow looking up at her. She anxiously paced the great cabin. She tightened her grip on her shawl. *No, it can't be!* Her body trembled, her legs became weak, and her knuckles were turning white gripping the window seal trying desperately to see outside. The wind seemed to be whispering, just as the whispering fog had that night she'd spotted the *Aeolus*, but she couldn't make out the words. Without warning the ship's bell began to toll giving off an eeriness in the dark night. Chills went down her spine remembering what Ian had said. "If the ship's bell rings in a storm someone aboard the ship will die." She shook her head. "No," she called out in the dark room, "it's as Johnny said, the tale of the ship's bell is just superstition – an old tale from sailors that they had made it up."

She sat in the chair shivering her eyes glued to the icy window. The night did slowly move on and the sun began to peek through the clouds as morning arrived. The storm had vanished and the sea was calming. She did a sigh of relief; they had made it and the worst was over.

She pulled her shawl up around her shoulders yanking her wool knit hat on, ready to check out the ship. She let Captain Monty leap from her arms and carefully stepped out of the cabin door, but stopped. A light layer of ice covered the top deck. She saw Sinjin, his back to her, his shoulders trembling and his eyes staring over the larboard side of the ship. He felt her stare and turned to face her. An extremely grave look covered his face and a cold sweat spotted his brow even in the freezing weather. She knew better than to walk over to him since she couldn't maneuver on the ice.

He cautiously made his way to her his face drawn.

She reached out her hand gripping his arm. "You need to come into the cabin and put some warm clothes on, you're soaking wet." His dark eyes were blurry with tears. "What's wrong? I can see it in your face." She stood frozen in fear and her body trembled. Her skin pricked and her pulse thudded loudly against her throat causing her voice to quake as she tried to speak. "What happened?"

"I will come in soon and change clothes." He sighed. "Belinda." Tears ran down his numb face. He grabbed both of her arms pulling her against his body. "Santos fell overboard last night and was lost at sea – we couldn't save him."

The air was sucked from her lungs and if it weren't for Sinjin's grip, she'd have slid to the deck.

"Santos lost his footing. I couldn't get him to stay in his quarters." Sinjin's head shook back and forth flinging his long black hair.

"No!" she screamed, her sharp voice echoed out in the icy air.

Sinjin took in a deep sigh. "I should have made him stay with you and never have let him on the slick deck."

Her body quivered. The bad feeling last night was real, the ship's bell ringing was true; it was Santos in trouble calling out to her in a whispering voice. "It can't be true – not Santos." She sobbed making her body quiver. "It's not right," she sniffed trying to breathe pulling in the icy air stabbing at her chest. "He was my best mate." Her eyes looked up into Sinjin's eyes. "I felt Santos' pain when he fell overboard." Her head moved back and forth. "Why did this happen?"

"I don't know," Sinjin answered, tilting his head to the side, tears raced dripping from his face. All the crew was supposed to have ropes tied to them, but somehow Santos' rope came loose.

Her throat tightened its grip chocking her. Santos was her best friend; he taught her how to fish, told her stories about Sinjin when he was a small boy and snuck her up to the crow's nest without Sinjin knowing. He was her old Jack and she was his Jackaro. He knew her better than anyone did, including her father. He knew she cared for Sinjin even before she did. He was teaching her to be a good Jackaro. He couldn't be gone – this wasn't for real. He had to be somewhere on the ship.

She looked up at Sinjin, seeing how painful this was for him, knowing it was true and there hadn't been a mistake. Sinjin had grown up with Santos on the ship when his father was Captain; he was as close to Santos as he was to his father.

Sinjin tightly embraced her and she wouldn't let go of him, afraid if she did she would lose him too.

"We'll miss Santos, but he wouldn't want us to feel sorry for him. He was doing what he loved and wouldn't want you to be upset." Sinjin lifted her face with his gloved fingers smoothing her hair from her eyes, wiping tears. "He cared so much for you, Belinda. He thought of you as his daughter and wouldn't want you to be sad; remember he is at peace now with his sea and his family."

Sinjin gently undid her arms and gave her a look that he had to see to the ship and they would be all right. He turned, going back to the men to talk to them. She didn't move, her feet seemed glued to the deck. She would remember all of Santos' tales, the good times they had, his laughter, his quick remarks that made her smile. How was she going to make it without Santos?

Sinjin hurried past her into the great cabin. She could see the hurt in his eyes, understanding he was going into the cabin to put on his uniform for a service for Santos' funeral before they set sail.

She pulled her shawl up tighter around her neck covering her face from the icy breeze. She looked over to the side of the ship and standing there in silence was Ian. She slowly and carefully made her way to him.

"I am so sorry," she whispered.

Ian grabbed her and both of their bodies shook with uncontrollable sobs.

"Santos is gone by the board, Miss Belinda," Ian gulped fighting back tears. "He was an old salt an' dear friend an' I am going ta miss him. 'Tis another sad day fer the *Aeolus*," Ian declared, tears rushing down his flushed cheeks not ashamed to show his feelings for his longtime mate.

"Yes, it is and Santos wouldn't want us to be sad." She patted Ian on the shoulder. "We will always remember his zest for life and his stories. Ian, Santos won't be gone as long as we remember him."

She stepped forward and looked over the side of the ship into the dark water, Santos' grave. She wondered how she was going to make it living on the ship without him; tears stung her face in the freezing air.

Ian wrapped his arm around her as they slowly and carefully walked back toward the great cabin. He might be old, but he had those steady legs of living on a ship.

The cabin door squeaked swinging open. Sinjin stepped outside with a bible clasped in his gloved hands. The crew stopped working and came to him.

Tobias walked up and she held onto his arm. He ducked his head; his wild hair covered his face not showing tears racing down. The grief crushed her heart seeing the young boy trying

228

inconspicuously to wipe the wetness from his face with the back of his hand. The Bible verse was read and the prayer was said. Sinjin said a few special words for his old and dear friend, his other father. She could see the pain on his face again, he had to say goodbye to another family member.

One of the mates added one prayer.

> *God grant that I may live to fish,*
> *Until my dying day,*
> *And when it comes to my last cast,*
> *I then most humbly pray,*
> *When in the Lord's safe landing net,*
> *I'm peacefully asleep,*
> *That in his mercy I be judged,*
> *As big enough to keep*

She knew it was a seaman's way to live and die by the sea. Santos loved his ship and the sea. He was now in the net of the Lord, would always have his sea, and was at peace. Santos was her friend her best mate. She would miss him teasing her about being a Little Jackaro. She could see him standing down below her on the top deck, when she was barrel man, his long gray hair flying in the breeze hearing his laugher rise up at her when she would be drenched by the sea. She was his Little Jackaro and he had told her they would always be family and she didn't think he would ever leave her. Now, she would remember all he taught her about being a great mate hoping to make him proud.

She was glad she'd known him even if it had been only a short time. She'd never forget his special weathered face, his gruffly looks, his kind smile that made so many creases in his face, and his laughter like the soft wind blowing across the wide blue sea.

The faces of the crew were strained not wanting to let their tears show as they paraded in a line looking over the edge of the ship saying their goodbyes. "We will miss ya mate," they each called out. Santos had helped and trained many of the crew just as he was helping her; this truly was another sad day for the *Aeolus*.

She fell in line behind the crew. It was now her time to say goodbye. Sinjin stood next to her, holding her arm tightly. Together they looked over the edge of the ship into the calm blue sea that Santos loved. It was as if the sea was at peace and had taken back one of its own.

"Santos, thank you my old Jack for all you did for me, and I will never forget you; God bless you in your new home. Goodbye my best mate and friend, peace be with you, Clarissa and Nora."

Sinjin not worried about showing his feeling in front of the crew whispered. "Santos is at peace like you said and the sea is taking care of him and we will be fine and that is what he would want." He stared down into the water. "Good bye, my dear friend, you will be dearly missed and may you be blessed by fair winds and following seas." Sinjin's voice flowed out in the air.

Sleep didn't come. She paced the small sleeping quarters hearing Sinjin moving around the great cabin. She opened the door slowly. Sinjin looked at her.

"You'd think we could sleep since we're exhausted from last night."

Her head nodded yes, her voice wouldn't work.

"Come, sit by the window, it's a lovely night, one Santos would love."

The pain of missing Santos had shattered her heart. She hadn't felt this much pain since her mom died. The loneliness was squeezing her body not letting her breathe. She wanted so dearly to go out onto the top deck, sit, and tell Santos her problems. He always had a solution and by the time he'd tell her a tale, she'd forgotten what was upsetting her.

Sinjin wanted to take her pain away, but he too was being overwhelmed with his loss. He now didn't have any family; he was alone in this world.

Belinda studied Sinjin's dark sad eyes and realized what he was thinking. She at least believed her father and Johnny were alive and doing well back in her time. Santos was her family too and taught her well. She moved over by the front windows and began to tell one of Santos' tales. Sinjin sat down in the other chair. His head leaned back listening to the tale she began to spin. Slowly his tired eyes closed and he began to breathe in a soft rhythm. She gently placed an old quilt over his long body, turned down the oil lamps, and left the room.

She lay in her bed. She could see Santos grinning at her as she drifted off to sleep.

CHAPTER TWENTY-ONE

THE TRUNK

Belinda made it through the next few days missing Santos every time she went up to the crow's nest. She thought about him as she held onto her new spyglass, its pouch hanging down from her neck. A sting of pain would appear stabbing at her heart when she'd think she heard his laughter down below, only realizing it was merely memories that wheeled in her mind. One day she knew she'd make it when she heard a commotion and roaring laughter from the crew. She looked down seeing Tobias and Captain Monty running around the ship playing, knowing Santos would have approved and life would go on for her.

One late afternoon Sinjin brought a rounded wooden top trunk up to his cabin. Her throat tightened seeing it was Santos' special trunk with Clarissa and Nora's things in it and all of Santos' possessions.

"Belinda, please, come and sit," Sinjin said as he pulled a piece of paper out of his pocket.

Tears flowed down her face. She scooted next to him on the old wooden floor. She now would be saying goodbye to Santos once more. Sinjin held the piece of paper in his hands.

"Ta my Little Jack, if ya are reading this then I have gon' ta Davy Jones' locker. Don't feel sad fer me, 'cause that is the life of 'n old mate. I am with my Clarissa an' Nora now, an' Zyanya, baby Mary an' yer father, John my best mate. I am at peace. Here is my trunk full of memories of my life – this I want ya ta have. Ya are the only family I have left in this great big sea.

Sinjin an' Belinda
God be with ya
Seas be calm,
Winds blow smooth,
Yer lives be long
My Little Jack an' Jackaro
My love forever
Yer old jack
Santos Barros

Sinjin handed her the note. She could see where Santos had added her name and Jackaro in his own handwriting, beside Sinjin's name, and she knew Santos had trouble writing and could see where Ian had helped him. Tears fell, dripping from her face dotting the note.

"This trunk is ours, Belinda. Would you like to go through it with me?" he asked bending down opening the trunk.

She nodded yes.

Belinda slowly lifted, from the cloth-lined trunk, all of Santos' memories. Baby clothes of Nora's, jewelry that he had given Clarissa, special notes that Clarissa had written to him when he would leave on his voyages, knowing John would read them to him. She was proud Santos had left everything to Sinjin and her. She would always cherish the trunk full of memories. When they finished, Sinjin laid the note in the trunk closed and locked it. He placed the trunk by his father's trunk on the sidewall. He took Belinda in his arms, caressing her face with his fingers. "Santos wouldn't want you to be sad."

She nodded and looked up into those dark eyes so full of love. Sinjin kissed her and whispered, "I love you."

She held onto his face and leaned her head next to his. "I love you too, please don't ever leave me."

"We will never be apart," he assured wiping her tears, then kissing her with overwhelming passion.

Days and nights went by and she knew the ship would be coming into Boston soon and she wasn't sure if Sinjin wanted to meet his family now, after losing Santos. She knew not to bring it up since he had been through a lot the last few days.

Tuesday, Ian pushed open the door to the great cabin carrying an arm full of women's clothes. "Miss Belinda, the captain said ya agreed ta wear these clothes an' go with him ta Boston. I don't know if this is a good idea or not, nonetheless he is determined. Especially now that Santos went back ta visit his wife an' daughters' graves. Ya will have ta be very careful."

"We will be fine, stop worrying Ian. When does he want to go?"

"Tomorrow, as soon as we dock. The crew will unload the ship an' prepare fer the next load ta Maine. Here are the clothes ya need ta wear. God be with ya," he said with a worried look on his face.

Lying on the bed was a brown paisley dress, a light brown apron on the front, and a white hat that looked like a nightcap.

At supper that night, she sat across the table from Sinjin. "Ian brought me some clothes and said you still want to go into Boston tomorrow."

"Is that alright with you?" Sinjin asked with a nervous tone in his voice.

"Sure, do you know where your grandparents live?"

234

"I've been by the home many times, but couldn't go in." His eyes looked up at her. "I'm still not sure if I'll be able to go in. I think of my mum and baby sister and how we were never welcome."

"We aren't going for you to be a part of this family. You just want to meet them and let them know you are around."

"They have a lot of money, Belinda, and they could cause me a lot of problems."

"I can handle them. I know the future remember. The newspaper that is around can cause them as much of a problem with your story as they can cause you. I won't let anything happen. I promise."

Sinjin smiled laying his hand on her hand. They finished their meal and Ian cleared the table so Sinjin could begin his paperwork.

Belinda snuggled in her chair by the windows pulling her shawl up around her shoulders and stared out at the calm sea. The image of Santos visiting with his family, a peacefulness falling over him, flowed through her mind, hoping Sinjin would find that peacefulness in Boston. The thought of the constable made her anxious, since she didn't have Santos.

She didn't want Sinjin to see how worried she was. She stood laying her shawl across the back of the chair. "Tomorrow is going to be a busy day," she said. "Goodnight, Sinjin." She crossed the room to him touching his arm. He leaned over kissing her goodnight. "Goodnight Belinda, I love you," he said gingerly turning back to his charts.

She snuggled in the squashy bed. Captain Monty curled up at her feet purring softly. She could hear Sinjin moving around in the great cabin, sleep wasn't happening for him; tomorrow would be an interesting day.

CHAPTER TWENTY-TWO

FAMILY

The next morning Belinda was up before the ship began to move. She slid on the undergarments and dress, her new black shoes, a couple sizes smaller than the other pair, and flung her long dark cloak over her shoulders. Sinjin sat on the top deck nervously tapping his fingers on the wooden box. His eyes locked in a stare looking toward the Boston Harbor. He hadn't called for the anchor to be raised. He smiled when she stepped out the cabin door; his dark eyes stared up at her.

"Is this alright – how I'm dressed?" she questioned, swirling around in a circle. "I still get a little confused about your time's clothes. There are so many layers of clothes I forget which one goes on first."

"Yay, you are perfect, but what does more layers mean?" he questioned, his eyes twinkling with a mischievous grin on his face.

"In my time women don't wear this many layers of clothes," she answered watching his grin grow wider.

"'Tis most interesting," his finger twitched on his chin as his eyes roamed slowly from her neck down her body. "I must hear more at a later time about the way people dress in your time, especially the women. Your time does seem to be fascinating."

Sinjin was dressed in his black shoes, stockings, long fitted breeches, and frock coat with tails. He had the height of his father and the dark look of his mother cutting a distinguished figure. He looked most handsome and elegant and she remembered how it felt to have his arms around her as they danced in the great ballroom of Drayton Hall making her body heat. She shivered turning her head quickly from him, as her face flushed not realizing how long she'd been staring.

His face lit, his eyebrow raised understanding she'd been daydreaming. "As soon as we dock we should be ready to leave, is that alright with you?" He asked placing his hand on her shoulder.

"No problem," she answered bringing her thoughts back to the present. "Just let me know when you are ready. Everything will work out. Remember Santos even told your father, his family was here on the ship."

"Thank you Belinda, and Santos would be proud of you." His hand moved from her shoulder to her face tenderly drawing his finger along her cheek to her chin.

"He would be proud of you to face your family and then move on." She stretched up on her tiptoes and kissed him.

Time went by slowly, as she sat watching out the cabin's windows, worried about what was going to happen when he met his grandparents, but she wasn't going to let Sinjin know.

The door to the great room swung open. "Are you ready?" Sinjin called out.

"Sure, let's go." Her dress swished as she sashayed out the door holding onto his arm.

"God be with ya both," Ian said standing by the side of the ship.

"We will be fine, Ian, don't worry," Sinjin assured patting him on the back.

The crew stood along the side of the ship worriedly watching. A carriage sat at the end of the pier. Sinjin kept his tri-corner hat on and it was hard to notice his dark skin. The carriage moved slowly along the roads of Boston, turning a few blocks from the harbor, then stopping in front of a huge brick house surrounded by a short brick wall and iron gates.

Belinda tenderly gripped Sinjin's arm. "Sinjin, you can do this for your father and for the peace it will give you."

He put his hands on her waist lifting her out of the carriage swirling her around. He leaned down. "I can do anything with you with me."

They strolled up the steps to the front door. Sinjin pulled a long rope and a bell rang inside the home.

A servant opened the door. "May I helps ya?" asked an older black man dressed in a nice black coat and breeches. His old wrinkled hand gripped the edge of the door, his deep black eyes twitched as he observed Sinjin.

Sinjin stepped forward. "We are here to see the owner of this home. This is – the Alvery family's home?"

The man's face tightened. "Yay, `tis de home of Mr. John H. Alvery an' his wife. Who do I says is calling?"

"I am Sinjin H. Alvery, Sir," Sinjin answered taking his tri-corner hat off bowing to the old man.

The man gasped. His hands quivered as he let go of the door and stepped back in dismay. "I'm sorry Sir, buts Mr. Alvery is busy right now. He's in a meeting in his office."

A beautiful older woman, gray hair twirled up in a tight bun on top of her head, with the bluest eyes came walking up.

"Jeremiah, is something wrong?"

The man turned around wiggling his hands nervously. "Dis young mans, Mrs. Alvery, woulds like ta sees Mr. Alvery. His name is Sinjin H. Alvery."

"What did you say your name was young man?" the woman snapped back.

"Sinjin H. Alvery, Madame, I am the son of John H. Alvery the second."

The woman's face paled and tears welled in her blue eyes.

"You – are John's boy?" she questioned in a crackled voice.

"Yay, Madame, I am."

"Jeremiah let this young man into the home. Now, who might you be – his wife?"

Belinda opened her mouth to speak, but Sinjin quickly interjected, "Nay. This is Miss Belinda Brady from Maine. She is a friend of mine."

Jeremiah led them into the drawing room, but his gaze remained on Sinjin.

The woman's blue eyes lingered for a few minutes on Sinjin's face. Tears gushed from her eyes. "You are John's son; you have the same look in your dark eyes. I would know my own son's eyes anywhere."

This was Sinjin's grandmother. Now, how was she going to treat her half-Indian grandson?

"You are John's mother?" Belinda questioned moving next to Sinjin.

"Yay, I am Coreen Alvery," the elegantly dressed woman replied sitting down on a red velvet settee, "so that makes you my grandson."

Sinjin anxiously cupped his hands together twisting them in a washing motion.

"Please have a seat," Coreen said kindly, holding an embroidered handkerchief in the air waving her delicate hand toward two striped wingback chairs across from the settee.

Sinjin ducked his head and sat down and Belinda maneuvered her long dress spreading it out trying to be graceful and sat down in the other wingback chair.

"Your grandfather John got so mad when he read your father's letter telling us he'd married an Indian woman, he didn't answer him and forbade me to." The handkerchief dotted her misty eyes. "I have worried all of these years about my son and you. Time seemed to go by and your grandfather got madder and madder at your father because we never heard from him. I guess they were both too stubborn…"

The drawing room door swung opened interrupting her. A tall thin, gray-haired man with gray-blue eyes and chiseled face, John Alvery, Sinjin's grandfather, walked into the room with two other men.

One of the men was plump with beady eyes hiding behind wire rim glasses, and the other man was short with blonde curly hair and radiant blue eyes.

Sinjin leaped from his chair.

John Alvery's voice was deep and full of anger. "Jeremiah said you are John's boy. What do you want? Money or the name?"

"Nay, Mr. Alvery." Sinjin stepped forward, confronting his grandfather. "I only wanted to see who didn't want me when I was a young boy," creases growing on his brow, "since I wasn't good enough for your family. I don't need your money or your family, but I had to see for myself who you were."

"Who might this young lady be?" John Alvery questioned, squinting his eyes tightly just as Sinjin was always doing.

"This is Miss Belinda Brady," Sinjin answered his dark eyes glaring at the man in front of him.

"Brady?" John replied taken aback.

The blonde-haired man standing next to Sinjin's grandfather, John stepped near Belinda. "I dare say I don't believe we have met before, my lady." The man bowed, his hat in his right hand swished to his chest. "Let me introduce myself. I am William Franklin Brady of Boston, you wouldn't happen to be relative to the Brady's of Boston?"

"Nay," Sinjin replied before Belinda could say anything. "She's from Harbor Towne, Maine."

Her breath seemed to whoosh out of her body not able to manage to draw any more air into her lungs. Her face paled, hearing the name William Franklin Brady, and the room seemed to be spinning in a circle. She stared at the man in front of her seeing her father's face, the same shaped face as hers. Sinjin stared down at her in a confused look. He grabbed her arm steadying her as her body became limp in his arms. He whispered, "are you all right, you look like you've seen a ghost."

Gulping she tried to get her voice to speak. "I have," she quietly uttered staring at her ancestor from the past.

"Did ya say Harbor Towne, Maine?" William's blues stayed on Belinda. "I'm an architect and I've been talking to some men from Harbor Towne, a Mr. Joe Smith and a Mr. Ben Hudson about building a lighthouse out on a cliff near the town."

This was more than Belinda's mind could take hearing William Brady talk about her lighthouse, town and the founding fathers.

"I have been drawing up plans for a tall stone lighthouse to be built in a few years in the small town. I will be moving there to oversee the building process, 'tis a beautiful area."

Sinjin gasped, his eyes became huge swinging from William to Belinda, understanding her anxiety. She was seeing a ghost; the ghost of her ancestor William Franklin Brady. The man who'd built her lighthouse on the cliff in Harbor Towne.

"My dear," Coreen stood from the chair, "are you all right?" She moved to the door. "Jeremiah, please bring this young lass something to drink."

"I'm fine," Belinda was finally able to say in a soft voice, fanning her hands in the air. "It's a little warm in here, but I'll be all right – you needn't fuss."

William Franklin Brady stepped closer and Sinjin's strong hands held onto her as she met her ancestor. "I didn't know any kinfolks lived in Harbor Towne," the man said in a soft voice his blue eyes staring into her same blue eyes. "My young lady ya do resemble my mum, God rest her soul. It's nice to meet ya and maybe we will meet again during my stay in Harbor Towne."

Jeremiah hurried into the room with a crystal glass in his hand carefully handing it to Belinda. She took a slow sip of the ale and her composure came back with her eyes glued on William Brady.

"Sir," William turned from Belinda back to John Alvery, "I must be going, Elizabeth is expecting me home. We will continue our meeting another day." William turned to Coreen, bowed, and then bowed to Belinda. He clasped her hand in his. "'Tis nice to meet you my dear and please send my regards to your family."

The other plump man said his goodbyes, bowed, and left the room following William Brady to the front door.

Belinda stood in a daze slowly sipping the ale in the crystal glass.

Sinjin's grandfather frowned, his bushy gray eyebrows arched and pulled tightly together. "Son, did your father send you here to plead with us to take him back?"

"Nay, my father died years ago with the knowledge that you didn't want me as your grandson, so that meant you didn't want him. He made his own family on his ship living a good life. It was hard in the beginning for him to lose my mum and baby sister, and then to lose you, but life went on for him. He was a great father, a great and fair man. It was nice to meet you and now we must be going."

Sinjin spun around and faced his Grandmother Coreen. "Madame, my father did talk of you and missed you very much. He would teach me songs and poems that you had read to him at night. I'm sorry I have caused you any pain. Thank you for taking the time to meet with us."

Sinjin turned to leave, but his grandmother Coreen stood from the settee and reached out her wrinkled hand taking his arm. "Nay, you aren't leaving like this," she said. "I want to know my grandson and learn what happened to my son. I haven't talked to my son in almost thirty years. Please stay for dinner and talk for a while to an old woman."

Sinjin looked over to his grandfather John sitting in a chair by the front window.

"If she wants you to stay I'm not going to stop her."

Grandmother Coreen held onto Sinjin's arm and led him to the dining room. "Jeremiah, we will be having company for dinner, please set two more places."

Sinjin's grandfather walked up to Belinda. "Why are you with a half-breed, young woman? You must be English."

"Sir, I'm not with a half-breed, but with a caring and considerate young man, that happens to have dark hair and eyes with dark skin. He's no different from you, except he has a very kind heart."

Sinjin let go of his grandmother Coreen's arm and hurried back to Belinda, leading her away from his Grandfather.

They sat at the dining room table and Sinjin's grandmother began to tell stories about Sinjin's father and his father's sister, Mary, growing up in this home. Sinjin chimed in telling tales of his father becoming a great sailor and his voyages up and down the coast. His grandmother asked about his mother. What was her name and what was she like?

Sinjin described Zyanya, the same as Santos had in his story, and told that she was a wonderful, caring woman and loved his father very much.

After the meal, the four sat in the parlor. Voices came from the vestibule and a plump, blonde haired woman came into the parlor and crossed the room to Sinjin.

Sinjin stood to greet her.

"I am Mary, your father's younger sister. It's good to meet my nephew after all of these years. I have just learned of my brother's death," she sniffed, wiping her eyes with a handkerchief resembling the one Grandmother Coreen held. "I hoped his life was a good one. I have missed him very much."

"Yay, Miss Mary, my father had a good life and he talked often of you. He loved you very much. My baby sister that died was named Mary Coreen after both of you. I have been told she had blue eyes, light hair and skin. I believe she would have been welcomed into the family."

The pain grew in Sinjin's eyes.

Mary reached out taking Sinjin's arm. "I am not Miss Mary, I am your Aunt Mary, and I want you to call me that every time you visit." She sighed. "And I hope it is often. You have some cousins and other family members to meet. Right father, Sinjin is welcome here anytime?"

Grandmother Coreen stood. "Yay, my son, you are welcome and I do hope you will visit often. I'd like to learn more about you and this ship that took my son away. What was it called?"

"Madame, 'tis called the *Aeolus*," Sinjin answered.

"Yay, the *Aeolus*. There was a story I used to read to your father at night about the *Aeolus*, the keeper of the wind. It was Greek mythology and he so loved the book and we read the story over and over." Tears filled her eyes. "I am also Grandmother to you," she said as she walked near him reaching her hand up gently touching his face.

"Thank you, Grandmother Coreen, and I will try to come back when we are in port. We must be leaving; I have the *Aeolus* to see to, she is now my ship."

Grandmother Coreen stepped near Belinda. "My dear, we didn't get to talk to you. Please come back with Sinjin."

"She will be back, Grandmother Coreen, thank you, and goodbye." Sinjin stood to take his leave. He leaned down and gave his grandmother a kiss on the cheek, and her old eyes lit up.

Sinjin and Belinda stepped down the front steps of the tall three-story brick home seeing that the carriage they'd arrived in had left, but another carriage pulled up and the man climbed down from his seat. "Mr. Alvery, please get in," the man said opening the carriage's door. "Now where is this ship of yers docked?"

"Sir, my ship is docked at the end of the harbor."

Belinda felt eyes on them. She peered out the carriage's window, seeing Sinjin's Grandfather John watching out the drawing room's window. He had a smile on his face with deep dimples, an older light-skinned version of Sinjin.

The carriage jerked to a stop at the dock and they made their way down the long boardwalk.

"Belinda, are you all right? Your face did become very pale when you met your forefather William Franklin Brady."

"It was a shock to meet my grandfather, the one who built my home and lighthouse. I remember the story my father used to tell about William Franklin Brady. He was from Boston and when the lighthouse was finished he moved his family into the old Victorian home." She smiled up at Sinjin. "How can this be? This is my family tree." she chuckled, "we must be from an old oak with its branches twisted and entwined together, since I'm meeting my family before my father was even born. Oh, this makes my head hurt."

"'Tis very strange to think about you meeting you own ancestor and 'tis more than my mere mind can handle."

"What's even stranger – William will be asking Mr. Smith and Mr. Hudson to meet my family in Harbor Towne and – he is my family that lived there," she said letting out a wild laugh. "That will stir up the small town and I agree this is bizarre for anyone to think about."

"Well, you might just get the chance to meet William again and his wife Elizabeth, what do you think about that? We will be back in Boston visiting my grandparents next spring. You know William Brady doesn't leave for awhile to go to Harbor Towne to build your lighthouse."

"Oh, and I could meet his children. He had two boys and one of them was," she grinned, "Samuel Brady, Finnegan's father. Remember, Finnegan was the man Ebenezer talked about in his tale of *The Black Shadow*. Aww, this is making my head spin – how can this be possible?"

"I dare say it might be fun to learn about your family." He grinned and whispered in a soft voice, "I wonder if William Brady is as headstrong as you?"

Her head tilted to the right and her mouth puckered. Sinjin draped his arm around her shoulder bringing her close and kissed her cheek.

Ian came running down the gangplank. "How did it go, Miss Belinda," he whispered.

"Come and sit down with me Ian and I will tell you another tale. A tale of a ghost, one you may not believe. I just wish Santos could be here to hear this too, but maybe he knows," she said, staring up at the white fluffy cottony clouds floating in the dark sky.

Ian nodded yes. She began her tale of Sinjin meeting his father's family. Ian's eyes grew wide as she told of meeting William Franklin Brady her ancestor from her past, the man who'd built the tall stone lighthouse on her cliff.

CHAPTER TWENTY-THREE

THE BROKEN MAST

The next day, Tuesday January 20ᵗʰ, 1789, the seas were calm as the crew prepared to sail from Boston.

Ernesto walked up on the top deck prepared to leave the ship to stay the winter with his wife and kids. "Ya my lady, I'm gonna miss. I will have stories ta tell my little rug rats about a lovely light-yellow haired sea angel. Most don't believe my tall tales, nonetheless I know that this tall tale is true," he said giving Belinda a kiss on the cheek.

The ship set sail moving away from Boston and she climbed up to her perch. It was peaceful sitting above the ship, but worry was coming over her realizing they would be at Harbor Towne in a few days.

A cracking noise began and her eyes grew wide seeing a line snap from one of the tall masts letting the sail swing directly at her missing her by only a few feet. Belinda cried out a piercing scream, "HELP!" Her eyes stayed on the mast watching it sway back and forth inching closer to her with each swing. The top mast jerked and the ship abruptly lurched to the right, throwing sails and riggings in disarray causing chaos.

Ashton leaped in the air trying desperately to grab the rope of the mast to secure the sail. Unexpectedly the ship wobbled to the left sending the sail wildly back, smashing him in the head, knocking him over the side of the ship!

"HELP!" she shouted, watching Ashton fly overboard landing in the dark water below. "Please someone help!"

Sinjin shoved the cabin door open crashing it into the cabin wall running out onto the deck. The crew dashed racing around the top deck.

"Sinjin, Ashton was hit in the head and knocked over the side of the ship!" she shouted.

"Hang, on Belinda," yelled Sinjin. "Tate, you help her and I am going after Ashton!"

She gasped watching in horror as Sinjin slipped his shoes, vest off, and leaped from the tall side of the ship into the frigid water far below. Tate began scurrying up the mast's ladder quicker than she'd seen anyone climb and his long, strong arms wrapped around her.

"Slowly, I won't let ya fall, jes try ta stay balanced," he assured.

When Tate let go of her, Belinda leaped from the ladder to the deck, and darted to the other side of the ship. She only saw the dark water rising in small waves. The crew quickly lowered the boat and accommodation ladder down the side of the ship. A few of the men dashed down the ladder jumping into the boat. Eli leaped into the water. Time passed feeling like hours going by, but finally she saw Ashton's body come to the surface and then Sinjin. Terrence grabbed Sinjin tugging him into the boat and one of the men wrapped a blanket around him. Eli, a large man, threw Ashton over his shoulders; carefully he began climbing the ladder. When he made it to the top, the mates grabbed Ashton's limp body laying him on some blankets on the deck. He wasn't breathing.

Belinda squatted down and began CPR. She wasn't letting another mate die on the ship. The men didn't say anything and just surrounded her watching her every move. All of a sudden, Ashton began to choke and spit water; his hazel eyes gradually opened and looked up at her. He would need rest and the bump on his head checked, but he'd be all right.

The men lifted Ashton carefully carrying him down to his quarters. Sinjin had changed from his wet clothes and was standing behind the men. He walked over to her. "You scared me to death when you screamed and I saw you sitting up in the crow's nest with the broken sail swinging wildly coming straight at you."

"Well, you did the same to me when you jumped from the ship and didn't come up to the surface for such a long time; I thought my heart had stopped."

"I have been jumping from this ship to go swimming since I was a small lad." He laughed. "Not in water this cold, but I learned to hold my breath and go down deep into the sea. I was relieved to see you were safe when I came aboard. You did a great job hanging on."

"It wasn't that hard, Santos taught me to tie myself to the mast with a sailor's knot. He showed me how to tie a knot so I could just pull on it and get loose very quickly. That way if the ship leaned too far and I wasn't watching I would be safe; so I guess, Santos saved my life."

"Let's get you warm and some dry clothes on. The mates will fix the sails and we will be underway soon, but I don't ever want to feel the pain again that I might lose you," he said in a soft voice, leading her to the cabin door.

She smiled up at him. "Me either," she whispered.

After she changed clothes, Belinda walked out to the great cabin and sat down on the arm of the chair by Sinjin. She looked into his dark eyes. "This has been some voyage, Captain."

He smiled. "I love you Belinda," he said kissing her as her body slipped down onto his lap cuddling close to him.

CHAPTER TWENTY-FOUR

THE WHISPERING FOG

With the excitement of the broken sails over, the next few days were quiet. However, the day finally arrived when she knew they would be getting close to her cliff.

Sinjin had taught her to read the old charts, how to use the azimuth circle, the instrument used to take bearings of celestial objects, and at night how to read the stars to find the ship's position. He was going to teach her everything about being a sailor. He was taking over for Santos.

She learned to steer and navigate the ship, understanding what a privilege it was to be able to steer his beloved ship. Between Ian and Sinjin, she was becoming a good Jack and knew Santos would approve.

Her feelings were mixed about going home. She wanted to see her father and the lighthouse, but she didn't want to leave Sinjin and the ship. She'd fallen in love with Sinjin just as Santos knew from that first day. Now, another question, how could she blend the two worlds?

Tomorrow the ship would be at Franklin's Cliff – her cliff, sailing pass into Harbor Towne, Maine. Night was coming on. She climbed into her bed, but tossed and turned all night. What was going to happen tomorrow? Would she be back in her time or would she stay forever here in this time of 1789?

Tuesday morning she was up early excited to see her cliff. She sat high above the ship scanning the horizon, wondering what destiny had in store for her. The great ship rounded the peninsular, its hull sunk low in the water under the weight of its cargo. In the distance, she spotted the tall rugged cliff so spectacular with its jagged rocks protruding from the sides. Her heart thumped like a drummer gone mad. She gripped her seat; there wasn't a lighthouse on top of the cliff. She had her answer; she was still in this time. Her eyes stayed fixed on her cliff for the rest of her watch, then she carefully and somberly climbed down from her post and sat at the bow of the ship.

Sinjin stood at the wheel, his hands anxiously gripping it tightly, watching her reaction knowing the lighthouse wasn't there. She turned around nodded her head and smiled at him. She was where she belonged. This was Sinjin's time and world and this is where she needed to be. Fate had brought them together, and she'd stay with him forever. She would follow her heart just as Santos had said.

Jessie yelled down. "Ahoy, Captain, an unusual fog bank is rolling in fast from far out ta sea."

Belinda saw worry growing on Sinjin's face and beads of sweat formed on his temple and across his forehead even in the cold temperatures. The phenomenon of the fog was happening again and the ship had to make it to the harbor quicker than was planned. As the ship approached Franklin's Cliff, the sea's waves grew massive in height, crashing against the ship throwing it from side to side just as it had done before. She felt a tug of pain in her heart and tears brimmed in her eyes watching Sinjin fighting to steer the huge ship.

The crew raced around the top deck preparing the ship, but the fog was coming in fast creeping toward them like a wild animal on the prowl.

"Belinda," shouted Sinjin, his voice flowed out joining the whispering fog, "get inside!"

When she grabbed the doorknob to the great cabin a touch of panic came over her making the hair on the back of her neck rise. She could see bands of dark clouds headed directly at the ship. Her body shivered as the whispering fog swirled in the air surrounding her, voices growing louder whispering her name.

The violent sea pitched the ship titling to its larboard side. She tried to stay balanced gripping her feet to the deck floor holding onto the cabin's doorknob. A gigantic wave towered over the ship. The monstrous wave knocked her to the side of the ship jerking her hand free from the doorknob. Her terrified eyes flew back to Sinjin. His dark face went pale watching the wave shove her body as it flew like a rag doll over the side of the ship. "Sinjin," her voice screamed fading away joining the whispers of the whispering fog.

CHAPTER TWENTY-FIVE

GOING HOME

I landed in the deep, dark seawater below the tall sailing ship. The ice-cold water kept covering my head as I fought to take in air, trying not to lose track of where I was in the black ocean. Coming to the surface, I couldn't see anything in the heavy mist and the dark water pounded furiously at my face. The solid wall of waves shoved me toward shore. I hit a smooth large rock and was able to pull my weary body onto the top of it. I stood on the boulder trembling. I was at the same spot Sinjin had saved me months before. I yelled for help, just as I'd done that night sliding down the cliff, but only the swishing and splashing of waves answered me back.

All of a sudden, the fog lifted and the light from the full moon was glistering on the water making the sea beautiful and peaceful. I shivered. My teeth chattered and I wrapped my arms around my body. I shouted as loud as my voice could yell. "Sinjin," my voice quivered resounding out to sea, but the only sound coming back to me was the sound of the whooshing of the calm waves splashing at the boulder sending icy sprinkles of water at me.

"Belinda!"

My heart started pounding. "I'm down at the bottom of the cliff," I yelled, searching for the tall ship.

"Belinda, is that you?" shouted the voice again.

My eyes swung up peering at the top of the cliff. In the light from the lighthouse that was swirling and circling in its constant rhythm, I could see my father stooped over the edge of the cliff looking down at me.

"Daddy, I'm down at the bottom of the cliff."

"Belinda, are you alright? I'll throw you a rope. Are you able to climb back up the cliff?"

"Yes, I'm fine; if you pull the rope, I can make it back up the cliff."

I tied the rope around my waist and started ascending the side of the tall cliff. As I slowly and carefully climbed the cliff, my eyes scanned searching for the *Aeolus*; there wasn't any sign of the tall ship.

I fell to the ground on top of the cliff and a wet lick swished across my face. "Oh, Neptune, I missed you so much," I shouted grabbing him smothering him in hugs.

I looked up; my father was standing over me, his hands swinging in the air. "Belinda, what happened to you? I've been worried out of my mind calling out for you." His eyes opened wide and his face frowned. "What are you wearing?"

"It's a long story Daddy and I will tell you in a little while."

"Yes, you can answer questions later. You're soaking wet. We need to get you into the house so you can get warm before you get sick."

He grabbed my arm and helped me from the ground leading me back to the house, but his eyes kept flashing back staring at my strange clothes.

I jerked to a stop. Standing so tall in the light of the lighthouse was my old Victorian home. Everything was as it had been that night when I fell from the cliff.

I hurried to my room, grabbed some clean clothes, and took a long hot shower. The shower felt so warm and inviting, but my mind swirled and I felt dizzy. I dressed in jeans and a sweater and slipped on my old pair of tennis shoes. I stopped by my dresser and looked into the mirror, or the looking glass as Ian called it and smiled back at my reflection. I was home whatever that meant, but how and why. My father would be able to help me figure out this dilemma. I quietly opened my bedroom door. My father stood in the living room talking on the phone to the doctor. I crossed the room and sat down on the hearth next to the warm fire.

He hung up the phone and sat down in his overstuff chair. His hand nervously rubbed his chin. "Belinda, I went to the lighthouse and sounded the foghorn, just as you asked. I hurried back to the cliff where you were standing, but I couldn't find you. What happened? I was so worried. I've been searching and searching the cliff – did you fall down the cliff?"

"Yes, I know I disobeyed you, but I had to find out what was at the bottom of the cliff. I thought I could make it down to the bottom, but the rocks were too slick and I slid down the cliff."

I then began my amazing story explaining how I'd fallen off the cliff and Sinjin had saved me from hitting the rocks below. I told my father about sailing on the *Aeolus*, the great sailing ship. The *Aeolus* was the ship I'd seen at the bottom of the cliff earlier in the evening. I told him how I'd somehow gone back in time to 1788 and was able to see our town when it was young. I explained how I rode a buggy out to our cliff and neither the lighthouse nor the home was here.

The story flowed about being the barrel man for the ship, fighting the pirates, the horrible storm, and the wonderful story about Charleston and going to Drayton Hall and seeing so many exciting cities. I even told about meeting William Franklin Brady, our ancestor, who was living in Boston. I thought my father would love to hear about my adventure, but I saw the expression of disbelief on his face. He didn't believe, or didn't want to believe my story. He had always believed anything I'd said, but not this time; he thought I'd gone crazy or mad. I saw a look in his eyes I'd never seen before and he didn't want to hear anymore.

His face paled and his hands swished anxiously together as he stood from his chair and paced the room. "You need to go and lie down in your room; Dr. Holt will be here in a few minutes to check on you."

I became quiet and my stories ceased. I did as my father asked and went to my bedroom and laid down on my bed. A few minutes later, I heard Dr. Holt talking to my father in the living room discussing what had happened to me. Dr. Holt had been my doctor since I was a baby and knew me as well as anyone in town. My father believed I'd hit my head and was telling him some strange stories. Dr. Holt agreed that was probably the answer of what had happened to me. He told my father he'd give me some sleeping pills and that would help me forget my dreams and I'd be fine by morning and back to my normal self.

My father and Dr. Holt came into my room. Dr. Holt sat down in a chair by my bed, cleaned his spectacles, and stared. He was surprised and confused to see my face and arms so tan, since it'd been cloudy for the last few weeks. I knew being the barrel man I'd been out in the sun for hours at a time, but wasn't bringing that answer up to the two men staring down at me. The doctor didn't see or feel any bumps on my head, but believed I'd lost consciousness for a while and dreamed my story. Dr. Holt did as most doctors and told me to rest, and I'd be fine tomorrow.

I heard the front door close and the motor on Dr. Holt's old pick-up leaving down the dirt road. My father's boots scrapped the wood floor crossing the hall coming into my room. "Belinda, the doctor wants you to take these pills and get some rest. He said you'll be fine tomorrow."

He handed me a pill and a glass of water. I did as my father asked and popped the pill in my mouth, but didn't swallow. My father said, "good night," and gave me a hug. "I'm so glad you're alright, I don't know what I would do if something happened to you." He stopped for a few seconds holding onto the doorjamb peering back at me with his tired blue eyes. "I was so worried about you." He closed the bedroom door and I could hear his boots scraping the floor as he walked back to the living room.

I spit the pill out of my mouth, reached down on my neck and felt the locket Sinjin had giving me. *"This wasn't a dream it was for real and I didn't hit my head and dream the entire tale."*

I slid a writing tablet out of the desk drawer, picked up a pen and sat down on my bed. My head leaned against the headboard and I began to write my story of what had happened that cold night of October 13th, when I met Sinjin and the *Aeolus*. The story of the whispering fog, how it called out to me and how I'd climbed down the steep cliff landing in Sinjin's arms. My story of meeting Ian, his plump body bouncing across the ship with a smile across his face, a man who took his job of being cabin boy seriously, but never could turn a person down who needed help. Santos, his mischievous grin, a scruffy bear who intimidated most mates; my counterpart, my best mate, a staunch friend I miss dearly. Tobias, his wild orange hair blowing across his freckled face, his crooked smile that would light up when he would read from a book, a sweet boy wanting to learn and venture out into the world. Lucky, a man who in this time, women would call a rich playboy, but I'd call a handsome man with love for life; a man I hope is enjoying life on his plantation and finds his love as I have. My love, Sinjin, a tall, dark-skinned man of few words, but a man whose eyes were kind, caring and showed so much love; a man I wanted to spend the rest of my life with.

I began to write all of the details about seeing the Right Whales, fighting and defeating pirates, sailing on the magnificent sea and seeing land along the shore as the ship traveled. I relived my journey to Boston with Santos finding his family's graves. The tale of going to Charleston and the great ball, the night I fell in love with Sinjin. Meeting Mamma Annie in St. Augustine, how Lucky had asked me to marry him and live on his plantation in Williamsburg. I even added the recipe for the special gingerbread cakes I'd learned from Quinnie. I described in detail the story of the ice storm, Santos slipping and falling overboard, dying at sea, and what an amazing jack, an old salt he was, and how I loved him.

I wrote of Sinjin finding his family in Boston and the tale that Santos told of his and John's family. How I was able to meet my ancestor William Franklin Brady, who lived near Sinjin's family and that he was working on the blueprints to build the lighthouse in a couple of years. I told of climbing to the top of the magnificent ship being the barrel man, and the story of how Ashton and I had survived when the sail broke loose. I told every fact about my dearly loved *Aeolus* and the magnificent dark sapphire blue locket that I wore around my neck, describing the locket as I clasped it in my hand. I added my undying love for Sinjin and that I missed him greatly.

I described every aspect of my journey not leaving any detail out, not even the tiniest of details. I had to remember forever everything about my adventure – the entire voyage.

The sun began to rise; its orange light flickered through the tall tree in the front yard sending a strobe effect flowing over my bed. I laid the pen down and read the story letting tears rush down my face. I didn't understand what had happened that night of the whispering fog or where the ship had come from and how I was the only one to see it. Before I closed the journal, I went to my dresser, slid the pocketknife and the turtle bone, my gift from Tobias, from the pocket of my canvas breeches, and placed the thin bone in the front of the journal. I clutched the leather book to my chest and paced the room. How could I get back to 1789? The phenomenon that had happened could it possibly happen again – but how?

I slid the journal into the bottom drawer of the dresser under a pile of clothes for safekeeping. I wanted to remember every detail of my adventure on the *Aeolus, the Keeper of the Wind.*

Morning had come, but I needed rest. I picked up the pill from the nightstand and swallowed it, climbed into the warm clean bed with my mind thinking of Sinjin. His dimples on his strong chiseled face, his warm smile, and those dark eyes that let me see into his soul. *I'll never forget you, and I'll love you for the rest of my life.* I promised him. I hugged my pillow and sobbed uncontrollably.

I woke later in the morning the smell of breakfast drifted into my bedroom. I believed I was onboard the ship until I felt the dampness of my pillow. I quickly realized I was in my own bedroom, in my time not Sinjin's time.

I dressed in my jeans and sweater. My father was busy in the kitchen fixing breakfast, his shoulders hunched over the stove. I knew my story of the whispering fog was worrying him.

"Oh, good morning Belinda." His head turned in my direction, a trying smile on his face. "Come sit down and have some breakfast. I made your favorite meal, blueberry pancakes and bacon."

"Thank you Dad." I sat down at the kitchen table taking a bite of the homemade pancakes stacked on my plate. "Dad, what day is it?"

"Why, it's Tuesday, Belinda, October the 14th." He gave me a puzzled look.

I gasped, dropping the fork onto my plate. This couldn't be true. I fell from the cliff on my birthday, Monday, October 13th, 1959 and today was only the 14th. But, I had been onboard the ship for months in the year of 1788. How could I have been gone only a few hours here in my time?

My dad's eyes squinted his face frowned. I wasn't asking any more questions.

After I finished breakfast, I went to my room. My feet slid to a stop at my bedroom door. My old clothes from the ship that I'd been wearing yesterday were gone. My father had thrown them away hoping all of the stories would disappear too.

Later that morning I sat on my round rock by the cliff's ledge looking out at the sea. I remembered a few months ago standing here with Ian not able to find my lighthouse or home.

Tears flowed through my fingers drenching my face. I felt alone; I began to tell Neptune my tale of the old sailing ship and he too looked up at me as if I'd gone mad.

I finally smiled thinking of Finnegan Brady's tale of the whispering fog he'd told the people of Harbor Towne. My smiled faded; no one had believed him and they sure wouldn't believe my tale. If only I could find his journal about his passage into the past. It might hold a clue of how to travel back into the whispering fog.

My fingers grasped my extraordinary locket. I believed my story of the tall sailing ship was real, nonetheless I'd never tell my tale again. If my father didn't believe my story, no one else would.

"Belinda," Dad yelled from the house, "Dr. Holt is on his way and wants to talk to you. He wants to be sure you're all right. Honey, it's getting cold out here – you need to come back inside."

About an hour later Dr. Holt showed up. He sat down in the living room. His wrinkled hands gripped his black bag; a large crease grew on his forehead. "Belinda, I'm amazed you didn't get hurt in the fall off the cliff. You sure are a lucky girl."

I ducked my head. Of course, I realized I had scrapped my arms, but Ian had taken care of the cuts. I smiled seeing the old scars on my arms. Quickly I pulled the sleeve of my sweater down so Dr. Holt couldn't see. I didn't answer the man.

Days went by and I sat each day and night out on my cliff watching for any sign of the *Aeolus*. I did as my father asked and agreed that during the day I'd finish my nursing classes in town, but every night I'd sit looking out into the sea Neptune always at my side.

I read all I could about the years of 1788 and 1789, Boston, St. Augustine, Williamsburg, and Charleston. I even learned the terminology about sailing on a tall sailing ship and was amused that I knew most of the facts, even some things that they weren't in the books. I wanted to ask my father about Finnegan's pocket watch, but knew like Finnegan's journal, the watch was hidden away.

I finished nursing school and received my nursing degree. Johnny would come by and visit me, at the encouragement of my father. We'd spend time sitting on my cliff and I'd tell him tales of the sea, the stories the crew had told me, however I couldn't even confide in my longtime friend my story of the *Aeolus*. Seeing the pain in his face I knew I was still the love of his life and he was planning to ask me to marry him, but that would never be since Sinjin was the love of my life.

Life moved on for me and the day arrived when I had to say goodbye to Neptune, my best mate. Now, I didn't have anyone I could confide in. Instead of days and months going by years seemed to fly by and there wasn't any sight of the *Aeolus*. All I had to keep me company were my memories, so each day I would write my thoughts down in my journal.

As my father aged, it was becoming difficult to take care of the lighthouse. I had a cousin, Marcus Brady, who loved the lighthouse almost as much as I did. When we were kids, Marcus had spent many summers learning about the lighthouse and the cliffs.

My father asked Marcus and his wife Ava to come live with us and help see to the lighthouse. He graciously agreed. The next month the couple moved into the old Victorian house. Our house became a home again and it didn't seem so lonely. Nonetheless, I never spoke to Marcus or Ava about my journal or what had happened that fall evening in the whispering fog in 1959. I knew in my heart that they would think I was crazy or that I'd been dreaming.

The next year we had company. Marcus and Ava had a daughter, Anita. She was a charming child and since I hadn't married or had any children Anita became like my child. I sat at night holding baby Anita snuggling her against my breast just as baby Langston had done so long ago at Lucky's plantation. I sat wishing and longing for a child of my own with Sinjin. I wondered what our child would look like, blending his dark skin and eyes with my fair skin and blue eyes. I could see our son that I would have named John Santos after two strong men, able to grow up on the *Aeolus*, just as Sinjin had done. Dreams of the life I wanted kept me going, believing the phenomenon of the whispering fog could happen again.

Every night, Anita and I took long walks and I taught her every path I knew to get around the steep cliffs. I showed her every place to hide on the sides of the cliffs. We would climb down to the water's edge and sit for hours. Of course we didn't tell anyone what we were doing.

Years swished by and my father became ill with arthritis. One warm spring day, Marcus and I helped him, his last time, climb the spiral steps up to the top of the tall lighthouse. He spent the entire day there. It broke my heart to watch him sitting quietly staring out to the sea knowing that was his last time to be in his deeply loved lighthouse. It brought back reality to me that I might not ever see the *Aeolus* and Sinjin again.

Not being able to go to the lighthouse finally wore on my father. It took the life out of him and the day did come, January 17, 1984, when I had to say good-bye. I stood at his bedside; his wrinkled hand reached out and gently touched my hand. He softly whispered, "Belinda, don't let the whispering fog take you like it tried so long ago." As he drew in his last breath, I caressed his hand. Tears raced down my face when his hand fell limp onto the bed. Marcus was confused about what my father said about the fog, but he didn't question me believing it was the gibberish of a dying man.

The house had an eerie chill. I left my father's bedroom and went to the living room to start a fire in the fireplace. I placed a log onto the grate but jerked to a stop. Lying in the ashes, charred around the edges, was a stack of yellowed papers. I laid the log on the hearth and reached my hand into the gray cold ashes lifting out each of the papers giving them a good shake letting the ashes fall to the floor.

My heart pounded as I began to read the scorched paper.

Finnegan Augustus Brady
Spring 1846.

I Finnegan Brady have to tell my tale of when I was a young man of twenty-two. It was the winter of 1846 my life was one planned out by my father, Samuel and mother, Sarah. I was to marry Ashlyn, a young beautiful girl who lived in the next county, an arranged marriage by all the parents. I had a free spirit and settling down with a wife wasn't a part of my dreams, nevertheless, I would do, as my parents wished.

That cold November night 1846, I stood on the porch of my parents Victorian home. My mother was busy in the kitchen cooking our evening meal and my father, just as he did each night was sitting in the parlor reading by the oversize fireplace. The house was quiet only hearing pots clanking in the kitchen. A strangeness was in the air, the barometer had been dropping for the last hour, and an eerie reddish glow was out to sea. It seemed even quieter than normal tonight. The air was still and muggy, a heaviness I'd never felt before making it difficult to breath.

I stepped down from the porch to do my usual constitution of my evening walk along the edge of the cliff. A sudden blast of cool air made me shiver tugging my sweater tight around me. I made my way down the long path to the lighthouse, to check on the oil lamps, but something caught my eye and I turned the opposite way and walked to the cliff's edge. Twenty miles out to sea in the light of the fading sun was an incredible size fog bank rolling toward the cliff I was standing upon.

I became paralyzed in my spot. I'd never witnessed anything of that magnitude. The fog bank continued to roll toward the cliff, but that wasn't what was intriguing. Voices began to whisper in the mist becoming louder as the fog neared. I wanted to turn and run to my home to fetch my father, believing I was going mad. But, for some reason my feet stayed glued to the top of the cliff. The whispers became louder flowing up from the deep sea below me, men's sad voices. I had now convinced myself I had truly gone mad and my father would find me later sitting here as a babbling idiot. I wasn't one to sit and ponder a situation so I forced my feet to move so I could peer down the side of the cliff expecting to see men shouting and waving at me.

I gasped. My eyes were now playing tricks on me just as my mind. Down below me in the dark water was a tall sailing ship. I instantly knew the name of the ship, a ship that'd sunk in the rough waters in the year of 1765, The Black Shadow. How could this be The Black Shadow standing tall in the misty *fog? I could plainly see its crew busily maneuvering around on the top deck adjusting the sails as the ship tried to get to port. I knew there was only one thing I could do, I had to help save The Black Shadow from the treacherous fog bank. How I was to accomplish such a large task was beyond my wildest thoughts, but I had a chance to change history and I would do my best to save the crew and beautiful ship. I began my decent down the side of the tall cliff literally into the whispering fog...*

I flinched, the rest of the paper was singed, and the words blurry and the other pages were scorched so bad I couldn't make out the words. Pacing the room, I held onto the blackened papers. Why did someone try to burn Finnegan Brady's diary? I sighed knowing my answer. My father had the papers the entire time. He did know what happened to Finnegan in the whispering fog. My father's last adventure of his life had been to make his way to the living room during the night and dispose of Finnegan Brady's papers by burning them in the fireplace. My father was frightened and afraid the whispering fog was coming back for me. I smiled to myself. I now had the proof that Finnegan Brady did enter the whispering fog into another period just as the tale Lucky told. I shivered. Was Ebenezer a sailor onboard *The Black Shadow* and a ghost? How did the whispering fog bring Finnegan back to his time?

"No, it couldn't be," I called out. I began to pace the room. Did the *Aeolus* sink in the water down below my cliff, as did *The Black Shadow*. I couldn't look up the information in the history books. I didn't want to know the answer. Thoughts swirled in my mind with so many questions but the answers Finnegan had of the whispering fog now had died with my father.

We buried my father Seth, next to my mom Rebecca in the family cemetery. I knew he was happy and at peace.

A few weeks after my father's burial, I went to his bedroom; it was time to clean out his things. I pulled out the top drawer of his chest. My heart began to race. Goosebumps grew on my neck. A small wooden box, etched on top with the image of the Mercator globe, sat next to my father's important papers. I lifted it and gently opened the lid. Lying inside the wooden box was the sterling timepiece with the initials *FAB, Finnegan Augustus Brady,* on it. I clutched the watch in my trembling hands hurrying to the lamp sitting on the nightstand. I held the pocket watch under the light seeing a small hinge. I summoned the courage to open the watch and carefully undid the clasp to find the case maker's mark. The watch was marked SP, meaning it'd been made in England, and the letter on the back marked F meant it was made in the 1700's. My heart vibrated faster like wings on a hummingbird. Finnegan Brady had brought the sterling pocket watch back from his time travels just as I had my locket hanging around my neck. I placed the small wooden box containing the sterling timepiece in my chest drawer next to my journal for safekeeping.

I thought many times about what my father said when he was dying, and wondered why he would never discuss the whispering fog with me. But like Johnny, the tales of the sea terrified many people.

Years moved on and Anita grew into a beautiful young women. I would sit on my rock next to the cliff and tell Anita my stories about the great ship *Aeolus* and Sinjin. She was the only person I trusted with the information and she'd sit holding my locket as I told my tales.

Late at night lying in my bed, I'd feel Sinjin's arms wrapped securely around my shoulders holding me snug against his warm body. I'd wake knowing it was a dream, but a dream of what I believed my life should have been. Many days I'd think my tales were a dream, not real. Maybe I was crazy and I had hit my head on a rock when I fell down the cliff, and had passed out as the doctor said, or maybe like Finnegan believed, I'd gone mad. Then, I'd touch the locket next to my neck. It wasn't a dream and I had to keep wishing with my entire being that I could be back with the man I love onboard the *Aeolus*.

Years flew by and Anita would sit at night in her bedroom working on her computer. I was fascinated with gadgets and the computer intrigued me. I learned quickly how to use the computer and I began to study online about the years of 1788 and 1789, gathering information to keep my tale alive. I never would look up the information about a sailing ship known as the *Aeolus*.

One cool windy evening, I sat in Anita's bedroom and entered the name Tobias Allen Langston into google. To my surprise a page came up along with a picture. The picture was in black and white, but I could see that wild orange colored hair and those baby-blue eyes so full of energy. I was thrilled as I read, Tobias had become a South Carolina representative in the early 1800's and a prominent lawyer in Charleston. He'd married, had three sons, and I was sure one of his sons inherited the turtle bones. He lived through the Civil War and died at the age of ninety-three (1775-1868). I sat back and thought about Tobias' story. Did he tell his sons about a young girl named Belinda, who lived on the ship called the *Aeolus*, and who taught him to read and write? I smiled to myself, my time on the *Aeolus* had to be real if Tobias was real; how else would I've known about him.

I wouldn't give up and sat each night on my cliff always believing the *Aeolus* would return. Anita understood why I spent so many nights all alone, and she always loved to hear about my journey when she'd come home to visit.

On the other hand, Marcus worried and tried to talk me out of sitting outside, especially on cold nights, but he couldn't change my mind and only Anita knew why. Nothing was going to stop me from my evening walks.

***

Tonight was one of the coldest nights of the fall, October 13th, 2009 my seventieth birthday. I notice the barometer in the living room dropping, and remember Finnegan saying the barometer dropped right before the whispering fog appeared.

It's been exactly fifty years since I stood on this cliff and climbed down falling and landing in the strong arms of Sinjin. I walk out of the warm old Victorian home; the gusty wind circles around me with a strange eeriness and a chill is in the air.

I grab my new red shawl; the one Anita had given me this morning for my birthday. The full moon is shining down lighting the path that runs along the ledge of the cliff. The sea has become violent swishing and hissing at the foot of the cliff, and a swirling thick fog is rolling toward land.

I look down into the dark waters. I knew my old eyes played tricks on me and many nights I'd thought I'd seen something sitting at the bottom of my cliff, or maybe hoping, but tonight I knew there was something there.

I pull my red shawl tightly around my shoulders, and walk closer to the edge of the cliff. My heart pounds in my chest. There, I saw it again, something tall down in the water near the bottom of the cliff. My eyes close and I listen hearing the sea calling out to me, whispering *Belinda,* so peaceful, so beautiful in soft voices.

I move close to the edge of the cliff and step down on the next shelf. I stand at that same spot that I stood 50 years ago. I wipe tears that are flowing down my face with the sleeve of my sweater. I remember that night, so many years ago, when I saw the *Aeolus* with her soaring beige sails flapping in the wind so magnificent and tall.

Oh....was I just dreaming or maybe hoping that I saw something in the water below or was there really something down at the bottom of the cliff. I knew there was only one way to find out. The mist hit my face. I knew what I needed to do. I had to follow my heart. I lean down and place my foot carefully on a rock; I begin slowly to step down the steep cliff.

My red shawl becomes tangled on a bush and slips off my shoulders. I didn't want to try and retrieve it, so I continue to move on.

I knew this was dangerous to do on a good day and at my age, it was foolish, but I had to find out what I had seen. I gradually and carefully make my way down the side of the cliff. My body jerks to a stop. I gasp.

Were my old ears playing a trick on me? I could barely make it out, but it was a bell ringing, an iron bell from a ship. I move down the cliff inching my way closer to the bottom. My heart thumps even louder. DING, DING, DING flows up the side of the cliff.

The night has become dark, the thick mist has covered the cliff, and I can't see the light from the lighthouse anymore. I use my hands to feel my way. I had to know the answer to what was at the bottom of the steep cliff. Was it the *Aeolus* or was I dreaming. The sea continues to softly whisper, "*Belinda.*" The tolling of the ship's bell becomes louder as my body shivers.

The rock under my left foot cracks giving way and I plummet down the side of the cliff. I gasp, knowing my fate, but I'm neither frightened nor afraid. I'm an old woman and I've lived my life. I begin to believe it was all a dream, hearing the ship's bell and seeing the tall shape out in the sea in the whispering fog.

My eyes close. I listen to the vicious waves down below me as I continue to slide down the cliff's side. If I'm going to die, then I'm going to die in the sea by my beloved lighthouse and cliff. I will die as a Jack, or a Jackaro. I smile thinking about Santos so long ago; a death at sea will be fitting for me, just as it was for him.

I stop falling; I feel arms holding me tightly. I open my eyes. I see my hands, touch my face and the wrinkles are gone. I'm young again. My eyes gaze up into those dark caring eyes that I had dreamed about for fifty years. Was I dreaming; did I die? Whatever the answer I didn't care.

I reach up and my fingers touch my locket. I'm home.

CHAPTER TWENTY-SIX

SAYING GOODBYE

Anita opened the front door to the old Victorian home walking out into the misty night and over to the rim of the cliff. She stopped; lying on the ground by the edge of the cliff tangled in a small bush was the new red shawl that she had just given Belinda for her birthday. She knew Belinda wouldn't have dropped it and just left it in the mist. She panicked pacing the edge of the cliff, calling out, "Belinda, where are you?" Anita held the shawl tightly in her hands twisting it back and forth, and ran back to the house.

"Daddy," Anita shouted running into the living room waving the red shawl in her hand, "I can't find Belinda, but I found her new shawl by the edge of the cliff."

Marcus grabbed his coat and raced out the door down to the cliff's edge. His voice echoed in the fog, "Belinda," but no answer. He kept calling "Belinda," letting the name resonate down the side of the cliff. His mouth pursed as he pushed the emergency button on his cell phone calling the sheriff.

That cold night of October 13th, the men from town, including Johnny began an extensive search along the cliffs next to the sea, but couldn't find anything. There wasn't any sign or trace of Belinda. It was as if she had disappeared into the fog.

Anita hurried back to the house and opened Belinda's bedroom door. She moved over to an old oak desk and slid the bottom drawer open. Lying there, worn from being held so many times, was the special journal that Belinda had written so long ago. Anita wrapped her arms around the journal remembering the stories told to her when she was a young girl.

She sat down on Belinda's bed with the lamp on the nightstand softly glowing on the old pages and began to read the journal word for word. When she came to the end of the narrative tears began to fall, joining the tearstains on the pages. Anita wasn't crying for Belinda being gone, but for herself. She was going to miss Belinda, but she believed she was back on her ship, the Aeolus, with the man she loved.

Anita picked up a pen and started writing the ending to the treasured journal telling the sequence of events of Belinda walking out to the cliff this foggy cold evening on her seventieth birthday, climbing down the treacherous cliff into the whispering fog to find her ship the Aeolus. She knew Belinda had heard the bell ringing from the ship just as she had heard in the fog over fifty years ago, and Belinda was now onboard the Aeolus with Sinjin. Belinda had followed her heart.

Anita closed the journal hugging it tightly. Going back to her bedroom, she slid the extraordinary journal into her chest drawer for safekeeping.

She walked out the front door letting the misty air blend with the tears on her face. Her mother was standing by the steps of the porch sobbing and the men were scattered throughout the yard. She could hear the men discussing how horrible it was for Belinda to have fallen to her death down to the sea.

Johnny's tired green eyes looked up at Anita. His head dipped, shaking his long gray hair. A smile spread across his face, somehow knowing Belinda's secret.

Anita marched in a hurried pace past the men making her way to the edge of the cliff. She snuggled the red shawl against her face smelling Belinda's perfume of fresh lilac. Her eyes panned out to sea looking into the dark foggy night; she smiled, but a lone tear ran down her face.

She leaned over the edge, whispering into the fog. "Good bye, my Belinda, I hope you have found peace." She turned to leave, "*no, that couldn't be,*" a lone bell from a ship was tolling out in the sea and whispering voices were floating in the misty air.

When her father Marcus died, Anita with her husband and little girl moved back to become keeper of the lighthouse. Time moved on and Anita taught her daughter, as Belinda had taught her, all about the cliff. At night, she would sit on the same round rock as Belinda did so long ago and read the journal about the voyage in the years 1788 and 1789 on the beautiful dark blue ship known as the *Aeolus*, *"Keeper of the Wind."*

On extra foggy evenings, Anita still walks out to the cliff's edge and listens for the bell of a ship, always wondering could the whispering fog return?

Today, fishermen tell tales that on very mysterious foggy nights, at the bottom of the cliff you can hear an old ship's bell bonging in a steady rhythm and the foggy mist whispering Belinda's name. The End

QUINNIE'S GINGERBREAD CAKES

18th Century

Take three pounds of flour, one pound of sugar, one pound of butter rubbed in very fine, two ounces of ginger beat fine, one large nutmeg grated, then take a pound of treacle, a quarter of a pint of cream, make them warm together, and make up the bread stiff; roll it out, and make it up into thin cakes, cut them out with a teacup, or small glass; or roll them out like nuts, and bake them on tin plates in a slack oven.

Glasse, Hannah, "The Art of Cookery Made Plain and Simple," 1796

21st Century
- 1 ½ lbs. all-purpose unbleached flour
- ½ lb. sugar
- ½ lb. butter softened to room temperature
- 2 tbsp. ground ginger
- 1 tbsp. ground nutmeg
- 1 cup molasses
- ¼ cup cream

Note: This recipe can be halved to make it workable in most kitchens.

1. Preheat oven to 375°
2. In a large mixing bowl, blend the flour, sugar, and spices thoroughly with your hands.

3. Warm the molasses and cream together in a small saucepan, stirring to blend. This is not to be hot but warm so that they blend together, not cook.
4. Work the butter into the flour mixture with your hands until it has a sort of grated bread look.
5. Add the molasses and cream mixture and work it up into a stiff dough with your hands. If it seems dry, add a little more cream to it. The dough should be stiff but not dry.
6. Roll out the dough on a floured surface about ¼-inch thick and cut cookies into whatever shapes please you. If you wish to form them into nut shapes as the recipe states they will look sort of button shaped when they bake.
7. Bake these in a 375° oven for about 8 to 10 minutes. They should still be soft to the touch before they come from the oven, not hard.

http://recipes.history.org/2013/04/to-make-gingerbread-cakes/
http://www.colonialwilliamsburg.com/

ABOUT THE AUTHOR

Diann Shaddox is a Native American Indian and a member of the Wyandotte Nation of Oklahoma and she has Essential Tremors. She's the author of "A Faded Cottage" and "Whispering Fog."

Diann was born on December 18th in a small southern town of Nashville, Arkansas, the youngest and only daughter of William and Mary Ann Shaddox. But, fate stepped in and William, a crop-duster, at the age of 25, died in a plane crash on November 20th, a month before she was born, therefore, Diann was never able to meet her father. Mary Ann, who grew up in Miami, Oklahoma, moved back to Miami after William's death, where Diann lived until her mother died when she was only 3 years old. Diann then moved to Nashville, Arkansas to live with her grandparents. At the age of 10, Diann's Granddad Holt died of a stroke, leaving her grandmother alone to see to her.

Diann learned from an early age about death and how life should not be squandered. Her Mamow Holt, who had lost her right hand in an accident at a factory in Nashville, Arkansas, taught her, you never give up. Her grandmother never let anything stand in her way. She taught herself to write, cook, and even how to sew and make quilts with her left hand, without any prosthetics. Being handicapped was a word she never used.

Growing up in a small town was wonderful, learning to fish, growing a garden and the most important thing, patience of a grandmother. Stories from the past evolved of family bringing many stories to life. Sitting out late at night on cool summer evenings, swinging on an old swing staring up at the stars helped Diann's vivid imagination grow.

She has an enthusiasm for travel and living life to its fullest. You have only one life and shouldn't waste it. The zest for meeting and getting to know people is a very important component in her life. She is a believer of herbs, natural and organic foods, and a big supporter of Bio-identical Hormones and keeping our planet green.

Diann has lived in eight great states, Arkansas, Oklahoma, Kentucky, New Jersey, Virginia, Texas, and Florida. South Carolina is now her home with her husband, Randy, her greatest supporter.

A FADED COTTAGE, a South Carolina love story about a man with Essential Tremors
A Mom's Choice Awards Honoree

A Faded Cottage is a powerful story blending fact and fiction about a famous artist whose life is turned upside down when he learns he has Essential Tremors and begins to shake uncontrollably. He leaves his life in New York and buys a faded cottage on the beach of South Carolina discovering his teenage love after thirty years. This is his journal of only two weeks, a story of endless love, and his tale of living with Essential Tremors.

DIANN SHADDOX FOUNDATION

Diann Shaddox Foundation is a Non-Profit organization, 501 c(3), committed to help people struggling in today's world with neurological conditions. DSF is bringing light to the darkened world of Essential Tremor & Joining Hands around the World.

Diann Shaddox Foundation was formed to support and add additional resources to the efforts of so many. DSF is dedicated to inspire, educate, enlighten, and increase awareness to the world about people living every day with neurological conditions such as Essential Tremor, Dystonia, and Parkinson's. Our funds will be used for awareness and will be distributed for research to help find the cause and cure for Essential Tremor.

Diann Shaddox Foundation is unwavering to bring awareness for Essential Tremor even if it is one person at a time. What is Essential Tremor? Essential Tremor is a progressive neurological condition that causes a rhythmic trembling of the hands, head, voice, legs, or trunk. About 10 million Americans have Essential Tremor. That's about 5% of all people in the United States. For comparison sake, 7.8% of the population have some type of diabetes. Most people though haven't heard about Essential Tremor and we are adamant to bring attention to the world.

www.diannshaddoxfoundation.org

CPSIA information can be obtained at www.ICGtesting.com
Printed in the USA
LVOW08s2236161015

458678LV00003B/117/P

9 780991 280537